Praise for books in the WORLD OF MORTAL ENGINES:

"Philip Pullman fans will love Mortal Engines . . .
I didn't want it to end"
Daily Telegraph

"Big, brave, brilliant"
Guardian

*"A staggering feat of engineering, a brilliant construction that
offers new wonders at every turn . . . Reeve's prose is sweeping
and cinematic, his ideas bold and effortless"*
Publishers Weekly

"Superbly imagined"
The Times

"The idea behind Mortal Engines *has other
authors crying 'I wish I'd thought of that!'"*
Geraldine McCaughrean

*"One of the most daring and imaginative science fiction
adventures ever written for young readers"*
Books for Keeps

"An absolutely must-read author"
School Librarian

"A ground-breaking futurama"
TES

"Philip Reeve is a genius"
Sonia Benster writing in The Bookseller

*"Reeve writes with confidence and power. He is not
only a master of visceral excitement, but at every turn,
surprises, entertains and makes his readers think"*
Books for Keeps

"Reeve is a master of young adult fiction"
Scotsman

PHILIP REEVE was born in Brighton in 1966. After school he went to art college, then returned to Brighton to work in a small, independent bookshop. Some years later he became an illustrator – providing cartoons for various books, including several of the *Horrible Histories* series. He has been writing since he was five, but *Mortal Engines* was his first published book. He lives with his wife and son on Dartmoor.

www.philip-reeve.com
www.philipreeve.blogspot.com
www.mortalengines.co.uk

By Philip Reeve

Fever Crumb
A Web of Air
Mortal Engines
Predator's Gold
Infernal Devices
A Darkling Plain

No Such Thing As Dragons

Goblins
Goblins Vs Dwarves

Here Lies Arthur

In the BUSTER BAYLISS series:
Night of the Living Veg
The Big Freeze
Day of the Hamster
Custardfinger

Larklight
Starcross
Mothstorm

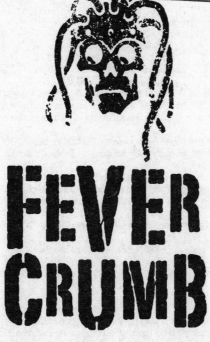

FEVER CRUMB

PHILIP REEVE

SCHOLASTIC

Scholastic Children's Books
An imprint of Scholastic Ltd
Euston House, 24 Eversholt Street
London, NW1 1DB, UK
Registered office: Westfield Road, Southam, Warwickshire, CV47 0RA
SCHOLASTIC and associated logos are trademarks
and/or registered trademarks of Scholastic Inc.

First published by Scholastic Children's Books, 2009
This edition published by Scholastic Children's Books, 2010

ISBN 9781407102436

A CIP catalogue record for this book is available
from the British Library

Printed by CPI Group (UK) Ltd, Croydon, CR0 4YY
Papers used by Scholastic Children's Books are made
from wood grown in sustainable forests.

5 7 9 10 8 6 4

www.scholastic.co.uk/zone

For Sarah and Sam

CONTENTS

PART ONE

1	The Girl From Godshawk's Head	3
2	An Offer of Employment	9
3	The Wind Tram	15
4	Stragglemarket	22
5	At the Sign of the Mott and Hoople	29
6	The Archaeologist's House	37
7	Under London	45
8	Skinner's Boy	53
9	The Scent Lantern	60
10	Summertown	67
11	Master Wormtimber	76
12	The Foldable Assassin	82
13	Morning After The Night Before	87
14	Skinners in the Brick Marsh	96
15	Hunting Fever	105
16	The Long Walk Home	111
17	Storm Coming	118
18	Chair vs Chair	126
19	Dr Crumb	135
20	At Nonesuch House	146
21	Nocturne in Blue	152
22	The Fifth Word	160
23	Under Siege	168
24	The Library	177
25	Heads Will Roll	187

PART TWO

26	The Flight North	195
27	Public Disorder	204
28	Under New Management	212
29	The Traction Castle	217
30	The Snow Leopard	223
31	Hidden Treasures	229
32	Technomancy	235
33	London Falling	244
34	Mayor vs Mayor	252
35	Mementoes	262
36	The Stalker's Question	269
37	The Magneto Gun	276
38	We Are the Dead	282
39	Crumbs of Comfort	289
40	The Passing Show	296

PART ONE

1

THE GIRL FROM GODSHAWK'S HEAD

hat morning they were making paper boys. Fever had gone down at dawn to the pressing room to collect fourteen of the big, furled sheets of paper, six feet square, which Dr Isbister made by pulping and pressing foolish old books which his library did not need. Then she had carried them carefully back up the winding wooden stairways of the Head to the chambers which she shared with Dr Crumb. There they had set to work.

Fever was just the right size now to lie on each sheet while Dr Crumb drew an outline all round her with his pencil. When that was done, she fetched two pairs of paper shears, and they carefully cut out the silhouettes. Soon fourteen of her blank, white selves lay stacked on the workbench. Fever stood at Dr Crumb's side, watching but not speaking while he spread out one of the cut-outs and laid a thin wire skeleton on top of it. He took care over the hands, with their complicated little mechanisms, and the dim white metal discs, like flimsy coins, which were the paper boy's eyes and brain. These were old-world mechanisms, and if they were damaged they could never be replaced, for no one knew the secrets of their making any more; they had been recycled from one generation of paper boys to the next ever since the Scriven first brought them down out of the unknown north.

When all the mechanisms were correctly positioned,

Fever helped Dr Crumb to coat the paper figure with paste. Then they took a second cut-out and stuck it precisely over the first, so that the two cut-outs formed a Fever-shaped paper sandwich with the metal parts hidden inside. Together, they carried it to the bath which stood in a corner of the room, and laid it in the solution. At first the paper boy just floated on the surface, like a dead leaf on a pond, but Fever took rubber-tipped tongs and gently pressed it down until the solution flowed over it and it sank. While Dr Crumb set to work on the next paper boy, Fever got her fingers under the edge of the bath and tilted it gently up and down, up and down, so that the solution shifted but did not spill, and the paper boy slid to and fro under the surface, his head and feet banging alternately against the ends of the bath.

Fever thought that it would be more rational to call the device a paper *girl*, since it had been drawn around her, but Dr Crumb said that it was not alive and had no gender.

"So why are they called paper boys?"

"A good point, Fever. The name is foolish, and was clearly not invented by a man of reason."

When all seven paper boys had been made and soaked, they lifted them out of the bath one by one and held them up so that the excess solution could drain off. Then, carrying the dripping figures on a rack between them, they left the workroom and went up the stairs and out on to the roof.

"This is a great waste of time," said Dr Crumb, as they pegged the paper boys out like laundry for the brisk west wind to dry. "Why the New Council do not just ask their Master of Devices to make paper boys for them, I

4

fail to understand. Master Wormtimber was once a member of our Order, and surely he cannot have forgotten *everything* he learned from us. . ."

"Perhaps the New Council knows you make them best, Dr Crumb," said Fever loyally. "And maybe they want paper boys they can be sure of, if there is really to be a war."

"There is not going to be a war," said Dr Crumb.

"But Dr Isbister told me that a nomad horde is approaching from the north—"

"As our Order's librarian, it is one of Dr Isbister's duties to read the city newspapers, and I'm afraid they fill his mind with rumours and scaremongery. This is not the first time one of the nomad empires has moved south. They will not dare to attack London. Though if they did, I doubt that a few paper boys could do much to stop them."

The drying paper boys flapped and crockled, a line of white dancers strung between two ventilator cowls. Specks of rust and dust blew against them and stuck to the still-wet paper, so Fever and Dr Crumb went to and fro patiently picking them off. After a while, as the boys began to dry, Dr Crumb went back below, leaving Fever to keep an eye on them. She walked to the roof's edge and lay down, enjoying the warmth of the sun. It was July, the height of London's brief summer. Bees droned past her, and the cries of hawkers came up faintly from the deep streets, where she could see people and carts and sedan chairs moving. Jackdaws called and squabbled around the strange old blue metal towers in Clerkenwell: wind-trams under their clouds of sunlit sail went rattling along their spindly viaducts. And somewhere beneath her, more as a vibration in her breastbone than an actual sound, Fever could hear the voices of old Dr Collihole and his assistants as they laboured in his attic workspace, assembling the vast paper balloon in which he planned one day soon to begin the reconquest of the skies.

Fever was the youngest member of the Order of Engineers, and the only female. Engineers did not have wives or children. But one evening fourteen years before, Dr Crumb had been called out to a dig on the Brick Marsh by an archaeologist named Chigley Unthank who wanted an opinion on some Ancient artefacts which he'd unearthed, and on his way back he had heard crying coming from an old weed-grown pit close to the road. There, among the bramble bushes, he had found a baby in a basket, with an old blanket laid over her and a label tied around her wrist upon which someone had written just four words:

HER NAME IS FEVER.

He had told Fever the story often and often when she was little. (Dr Crumb did not believe in telling lies, not even white lies, not even to little girls. He had not wanted her to grow up thinking she was *his*.) She knew how he had stood there in the twilight staring down at the baby in the basket and how finally, not knowing what else to do, he had carried her back with him to Godshawk's Head.

In earlier years he might have taken her to the civic orphanage, but that was the summer of the Skinners'

Riots, and the orphanage had been wrecked and looted, along with much of the rest of the city. In London's rougher boroughs, like Limehouse and St Kylie, the skins of murdered Scriven still flapped like speckled flags from poles which the Skinners had set up at street corners. The collection of merchants and lawyers who called themselves the New Council had not yet completely restored order.

Dr Crumb made up a little bed for the foundling in a spare drawer of his plan-chest and fed her watered-down milk through a laboratory pipette. Looking into her eyes, he noticed that they were different colours; the left dark brown, the right soft lichen grey. Was that why she had been abandoned? Had her mother been afraid that her neighbours would take that small oddity for a sign that the child was a Scriven or some other sort of misshape, and kill her? There was a small wound on the back of her head; a thin cut not quite healed. Dr Crumb, who had seen for himself the savagery of the Skinners, imagined some crazed Londoner slashing at her with a knife. . .

The other Engineers, gathering round him to peer at the tiny refugee, had all agreed with him; the child must not go back to live among those savage, superstitious Londoners. She would stay with the Order, in Godshawk's Head, and Dr Crumb would act as her guardian. Girls had never been admitted to the Order before, since it was well known that female minds were not capable of rational thought. But if little Fever were to be brought up in the ways of the Order from infancy, was there not a chance that she might make a useful Engineer?

*

So here she lay, fourteen summers later, in the sunshine on the Head's roof. She had grown into an odd-looking girl, and her clothes made her look odder still. Only someone who had spent fourteen years being told that appearances don't matter would dress in clothes like those. Big digger's boots, skinny black trousers, an old grey shirt, a white canvas coat with metal buttons. Then there was her hair, or rather, her *lack* of hair. The Order were keen to hurry humankind into the future, and they believed that hair was unnecessary. Fever shaved her head every other morning, and had done so for so long that she didn't remember what colour her hair would be if she were to let it grow. And below the bald dome of her head she had a curious face, with a short, sudden nose and a wide mouth, thick fair eyebrows and, oddest of all, those large eyes that didn't match. Yet somehow it all worked. It was one of those rare faces which bypassed pretty and went straight to beautiful.

Of course, that would never have occurred to Fever. She attached no importance to her looks. But she *was* beautiful, all the same, as she lay there watching the city and waiting for the paper boys to dry and idly tracing the raised line of that old scar that she could feel but never see; a slender silvery thread which curved along the base of her skull.

8

2

AN OFFER OF EMPLOYMENT

odshawk's Head was not a building; it really was a head. Auric Godshawk, the last of London's Scriven overlords, had planned to commemorate his rule with an immense statue of himself, but he had got no further than this metal head, seven storeys high, which stood near Ox-fart Circus on a patch of waste ground surrounded by the huge, abandoned smelting and rolling sheds where it had been constructed.

The Scriven had arrived in London two hundred years before. Driven out of their northern homelands by some power shift among the nomad empires, they swept south in search of a city to conquer, and London, rich in trade and archaeology, had drawn them like magpies. After smashing London's army at the Battle of Barnet they dragged their mobile fortress on to the summit of Ludgate Hill, tore off its wheels and converted it into the Barbican, the stronghold from which Scriven kings would rule over the city for the next two centuries.

They were brilliant, cruel and party mad, and they were not exactly human beings. In the black time after the Downsizing all sorts of mutations had come whirling down the helter-skelter of the human DNA spiral, and the Scriven claimed to be a new species entirely. *Homo superior* they liked to call themselves, or sometimes *Homo futuris*, the idea being that they had come into the world to replace dull old *Homo sapiens*.

They were strange in a lot of ways you couldn't easily put your finger on, and in one way that you could: their pale skin was blotched and dappled with markings, like leopards' spots. Some Scriven's spots were freckle-coloured, others were dark as spilled ink. The Scriven prized dark markings most. They believed that they had each been written on by a god called the Scrivener, who had inscribed the future history of the world upon their skins. Scriven scholars spent whole lifetimes making drawings of other Scriven in the nude, and trying to decipher the Scrivener's sacred ideograms.

But like most mutant strains, the Scriven hadn't thrived for long. The genetic peculiarities of which they were so proud turned out to be their downfall. All London's previous conquerors had intermarried with native Londoners and had children who were Londoners themselves, but although some Scriven took human wives and lovers, no children ever came of those unions. Even Scriven marriages were often barren. By the time Godshawk began work on his giant statue there were only a few hundred Scriven left, lording it over a city of sixty thousand. The taxes needed to pay for it, and the slave labour used in its building, helped spark the Skinners' Riots, in which Godshawk and all the other Scriven had been slaughtered.

The rioters had swirled all through London, burning and smashing anything connected with the Scriven, but they'd not been able to do much damage to that titanic head. When the smoke cleared it was still standing, its stern face dented and daubed with angry slogans.

There had been a housing shortage after the riots – the burning down of buildings, it turned out, had been a bad idea in a city made mostly of timber and thatch – and the unpopular Order of Engineers (who had taken no part in the uprising, and many of whose members had worked for Scriven masters) were thrown out of their big Guildhouse on Ludgate Hill to make room for displaced families. It seemed logical that, rather than waiting for a new Guildhouse to be built while their valuable collections sat mouldering in makeshift huts, they should just move into Godshawk's Head. It was hollow, mostly weather-tight, and very big. The builders had left scaffolding inside which formed the basis of floors and walls and stairways. The Engineers glazed Godshawk's eyes, and poked dozens of smaller windows in his cheeks and forehead. They gave him a tar-paper roof like a bad hat. The Head was only intended to be a temporary accommodation, but it became permanent. After all, as the Engineers liked to joke in their dry, unfunny way, it was most appropriate that they should live in a head. Hadn't they always said that they were the brains of the city?

That night, when the paper boys had been taken down and packed in boxes and sent up to the Barbican, and Fever was washing up after the evening meal in the tiny kitchen which adjoined Dr Crumb's workspace, there came a tapping on the door. She put down the dish she had been wiping and reached for a towel to dry her hands, but Dr Crumb had already left his workbench and gone to see who their visitor was. Fever could not see the door from where she stood in the kitchen, but she heard it open, and heard the voice of Dr Stayling.

Fever wondered what could have brought the Chief

11

Engineer to their quarters at such a late hour. She was almost tempted to eavesdrop on what he and Dr Crumb were talking about, but she reminded herself to be reasonable. *There is no profit in wondering why Dr Stayling has come here,* she thought. *It may be nothing to do with you, Fever Crumb, and if it is, you shall find out about it in good time.* So she made herself go on with her chores, carefully wiping and drying each plate, dish and utensil and putting them back in their places on the kitchen shelves. *A place for everything, and everything in that place,* was one of the rules which Dr Crumb had taught her when she was very little.

She was just emptying the dirty water out of the kitchen window when Dr Crumb called to her. "Fever. Dr Stayling would like to speak with you."

So it did have something to do with her! She put the bowl upside-down on the sill to drain, then shut the window. She ran a hand over her head, glad that she had shaved that morning. Then she went through into the workroom.

Dr Stayling was a tall, broad-shouldered old man. He shaved his head, like all the Order, but he didn't bother to clip the hairs in his nostrils, which were long and steely grey and quivered when he breathed. Fever, facing him, reminded herself that it would be childish to find that distracting.

"Fever," said Dr Crumb, looking worried, "Dr Stayling has a proposal for you."

"It is not my proposal, you understand," said Dr Stayling, with that North Country accent of his which grew stronger when he was excited. "Kit Solent, a minor archaeologist, has asked me to supply an Engineer to live at his house on Ludgate Hill and help him to study artefacts from a new site he has discovered. He has requested you, Fever."

Fever, like a good Engineer, showed no emotion, but beneath her white coat her heart began to beat very quickly.

"Fever is very young, to be sent out on such a placement," said Dr Crumb.

"Nevertheless, Crumb, you're always telling us how rational and capable she is. And it is perfectly usual for young Engineers to be sent out into the world. Only then do we find out if they are truly men of reason, or if they will fall prey to the world's temptations. You did it yourself, Crumb."

"Yes," said Dr Crumb, looking suddenly flustered. "Yes, I did, and it was a . . . a troubling period. Difficult. . ."

Dr Stayling went and stood at the window, gazing out across the great, smoky, unreasonable city. He said, "I always had high hopes for young Solent. As a young man he struck me as having a very rational mind. Made some interesting discoveries. Remember that old underground railway station down by the Marsh Gate? That was one of his finds. Remarkable state of preservation. Then he went and married some digger's daughter, and that was the end of his usefulness. They busied themselves mooning about and having babies for a few years, and then the girl died, and ever since he's just looked after the children while living off his savings, which I should imagine are getting pretty low by now. I'm pleased to hear that he's digging again. It is rational for the Order to encourage him in any way we can."

13

Fever thought that she liked the sound of Master Solent, although she knew it was irrational to form an opinion based on such little knowledge of him. Still, she looked hopefully at Dr Crumb, wondering if he would let her go.

Dr Crumb still looked troubled. He said, "Fever is a great help to me here, Dr Stayling. What shall I do without her?"

"Oh, I'll ask young Quilman to come up and assist you, Crumb. He's highly rational. And it is only for a short time; three weeks or a month. So pack your bag, Fever Crumb. You will be leaving for Ludgate Hill tomorrow."

3

THE WIND TRAM

he main entrance to Godshawk's Head was not through its mouth, as you might expect, for annoyingly Godshawk's sculptor had chosen to represent him with his lips firmly closed. Instead, the Order and their visitors came and went through a door at the top of a flight of steps which led up the Head's left nostril.

Out of that door and down those steps next morning came Fever Crumb, in the pearl-grey London daylight, pushing open the gate in the high fence which ran all round the Head and walking out on to the tram stop, which was a timber platform built on piles against Godshawk's upper lip.

Dr Crumb came with her. He had carried her cardboard suitcase from their quarters, and he would have liked to carry it further. He would have liked to go with her all the way to Solent's house and see what sort of place she was to live in and among what kinds of people. Fever would have liked that, too. But neither of them dared suggest it, for fear the other would think them irrational.

So they stood on the Head's wooden moustache in the gusty, biting wind and wondered what to say. The tram was due, but as yet there was no sign of it. The wire-link fence sang thinly in the breeze.

"The wind is still from the west," observed Dr

Crumb at last. "You will have a good, brisk run to the Terminus, and from there I believe it is but a short walk to Solent's place."

Fever agreed. They stood facing each other, the collars of their white coats turned up against the wind. On Fever's head was a wide-brimmed straw hat which Dr Crumb had unearthed from somewhere, saying she would need it to protect her scalp from the sun. She held it on tightly and watched the thick, gunmetal clouds sweep above the city and thought about sums, angles, anything that would take her mind off what she was feeling.

She didn't want to go. She wanted to stay in the Head for ever. She wanted Dr Crumb to hold her hand and lead her back inside. She felt afraid of living without him, and angry at him for not standing up to Dr Stayling and insisting that she stay. But she knew, too, that those feelings, like all feelings, were irrational. They were the frightened instincts of a small animal leaving the nest for the first time. Everyone had instincts, just as everyone had hair; they were another vestige of humanity's primitive past. A good Engineer learned to suppress them.

The tramlines began to chirrup, and then to hum. She glanced to windward, and there was the tram coming down the long sweep of the viaduct which carried it above the roofs of Wary Edge. In another half minute it would be at Godshawk's Head. She turned back to Dr Crumb, and almost lost control and hugged him, but by then a whole crowd of Engineers were coming out of Godshawk's nostril like a highly educated sneeze, and what would they think of her if they saw her

16

acting on her feelings? They would think that they had been right all those years ago, and that girls were not suited to the ways of reason. So she held tight to the handle of her suitcase with one hand, and kept that farm-girl hat in place with the other, and just nodded to Dr Crumb, and Dr Crumb nodded back, and wiped his eyes with his coat cuff and said, "Bother this wind. . ."

"Farewell, Fever Crumb!" called the other Engineers. "Good luck! Be reasonable!" And she bowed to them too, and then the tram was almost alongside the platform and there was nothing to do but turn and run for it while Dr Crumb in a voice too small for her or anyone else to hear, said, "Take care, little Fever! Take care. . ."

Fever had often watched wind trams pass the Head, but she had never boarded one before. There was a worrying gap between the platform's edge and the tram's deck, but her legs were long and strong and she leaped it easily and dumped herself on one of the slatted wooden seats behind the main mast. The tram did not slow, but kept trundling past the tram stop at a steady twelve miles per hour so that the Head fell quickly astern, and was soon hidden behind a terrace of thirtieth-century villas.

Fever set her suitcase down on the deck between her feet and groped in her pocket for the coins which Dr Crumb had given her. The tram conductor, a squat man with a wooden leg, came stumping aft, and she said, "The Central Terminus," and put the coins in his hand. In return he gave her an oyster shell and an expectant stare, as if he was waiting for a thank you, but Fever did not see any reason to say "thank you" – he had not done her a favour, merely his job. After a moment he stopped waiting and went on his way, muttering something to another of the tram crew, who laughed nastily.

The oyster shell hung on a cord threaded through a hole bored in its edge. Everyone who travelled by London Transport wore one. Fever took off her hat and looped the cord over her head and put her hat back on and sat on her uncomfortable seat and watched the city slide by. The cloud cover was breaking and a stook of sunbeams stood on Ludgate Hill, gilding the wet roofs of the Barbican and the copper-topped towers of the Astrologers' Guild.

For the first time the bad, breathless feeling which had seized her when she was saying goodbye to Dr Crumb began to fade, and in its place came something which she thought of as *positive anticipation*, but which someone who had not been brought up by Engineers would have called *excitement*.

More houses went by, their top floor windows level with the tramline. Then the weed-grown summit of a digger's spoil heap, with goats grazing among the buddleia. They passed other stations where people jumped nimbly aboard carrying children and shopping and cumbersome packages, squeezing into the seats on either side of Fever's. The wind died a little as the tram nosed its way deeper into the built-up heart of the city, passing into the lee of tall buildings. Ahead, flocks of dust-grey pigeons wheeled around the thatched roofs of the Central Terminus, in the shadow of Ludgate Hill. The tram crew furled their flapping sails, took up long poles and quanted the rest of the way, only stopping when they reached the incline outside the terminus, down which the tram coasted until it fetched up with a jarring thump against the straw buffers.

"Central Terminus! Alight 'ere fer Ludgate Hill, Liver Pill Street an' the Stragglemarket! Change 'ere for stops to 'Bankmentside, St Kylie, 'Ampster's 'Eath, and Effing Forest!"

And oh, the noise of it! Fever was pummelled by the din and stink and bustle that greeted her as she climbed down from the tram and made her way along the platform, which was spattered with pigeon droppings and clumps of filthy straw fallen from the high, thatched canopy overhead. Stevedores shunted trolleys piled with crates and barrels at Fever, and left it to her to decide whether she would leap aside or be crushed under their wheels. Men shouted to one another as they ran up the masts of lately arrived trams to furl their sails. Doors slammed and handbells rang as other trams pulled out, laden with freight and passengers.

She clutched her little cardboard suitcase to her chest and hurried on until she reached the wooden turnstile at the platform's end. There she held up her oyster shell while the eyes of the turnstile keeper flicked over her in a bored, faintly aggressive way before letting her through.

At once she found herself caught up in a river of Londoners which was swirling across the concourse and down a broad flight of wooden stairs and out into the street to join a still larger river outside. Drovers were herding sheep towards the meat market, barrow boys and news-sheet vendors were shouting their wares and dozens of sedan chairs were being carried past, bobbing on that tide of hats and heads like over-decorated cupboards washed away in a flood.

Fever fished in her pocket for the directions which Dr Stayling had given her, while keeping tight hold of the handle of her suitcase. Dr Crumb had warned her of the sneak-thieves and dip-pockets who haunted London's busier streets. She peered at Dr Stayling's sketch map, but she could not relate the neat lines he had drawn to the complex, busy, jagged streets in which she found herself. She looked about for a street name or a signpost, but there were none. The river of people swept her on. The low sun was lighting the upper parts of the buildings and a window flashed as a maid leaned out to empty a chamber pot. Fever jumped aside just in time to dodge the shower of urine, and stumbled into the path of a religious procession – celebrants in robes and pointed hats whirling and clapping and chanting the name of some old-world prophet, *"Hari, Hari! Hari Potter!"*

Disgusted, Fever veered away. But all around her now were the signs of unreason; temples to Poskitt and Mad Isa and dozens more of London's shabby gods, with the ramshackle copper-domed towers of the astrologers poking up over their roofs. Shops and stalls sold scents and prayer flags and dreamcatchers and impractical hats and cheap storybooks with lurid covers. Barrow boys swore and squabbled. Women passed by with painted faces, wearing skirts so wide that small wheels had been attached to the hems to stop them dragging in the street-muck, while little gas balloons held up the points of their flamboyant, lacy collars.

It was small wonder, Fever thought, that the Order of

Engineers had long ago decided to cloister themselves away from such a world, with all its disorder and distractions. Round a corner she went, and down steep, cobbled streets that kept turning into stairways. Down? No, that must be wrong! She looked at the map again. She should be going *up*hill.

She was growing confused and panicky, but she was still rational enough to see the truth. She had been alone in the city for barely five minutes, and already she was lost.

4

STRAGGLEMARKET

rying to think in the calm and scientific way that Dr Crumb had taught her, Fever turned her back on the sun and started following a nearby viaduct, hoping that it would lead her back to the Terminus. But the viaduct was not easy to follow. Scruffy buildings leaned against its supports, archaeological digs opened in the middle of streets, and in detouring round them she soon lost sight of the tramline altogether.

(She did not notice the black sedan chair which cut through the crowds a hundred feet behind her, dogging her path like a large, square shark.)

She took wrong turning after wrong turning, and ended up on a street with high, abandoned-looking warehouses on either side. In front of the buildings small-time scavengers and archaeologists had set out their wares on trestles under canvas awnings, or spread them on blankets on the cobbled ground. Fever tasted a sudden tang of homesickness as she looked down into a hamper filled with old mobile phone carapaces just like the ones she had so often cleaned and polished for Dr Crumb. On other stalls she glimpsed intriguing knots of old wiring and circuitry, and once a whole engine, but most of the traders were simply selling junk; shapeless old clots of crushed plastic and rust whose purpose not even an Engineer could hope to guess.

"'Allo ducks!" called a toothless old woman, seeing Fever glance at the rust-stained stones which were spread on her blanket. "Treat yourself to a bargain, dearie!" She snatched at Fever's sleeve and Fever looked round into her mad old face. The woman's eyes widened. Her grin turned into something different. "What are you?" she asked. She started to back away, pointing with one arm at Fever's face while she used the other to elbow a path for herself through the crowd. "Her eyes!" she squealed. "Her eyes! She's one of them!"

"Please, do stop it," said Fever, but her voice was small, no more than a whisper really, while the old woman's had risen to a wheezy shriek.

"Scriven! She be Scriven!"

Heads were turning. People were noticing Fever, and they weren't the sort of people she wanted to be noticed by. Burly barrow boys, rag-robed scavengers, crop-headed London roughs with tattooed necks. With startling speed a ring of gawpers congealed around her, attracted by the scent of coming violence. Someone knocked Fever's hat off, and as she stooped to pick it up she heard them muttering, "Look at her! She's got no hair! *No hair!*"

"I am an Engineer," said Fever, straightening up. "I shave my head. Hair is unnecessary, and provides a home to lice and fleas. It is a vestige of our animal past. . ."

But none of the people round her looked as though they'd know what "vestige" meant, or believe that mankind was descended from the animals. They weren't listening anyway.

"She's tall enough, but she ain't got no speckles," said

23

one man, peering into Fever's face. "She ain't no Scriven."

"But look at them *eyes!*" another urged. "She's some sort of misshape all right. 'Ow could she be human yet 'ave eyes that don't match?"

"Of course I am human!" said Fever weakly, but the men were all suspicious now, and that word "misshape" had been enough to rouse a wary hatred from deep in their folk memory. Mutations were rare, and not many had been as long lasting or as dangerous as the Scriven, but most Londoners still believed in stamping out misshapes wherever you found them, just in case.

Fever looked around, hoping to find someone in the crowd she might appeal to. There was no one. Some were jeering and laughing at her, while others looked ready to murder her. "Your behaviour is irrational," she told them, hoping to calm them, but she could not seem to make them understand. They clumped closer, leering, one man reaching out to prod her. Behind their faces, like something in a dream, a black sedan chair slid towards her, swinging side-on. As the crowd sensed it and turned their heads to look, Fever saw her chance and fled. She found a side alley and darted down it, her cardboard suitcase banging its corners against her legs, shouts breaking out behind her, a rotten cabbage bursting against the damp brickwork of the alley wall.

For a moment there was panic, and wet cobbles, and the slap of her running feet. Then she rounded a corner into another alley and there was the black chair again, blocking the way ahead.

"Miss Crumb!"

A man was leaning from the chair's open door, calling out to her as she turned to run back the way she'd come. He opened the chair's door and reached out a hand to Fever.

"Come on, Miss Crumb," he said. "The Stragglemarket's no place to hang about. Not for a stranger." He smiled, and his smile made her feel safer. "I'm Kit Solent," he said. "Stayling told me you weren't used to being out alone, so I decided to come and meet you at the station. I called, but you must not have heard me. Not your fault, of course. Once you get caught in the crowd, you end up going where it takes you. . ."

Another crowd, the angry Stragglemarket mob, was approaching fast along the same alley Fever had just run down. She could hear their voices, harsh as animals'.

"Come on, hop in," said Kit Solent.

Fever decided that the rational thing would be to do as he asked. She passed up her case to him and clambered inside, feeling the chair dip beneath her as the bearers adjusted to her weight. Then Kit Solent tugged shut the door and rapped once with his knuckles on the wall behind his head. The chair set off at a brisk walking pace, back up the alley Fever had just run down, herding her pursuers ahead of it. Solent gestured to Fever to keep her head down and leaned from the window, calling out, "She's not come this way."

Crouching between the two bench seats, Fever's eyes grew used to the shadows of the chair. She saw that two children were sitting beside Solent; a boy of about eight years and a little girl, much younger. They sat close together and watched Fever solemnly, like a pair of owls. The girl was clutching some sort of pretend animal; a blue dog made from fluff and wool.

"There!" said Kit Solent, helping her up, and grinning at her as she settled herself on the seat opposite him. The Stragglemarket was behind them; the chair was climbing through quieter streets, up the side of Ludgate Hill. "Miss Crumb, I do believe you are the most exciting employee we've ever had. We have had a sedan-chair chase and a near riot, and it's not yet time for elevenses. You must have a perfect genius for getting into trouble!"

Fever blushed. "It was no fault of mine," she said, peeking through the tiny window behind his head to make sure they were not being followed. "Those people were most irrational!"

"They were *scared*, Miss Crumb," Kit Solent replied. "Don't you know your history? The Scriven used to run this city, and they were cruel and wicked and not altogether human. Anybody who looks a bit different tends to remind people of them."

He smiled at Fever. He was older than Dr Crumb but not nearly as old as Dr Stayling; a large, handsome man, slightly overweight, with an intelligent face, blue eyes, long, chestnut-coloured hair tied back with a silver clasp, scruffy clothes, an ink stain on his shirt cuff. Fever remembered him now; he had visited the Head several times, and she had looked down from the window of Dr Crumb's chambers and watched Dr Stayling greeting him when he stepped off the wind tram.

The little girl tugged at Solent's sleeve and he leaned down to listen to what she whispered. "That's right, Fern. She's got no hair."

The girl went back to staring at Fever, her small chin

pressed against the head of the toy animal. Kit Solent said, "This is my daughter, Fern, and my son, Ruan."

"Good morning, Miss Crumb," said the boy.

Fever nodded warily. The only child she had ever known was her own younger self. All she remembered about childhood was longing to grow up so that she would understood things as well as Dr Crumb and be a child no longer. She had no idea what she should say to these two, who were staring at her so expectantly. She felt her ears turning pink. It occurred to her that there *was* a purpose to hair – it hid your ears, so that nobody could see them flush when you were embarrassed.

"Your Order has kept you something of a secret, Fever," said Kit Solent chattily. "A girl Engineer? I had no idea that there were such animals until Dr Stayling mentioned you. He tells me you're the best of their apprentices. I decided at once that you were the girl to help me with my project. So much nicer for the children to have a young person about the house, instead of some stern old man."

Fever's ears felt hotter and hotter. One of the Order's best apprentices? Dr Stayling would hardly have called her that if he had seen the unreasonable panic she had got into simply trying to find her way to Solent's house. . . To avoid having to look at Kit Solent she stared out of the window instead, and saw that the chair was turning on to a shabby street that curved along the south-eastern flank of Ludgate Hill. The tall houses, which had been the homes of the Scriven and their wealthy human collaborators, still showed signs of damage from the Skinners' Riots. Many were burned out shells. Even those that were still standing had

27

boarded windows, and the summer weeds waved head high in their gardens. Fever knew that London's population had dwindled in the years since the Riots, as people moved south to warmer, safer, richer cities, but she had not realized that whole streets of houses lay abandoned so close to the Barbican.

Or perhaps not quite abandoned. Outside one of those gaunt, derelict villas the chair slowed, then turned in through the rusted-open gates to stop on a stretch of weedy gravel outside the front door.

"Here we are!" said Solent brightly, and stepped out of the chair as the chairmen set it down, lifting Fern out after him and leaving Fever and Ruan to make their own way out while he rummaged in his purse for coins to pay the panting bearers.

Fever stood on the gravel and looked up at the place where she was expected to live. It was a tall building, standing alone in what must have been gardens back in Scriven times, but were now a wasteland of brambles and overgrown topiary. Tall clumps of nettles swayed in the breeze, releasing their clouds of pollen like faint breaths of smoke. Most of the lower windows were boarded up, but some on the upper floors still had glass; dusty, dirty glass behind which swags of coloured material had been pinned up as curtains. High above she saw a battered roof, and some listing chimney pots.

Solent caught her by the arm and propelled her up the front steps. "Welcome, Miss Crumb," he said, bending to unlock the heavy door. "Welcome to Number 17 Ludgate Hill Gardens, my humble home. . ."

5

AT THE SIGN OF THE
MOTT AND HOOPLE

f all the pubs in many-taverned London, the Mott and Hoople on Ditch Street was the dimmest, the dingiest, the darkest and the most dangerous. There had been a tavern on that spot for centuries, and the centuries seemed hardly to have changed it; it still held the same stale smell, still wore the same bullseyes of bottle-bottom glass in its stingy little windows, still had the same sick-and-sawdust floors and the same old jar of ancient gherkins standing by the beer pumps on the bar. And behind the bar, the Mott's landlord, Ted Swiney, who grinned, and joked, and acted the jolly host, and stayed sober always, watching with mean, cunning little piggish eyes while the customers squandered their last few farthings on his booze.

That morning the talk in the Mott and Hoople was all about the news from the north. London's two newspapers, the *Standard* and the *Alarmist*, which could usually agree about nothing at all, both claimed that a nomad outfit called the Movement was pushing south. The *Standard* said they were refugees, dislodged from their own holdings up north by the deepening ice, while the *Alarmist* reckoned they were invaders, bent on taking London for themselves. Both papers wanted to know why the Trained Bands, London's part-time militia, had not been sent north to reinforce the guards and lookouts who manned the Orbital Moatway.

The drinkers in the Mott and Hoople wanted to know, too. Ted listened to their grumbling while he wiped the glasses clean. He was pleased by the edge of worry that he heard in their voices. When people got worried they started looking to the New Council to do something, and the New Council were a bunch of hapless do-gooders who were completely incapable of doing anything. Frustration and anger and violence would result, and it seemed to Ted that a man who understood the needs and workings of the London mob might use that anger to his own advantage.

Because Ted had ambitions. He'd come from nothing to make himself a big man in that part of town. As well as the Mott and Hoople he had two other pubs, the Blogger's Arms on 'Bankmentside and the Polished Turd in B@ersea. He owned the Brimstone Brewery, too, and a row of tenements in Lemon Heel which he let out at fearsome rents to low-end archaeologists and bar girls. It seemed to him that it was only Lord Mayor Gilpin Wheen and them other do-gooding poofs on the New Council who were stopping him from being bigger still. Secretly, down in the basement of his mind, he stored a sly and precious dream: Tedward Swiney as Mayor of London.

"Those nomad empires are tough," a digger at the bar was saying. "And they're tooled up with all kinds of old-tech, and terrible ancient weapons what they dig up out of the Ice Wastes."

"Everyone knows the Movement's spies come in and out of London as they please," said another, a man with the stained hands and leather apron of a plasticsmith.

"Dressed up as merchants and riding on them foreign land barges. . ."

Ted shook his head, coming round the bar's end to kick fresh sawdust over a mound of last night's vomit and put the latest smell by Prince Nez into the pub's battered scent lantern. The men fell silent, waiting to hear what he thought of it all. "You're right," he said. "The New Council are too weak to stand up to this foreign muck. They never stood up to the Patchskins, did they? While us poor folk was suffering and dying, Gilpin Wheen and his like was sitting quiet and building up their businesses and bowing and scraping; "Yes my lord Scriven, no my lord Scriven. . ." It was us who risked our necks to throw the Scriven down, but it was them who picked up their power; all them lawyers and antiquaries and do-gooders. And you think they're going to raise a finger to save us from these nomad 'nanas? They're probably in league with the Movement themselves, half of 'em."

His listeners nodded wisely, pleased to have their worst fears confirmed.

"Still," said Ted, brightening a bit, "this is London. Eh? We sorted out the Dapplejacks, didn't we? And we'll sort out these new cloots if they try and get across the Moatway. All we need is a good hard man to lead us." He stumped back behind his bar and started refilling a mug which one of the men held out to him. "Let 'em come. One proper Londoner's worth a hundred foreigners."

At which point, right on cue, the door banged open and a proper Londoner came in. A gaunt old man, dressed in a quilted coat so long that it brushed his boot heels and so black that it seemed to suck the colour from his long, hollow face, leaving it white as a paper mask. His hair was white too, trailing in greasy rat tails over his coat collar. In his right hand a thick black staff. On his head a black bowler hat, gone greenish with age, the binding of the brim come loose and hanging down in tatters.

He paused, leaning on his staff in the lit oblong of the doorway, and announced his arrival with a long fit of wet, wheezing coughs.

"It's Creech," said Ted Swiney. Men whispered, nudging one another, until all heads had turned to stare at the newcomer. "It's Bagman Creech!"

Space was hastily made for him at the bar. A stool was dusted and pulled out for him. Men whipped their caps off. Bagman Creech was a hero. When the Skinners' Guilds rose up to rid London of the Scriven tyrants, Bagman Creech had been their general. You could see paintings of him even now, done thirty feet tall on the walls of tenements in Limehouse and St Kylie, holding up a Patchskin's head and shouting out the Skinners' war cry in curly-whirly script:

This Ain't Genocide!
This is Rock 'n' Roll!

Of course, he'd aged a bit. The New Council which had been formed after the riots had taken steps to stamp out the Skinners' Guilds. They were glad to be rid of the Scriven, of course, but order had to be restored. Bagman Creech had objected, so they arrested him and chucked him in the Clink prison. You could see how he'd suffered there by the pained, rheumatic way he walked. You could hear it in the steady wheezing of his breath, and the cough that rumbled endlessly down in the wet cellars of his lungs.

"Morning, Ted Swiney," he rasped, reaching the bar and propping his black staff against it.

"Bagman," said Swiney, with a nod. "What do you say to a pint of Brimstone Best?"

"I'm not stopping," said Bagman Creech. His voice had been sanded away until only a whisper remained. The men at the bar leaned closer to hear. "I'm working. I heard a misshape was seen up the Stragglemarket this morning."

That was the other thing about Bagman Creech. Unlike the rest of London, he'd never been convinced that the Scriven were gone for good. He'd always believed that some had escaped, and were lurking somewhere, out on Tyburn Waste or deep in the mazes of the Brick Marsh, waiting for a chance to take revenge. Old and ill as he was, he still spent his days a-googling for them wherever they might hide.

Ted wiped a mug and shook his head. "I heard that too. Lily Dismas said she saw a Dapplejack. Mad as a spoon, she is."

Bagman Creech had pale, hooded eyes with a winter light in them. "If Lil's mad it's because the Scriven drove her mad," he said. "Ten years she spent in their lock-ups. If she says this girl she saw was Scriven, she was Scriven. And it falls to me to track her down and do what's needful. People are scared, Ted Swiney, and if you won't help 'em then I will. . ."

Ted set the mug he'd been polishing down on the bar

and returned the old Skinner's stare. Not many men could have spoken to him like that and got out of the Mott alive. Creech was different, though. A man in Ted's position had to show respect for the old Skinner. He said, "What I heard was, that girl in the Stragglemarket got took away in a chair. "

"I heard that too," said Creech. "You know whose chair it was?"

"Search me, Bagman. A taxi prob'ly. I don't know."

"I'll keep asking then." Bagman turned, suppressing another gust of coughing, and started back towards the doors.

Ted watched him go. He had the uneasy feeling that he might have made a mistake. If the commons were getting panicky about a Scriven on the loose, he had to show them that Ted Swiney took their fears seriously. "Creech!" He threw out the word like a fish hook. Creech stopped as if it had snagged the back of his coat. Turned.

"You need a hand?" asked Ted. "You don't sound well. I bet you could use a boy to do some of the legwork. . ."

He was stamping as he spoke on the trapdoor behind the bar, which led down to the cellar where the beer was stored. It yawned open and a shabby boy of eleven or twelve came scrambling up, clutching a mop in one hand and already cringing in readiness for a blow from the back of Ted's hand.

"Charley Shallow," said Ted Swiney, "you're about bright enough to run an errand, ain't you? Carry a letter, knock at a door, maybe cook up Master Creech's supper of an evening?"

34

"Yes, Ted," the boy said meekly, looking at the floor.

Ted turned in triumph to the old Skinner. "There. You take him, Bagman. Borrow him for as long as you like. Compliments of all at the Mott and Hoople. A man of your advancing years could use a servant, and I've got plenty. You take this one."

Charley Shallow hung his head, too meek to meet the Skinner's gaze. Creech coughed softly, deep inside himself. He was about to say that he worked alone, always and only alone, and that hunting Scriven was no job for a kid. But something about the boy – maybe his wan, weazen face, or the way his whole thin body leaned away from Ted Swiney, still waiting for a blow – something made him change his mind. Anyway, the publican was right. He wasn't as young as he used to be. He could use some help.

"That's highly 'preciated, Ted," he said.

"There you go, Charley," said Ted Swiney, grabbing Charley by his scuffled hair and shoving him round the end of the bar. "You go with Master Creech. You do as he tells you."

Charley Shallow stumbled across the sawdust floor and looked up into his new master's face. Lean as a skull it looked, and those deep-set eyes were like windows into somewhere where you wouldn't want to go. But he couldn't be any worse than Ted Swiney, could he?

Some of the men at the bar, who had never noticed Charley Shallow before, reached out now to tousle his hair and thump him on his bony shoulders. "Brave kid," they mumbled, and, "Good luck!"

Bagman Creech just turned towards the door again and said, "Fetch your stuff, boy, and follow me." He walked to the doorway and out into the street, waiting there in the sunshine, away from the reek of sick and scent lanterns.

Charley, who had no stuff to fetch, was about to follow him when Ted Swiney suddenly reached across the bar and lifted him up by his coat collar. His amiable act had ended. He growled softly into Charley's ear. "Anything the old cloot finds out, I want to hear about it. You understand?"

Charley nodded eagerly, and Ted dumped him on the floor, grinning round at his customers to show he'd just been having a bit of harmless fun with the boy. His smiling cheeks were red and round as two wax apples. He leaned over the bar to straighten Charley's coat and pat his hair flat. "Now hop along. Don't keep Master Creech waiting."

Charley hopped. He scurried out into the daylight, and Bagman Creech nodded once at him and set off up Ditch Street with Charley trailing after him and the tip of his black staff going *clack, clack, clack* upon the cobbles.

6

THE ARCHAEOLOGIST'S HOUSE

ever was perplexed by Kit Solent's home. It was so rich and so poor, and there were so many things there which didn't seem to have a purpose. The high ceilings were crusted with swags and swirls of plaster which hung down at the corners of the rooms, formed into the shapes of birds and leaves and bunches of fruit and stained with yellowish dribbles where water had seeped through from the floor above. There were heavy, dusty drapes to curtain the boarded windows, and threadbare carpets on the floors. One room was paved with hundreds and hundreds of tiny tiles, and when she looked closer, in the slatted light which tilted through gaps between the window boards, she saw that they were letters from the keyboards of Ancient computers. Fern's and Ruan's toys lay scattered about on the carpets and on the heavy, decorated furniture. There were portraits of Kit Solent and his children on the walls, and in the drawing room hung a painting of a woman with long dark hair and an absurd, frilled collar. A cluster of candles stood on a table beneath it, among plump puddles of dried wax.

"My wife, Katie," said Kit Solent, when he saw Fever look at it. "She died of the blue flu soon after Fern was born."

Fever could not think of anything to say.

"She's our mummy," said Ruan importantly. The children had followed Kit and Fever in from the garden and stood now on either side of Fever to look up at the portrait. Ruan said, "We burn candles for her, so that she'll have some light down in the Sunless Country."

Fever wondered if she should point out that there was no such place as the Sunless Country. She was shocked that the children's father let them believe such superstitious nonsense. And surely all those candles were a fire hazard? But she was a guest in this strange house, and she did not want to offend.

Ruan went over to a small side table on which stood a little brass lantern with a pointed roof pierced by patterns of star-shaped holes. Fever wondered if this was another religious ritual, but then recognized the thing as a scent lantern; she had seen others like it in the windows of shops near the Head. Ruan chose a phial of perfume from a drawer beneath the table, opened the lantern's door and let fall three drops on to a lint pad resting on a turntable inside. While he stoppered the phial and returned it to its drawer, his father took out a box of matches, reached into the lantern and lit the wick beneath the turntable. The rising heat made it start to revolve, wobbling slowly around on its spindle. Ruan closed the door, and smiled shyly at Fever as the smell of the perfume began wafting from the holes in the lantern's roof.

"That was Katie's favourite scent," said Kit Solent, looking kindly at his son as he shook out the match and laid it on a little shell-shaped dish beside the lantern. "*Nocturne in Blue*, by Eldritch Hooter. It's a sentimental old smell from Scriven times. Not like the stuff that gets into the scent parade these days; all those ghastly stinks by Prince Nez and Sniffa Dogg. Are you fond of scents, Fever?"

Fever shook her head. She knew nothing about scents except that they were foolish and unnecessary and Londoners wasted a deal of money on them. Even so, as the smell from the lantern grew stronger, she had to admit that it served to mask the odours of mould and mildew which hung about the old house. It was a subtle scent, and achingly familiar. For some reason it made her think of lawns at twilight, and big trees standing silent in that time at the end of a summer's day when the breeze fades and all is still. The lagoons, calm as mirrors, held the last of the light, and shadows stretched across her lawns. . .

She shook her head to drive away the image, so intense that for a moment it had felt more like a memory than an imagining. *How strange*, she thought. She was not usually an imaginative girl. She hoped that her adventures on Stragglemarket had not disarranged her wits.

Kit Solent, watching her, said, "Are you all right, Miss Crumb?"

"Perfectly," said Fever quickly.

"Tired from your journey, I expect. Come and sit down. . ."

The scent went with them as he led the way through into another room, a large conservatory with glass walls and a glass roof, looking out into a jungly garden behind the house. It was littered with books, papers, cast-off clothes and muddy shoes. A cat was sunning itself on a wooden table among plates which still held the remains of breakfast. "Sit down, sit down!" said Kit Solent amiably, dumping the cat on the floor and placing a kettle on a stove which stood in one corner. "I expect you'll want a cup of tea after your journey?"

Fever shook her head, and tried not to feel shocked. "It is deeply irrational that dried leaves should be transported halfway around the world aboard ships and land barges simply to flavour water. Besides, tea is a stimulant, which leads to nervousness and irrationality."

"Oh," said Kit Solent, slightly surprised. "Coffee, then?"

"Just a mug of boiled water, please."

Fern giggled. Kit frowned at her. Fever watched as patiently as she could while her new employer wiped two mugs and set them ready, then filled a silvery infuser with tea leaves for himself. As politely as she could she said, "Master Solent, a conservatory is not a rational place to keep a stove. The heat will be lost through all this glass, instead of helping to warm the house. . ."

"Ah, but the view of the garden is so nice," said Kit Solent, grinning at her foolishly. The kettle grumbled, coming to the boil. He filled the mugs and brought them to the table, saying as he sat down, "It must feel strange, coming here after the Head. We're not very rational, I'm afraid. But you'll grow used to it."

"Miss?" said Ruan. "What *happened* to your hair?"

Fever felt herself tense, wondering how to speak to these unreasonable small people. "I shave it off," she said. "Hair is unnecessary. It is a vestige of our animal past, and provides a home for lice and fleas and other parasites."

40

The boy nodded, and his eyes crossed as he peered up at his own tufty fringe, hoping to see some parasites there. "Fever," he said. "That's a funny name. . ."

"Ruan!" his father warned.

"Not at all," said Fever. "During the Scriven era there was a fashion for women to name their children after whatever ailments they suffered from while they were pregnant. I have heard of people named 'Backache', 'Diarrhoea'. . ."

"I knew a man once called Craving-For-Pickled-Onions McNee," agreed Kit Solent. Ruan giggled, and Fever looked disapprovingly at his father. Was he joking? She didn't see the purpose of jokes.

The little girl, meanwhile, had decided that Fever was now safe to talk to. She held out the toy dog to her and said, "His name's Noodle Poodle. He's three."

Fever was not sure how to reply to that. She turned to Kit Solent instead. "You have work for me, I believe? Dr Stayling said that you have uncovered an Ancient site, and that you have asked for an Engineer to help you study the artefacts it contains."

Kit Solent took another slurp of tea and then sat back, lifting Fern on to his lap. He looked slightly embarrassed. "I may have misled old Stayling slightly. The site which I've uncovered has not yielded any artefacts yet, but I believe it soon will. Until it does, I'm keen to keep it secret; I should hate one of the big archaeological combines to nip in and steal it from me."

Fever nodded. Archaeology in London was a cut-throat business, so it was rational that Kit Solent would wish to keep his find a secret. She said, "What is this site? An Ancient building?"

"Not exactly. . ." Kit looked wary. "I'll take you there, so you can see for yourself. But first we must wait for Mistress Gloomstove to arrive. Mistress Gloomstove is my housekeeper. She will take the children to school, and then we can go exploring."

Mistress Gloomstove arrived not long afterwards; they heard her open the front door just as Fever was finishing her hot water, and the children went scampering to meet her, Ruan telling her loudly about their new, bald-headed visitor. She emerged into the conservatory a moment later, weighed down by bags and shopping baskets, the children orbiting her like eager moons. A large, red-faced, breathless-looking woman in starched white aprons and an irrational hat; she looked suspiciously at Fever, and muttered, "Charmed, Miss, I'm sure," when Kit Solent introduced them.

"Fever will be staying," Kit told her, taking one of the baskets from her and nodding for Fern to take the other. "Will you make up a bed for her in the room on the top floor? The one that still has its ceiling all intact?"

"Of course, sir," said the woman meekly, with another look at Fever. She carried her bags through into a kitchen which opened off at the conservatory's further end, and the children went after her with the baskets, Fern saying loudly, ". . .and I want all *my* hair cut off, because it gives you *pastarites*. . ."

After that came five minutes of din and confusion while the children found their school things. "They attend Miss Wernicke's School for a few hours every day," explained Kit Solent, through the noise. "It's a jolly place; just a single room above a tech shop on Endemol

Street. Miss Wernicke teaches them reading and writing, drawing, singing and so forth. . ."

Fever tried to look interested. She had not heard of Miss Wernicke's establishment. She did not think that Dr Crumb would approve of it.

And then, at last, the children were gone; the house was quiet; she was alone with Kit Solent.

"There!" he said. "Now, Miss Crumb, I shall lead you to my excavation."

Fever followed him. To her surprise he did not take her back outside into the streets, but deeper into his house.

When she thought about it, it was not altogether strange. Ludgate Hill was not a natural hill, but the collapsed and compacted wreckage of a district of immense towers which had stood in this part of London in the twenty-first century. It was known to be honeycombed with diggers' tunnels, so it seemed quite possible that Kit Solent might have stumbled across some cache of wonders beneath his own floor.

They came to a dead end; a corridor which stopped at a large mahogany bookcase, the shelves crammed with worthless novels. Kit Solent walked straight to it, and reached up to press a stud concealed in a swag of ornamental carving. Behind the rows of books machinery grumbled like a tetchy librarian, and the whole case slid sideways into a deep recess in the wall.

"A secret passage," he said, looking expectantly at Fever, certain she must be excited by such a romantic thing. "Rather a cliché, I'm afraid. . ."

"Ingenious," said Fever, allowing herself to raise one

eyebrow just a quarter of an inch. "Operated by a system of pulleys and counterweights, I presume."

They stepped through the gap where the bookcase had stood and it rumbled back into place behind them while they went down ten steps into a windowless, whitewashed chamber. It had the feel of underground; that damp brown smell. There was one door, a very small one, opposite the foot of the steps. Lanterns were ranged along a stone shelf.

Fever wondered suddenly if she were entirely safe in this strange place, with this strange man. But she could see no way now of turning back. Solent handed her a lantern, and used his tinderbox to light it before lighting another for himself. Then he opened the narrow door.

It revealed a dark opening; a man-high passage shored with timber baulks. Stale air came out at them, and the sound of water trickling somewhere far below, and a wet, raw-dough smell of secret places deep beneath the city.

7

UNDER LONDON

here was a tunnel beneath the house. She squeezed after Kit Solent along the narrow, wood-walled passage which looked as if he had dug it himself, and after a few yards they emerged into a much broader, older working. The prints of his boots were stamped in the damp earth underfoot, as if he had come and gone along it many times.

"Not scared of the dark, I hope?" he asked cheerfully.

"Of course not!" said Fever. What did he take her for? Another of his children? But she walked a little faster, all the same. It was very cold in the tunnel. The light from their two lanterns lit up the low brick roof, the timber buttressing which lined the walls. Before long the timber gave way to rusty metal, ribbed like the throat of a whale and slick with moisture. Not so much a tunnel as an enormous pipe.

"This passageway was dug by Auric Godshawk, I believe," said Kit Solent. "It linked the Barbican with a house he owned outside the city. The Barbican end of it is all filled in now. Katie and I heard rumours about it years ago. Then, two summers back, there was a cave-in in one of the streets higher up the hill. A section of pavement collapsed into what people thought was just an old digger's working. The hole was filled in, but I guessed at once that it was Godshawk's tunnel, and I worked out the likely course it took beneath the city. I took the house in Ludgate Hill Gardens because its cellar was as close as I could get to the line of the old tunnel. Then it was just a question of digging until I hit it. The tunnel itself was in pretty good repair; just a few roof-falls to deal with, a few leaks to plug."

"How far does it go?" asked Fever, peering into the darkness ahead.

"About two miles. I hope you're feeling fit. . ."

Two miles, thought Fever. That would put their destination well outside the southern edge of London, deep in the Brick Marsh.

"Does anyone else know about it?" she asked.

"No," Kit replied. "Godshawk had the labourers who built it put to death, and any of his Scriven friends who knew about it were murdered in the Skinner's Riots. You're honoured, Fever. Apart from me, you're the only person in London who knows this is here."

For some unreasonable reason, that made Fever uneasy. As they walked on she began to feel more and more aware of the darkness that was pressing in behind her. She looked back once or twice and saw it flooding after her along the tunnel, repossessing the places which her passing lamp had briefly lit. She remembered accounts which she had read about the London under London; a midnight maze of tunnels dug by generations of scavenger-archaeologists, linking up in places with far older networks, the winding processional Deepways of the Raffia Hat Culture and even sections of the Ancient underground system. There were tales of blind white savages living in the deepest shafts, the descendants of people who had sought shelter there from the Downsizing and never found their way out.

Fever did not believe such yarns, of course. But each time a stone fell in the dark behind her she started, and walked a little faster, anxious not to be left behind.

After a long while the tunnel started to rise, and they stepped through a doorway into a big underground space. It was brick-built, this place, and flagstone-floored, like the deep cellar of some important old building. There was a toolbox standing in the middle of the floor, along with some spare lanterns and an oil-stained rag or two. In the far wall a big steel door was set. Around the edges, where it met the heavy door frame, bright scars and gouges showed where someone had tried with a variety of tools to prise it open.

"Impressive, eh?" said Kit Solent, holding his lantern up to light Fever's face and watching her reactions as she studied the strange door. "I've been trying for months to get that open. I finally got a drill through it, but it looks as if there's another door behind it and likely a third behind that, and they're all reinforced and made of something that grinds my drill bits flat in no time."

Fever glanced quickly around the underground chamber. It was empty except for Kit's tools and lamps and that great steel portal, like the door to a colossal safe. "What's in there?" she asked.

"I'm not entirely sure," said Solent, with a shrug that made the lantern light shrug too. "But the old villain must have been keeping *something* in there, to make it worth erecting such a door."

Fever looked at him. He was still watching her. "This was Godshawk's?"

Kit Solent nodded. "Look closer. Please."

Fever was surprised to be asked. She put down her lantern and went over to the door. She saw the places where drills had gnawed at the metal. Otherwise, it was in good condition, unrusted and undented, shining coldly in the lamplight. It was not new, but nor was it very old. There were no handles or hinges, so she guessed that it was meant to slide open. On the heavy frame to the right of the door, on the same level as her eyes, she saw a row of ivory studs or buttons, each printed with a single number.

"'Lectronics?" she said to herself. She had heard of 'lectronic locks, but never seen one. They were deep old-tech. No one nowadays knew how to create the minute chips and circuits which controlled such a device, so to make one you needed a piece of Ancient technology which still worked, and such treasures were rare and wildly valuable. . .

She turned, and found Kit Solent watching her with an expression she did not know how to read. It looked almost as if he were afraid of her. "This is a 'lectronic keypad, Master Solent," she said awkwardly. "You would have to know the code. Without it, I don't see any way of opening this door. If you keep drilling at it you might damage it. You might make it impossible to open even *with* the code."

"And what *is* the code, Fever?" Solent asked.

It was an absurd question. But strangely, it did not *feel* absurd. For a second, Fever actually thought about it, as if she might know, while Kit Solent watched her

48

steadily with his eyes shining in the light from the lanterns. Then the moment passed; he laughed and said, "Come, let's get some fresh air, and I'll explain."

There was another door in that underground room, so small and ordinary that Fever had not noticed it. It was made from planks of wood, and its handle was a worn ivory egg which seemed to her peculiarly familiar.

Kit Solent turned the handle and opened the door, and held it for Fever to go through, then followed her up a long wind of brick stairs with Fever's shadow, cast by the light of his lantern, laid up them like a carpet.

"Can you guess what lies behind that door that we have been trying to open, Fever?"

"No, Master Solent."

"It is a workroom. It is Godshawk's room, where he worked on his secret inventions. It was a secret itself, even during the rule of the Scriven."

"Godshawk. . ." said Fever, and for some reason she imagined a low, unwindowed room ribbed with stone buttresses, and brass lamps shaped like lilies hanging from the roof. "I did not know Godshawk was an inventor. I thought he was insane. . ."

"He was a Scriven. They were all insane, judged by our human standards. But they loved tinkering with the old machines, and making new ones. Your Order never approved. The Scriven were too playful; not scientific enough. Perhaps to them engineering was a sort of art. And Auric Godshawk was a very great artist indeed."

They came to the stairs' top, and another door. This one of metal, sealed with immense bolts. They were old and rust-stained but they had been recently oiled, and

Fever slid them open and leaned against the door and was dazzled by daylight. She stepped out into long, wet grass. The door was set into the side of a low, squarish hill, and almost hidden by evergreen shrubs which someone must have planted all around it. Pushing her way out through their wet needles, Fever turned and shielded her eyes against the brightness of the day and looked about, trying to understand where she was. Up on the hill's top stood the stubs and shards of a ruined building. Around the base of the hill the sun shone wanly on the waters of the Brick Marsh, formed during the earthstorms of the previous century when the old river Thames had changed its course and spilled away southward, drowning London's southern boroughs in a wide wilderness of reed beds, wetlands and lagoons.

Kit propped the door ajar and started to climb up the hill's side, and Fever followed.

"Godshawk built his home on this hill," said Solent. "It was called Nonesuch House. Long before the Scriven chose him as their leader, he had his villa here. Even then, when he had his royal apartments in the Barbican, this was always the place he loved the best."

The hill went up in grassy terraces, a green ziggurat. They passed fallen statues flocked with moss, and skirted strange, shallow pools. At the top stood what remained of Nonesuch House. Fire-scorched jagged crusts of wall, a mass of charred timber and smashed rooftiles and tangled weeds filling the spaces between them. A blackbird clattering in a bramble bush. But Fever, as she looked in through the empty windows, saw Scriven nobles in evening robes and their women in gowns like vast, blowsy flowers, crowding the big rooms, spilling out on to the

50

lawns to watch glowing paper lanterns loft into the air. She shut her eyes and forced the vision away. What was wrong with her today?

"It is very unfashionable now to say that the Scriven created anything of worth," said Kit Solent. He picked up a shard of floortile, looked at it, and let it fall. "And it's true that most of the things Godshawk tried to invent were crazy – new colours, flying machines, devices for recording dreams. He spent most of his spare time tinkering with Stalkers' brains. He dissected the last of the Scriven's Stalker warriors in the course of his researches, which is one of the reasons they could not defend themselves when the riots began. But he worked on other things as well, and I believe that one of them still exists, buried in that vault down there beneath us."

Fever turned around, taking in the view and trying to ignore the strange feelings that the place aroused in her. *Feelings mean nothing. Stop feeling and* think. . . A wash of sunlight silvered the far-off roofs of Ludgate Hill. "I am surprised that no one has found this place before," she said.

"The causeway which linked this hill to London has been cut," said Solent. "The way across the lagoons is hazardous. The vault was a secret even in Godshawk's day. No one knows that it is here. And the door in the hillside was completely overgrown; I could never have found it from outside."

"So how did you learn of it?"

"Stories. Rumours."

"It seems irrational to buy a house and dig a tunnel simply because of stories. . ."

"But I found the vault, didn't I?" said Kit Solent triumphantly. "Now it is just a question of getting inside. Of course I could announce my discovery – I know people who would be happy to take the top off this hill and use brute force and gunpowder to get into Godshawk's inner sanctum. But I don't like such methods. I want to try a subtler approach. And I think you can help me, Fever Crumb."

8

SKINNER'S BOY

oo shy to speak, Charley went silently after Bagman Creech through the busy Stragglemarket. He hung back quiet and watchful while the Skinner talked to some of the stallholders there, listening to their accounts of the strange-looking girl who had come their way that morning, and the sedan chair which some believed had smuggled her away.

"It was Bert @kinson's chair," said one man. "I'm surprised at him, aiding a dirty Patchskin like that."

"We have no proof that she was a Scriven," Bagman Creech reminded him. "That is for me to find out. And it was not the chairmen who aided her, but their passenger, the man who hired them." He glanced upward, judging the time by the way the sun hit the tops of the old warehouses above him. "I'll be taking a little refreshment at the Scary Monster. Pass word for this @kinson to come and find me there."

The Scary Monster and Supercreep was a big tavern halfway down Cripplegate. It was set back from the street, with tables arranged outside under a dim see-through canopy made from salvaged plastic. It wasn't the class of place where Charley thought he would be welcome, but Bagman Creech looked back at him and jerked his head to show that Charley should come with him. They sat down together at one of the tables and studied each other in the brownish light that came through the plastic roof.

"You look hungry, boy," said Bagman Creech. "Ted Swiney given you any breakfast today?"

Ted Swiney hadn't, but Charley wasn't going to admit it, in case word of his disloyalty got back to the publican. "I'm all right, Master Creech," he said.

A soft cough rumbled like far-off thunder down behind the Skinner's ribs. He blinked his pale eyes at Charley. "I remember being mostly hungry when I was a boy."

Charley, caught off-balance by the sudden notion that Bagman Creech had once been a boy, said, "That must have been a long time ago, Master Creech."

Bagman Creech started to laugh, and kept on laughing until the laugh turned into a long choking spasm. He retched like a cat with a furball and coughed up a big, blood-veined pearl of phlegm which he spat on to the flagstones under the table. "It was that, Charley," he whispered hoarsely, wiping his eyes with his shirt cuffs. "It was a long, long time ago. And food was scarce for normal folks in them days, for the Scriven ruled this town, and took all the good things for themselves and their cronies. And that's why I was mostly hungry, then."

Meanwhile, the serving girls, looking like white hens in their crisp aprons and bonnets, had been gathering at the tavern door to gawp at their famous guest and whisper about who would take his order. ("*You* go, Gertie," "No, *you* go!") Now their mistress, the Scary Monster's fat landlady, shoved her way between them and hurried to Bagman's side to curtsey and twitter.

"Oh, Master Creech, this is an honour, how can we serve you, good Master Creech?"

"Well, Mistress," said Bagman Creech, "I'll take a mug of your porter, and a stack of pancakes for my young assistant here."

"Oh yes, sir," fluttered the landlady, looking at Charley in a way no one had ever looked at him before, as if he meant something.

"And honey!" called Bagman Creech, as she hurried off. "Plenty of honey." He looked at Charley again, and smiled. His lean old face was so unused to smiling that Charley was afraid it might crack and drop off his bones like plaster off a wall. He had long teeth, scuffed and yellowed as the keys of a pub piano. "Pancakes was my favourite, as I recall," he said. "Honey pancakes 'specially."

"Thank you, Master Creech," said Charley, whose mouth was watering at just the thought of pancakes.

The old man shrugged. "I generally work alone," he said. "But. . . Well, Ted Swiney's a bad man, but there's truth in what he said. Maybe it is time I had a youngster to help me out. How old are you, Charley?"

"Eleven, Master Creech. Maybe twelve."

"Old enough, then. Got a mum and dad, have you?"

Charley shook his head. For as long as he could remember he'd just hung around the Mott and Hoople, sleeping in the cellar or the yard out back, doing odd jobs for Ted Swiney, eating what scraps he could find. Probably his mother had been one of Ted's servant girls, but he didn't remember her. Who his dad was, only the gods of London knew.

Bagman Creech coughed thoughtfully. "And you wouldn't be too brokehearted, I'm guessing, if you never had to go back to Ted Swiney's employ?"

55

"Oh no, Master Creech!"

"'Cos I'm like you, Charley, all alone. And it seems to me that maybe it's time I started training up some young fellow to take over my job, when I'm too old to do it any more. How would you like that, Charley? To sign on as my 'prentice?"

"What, and hunt Patchskins, Master Creech? I don't think I'd be brave enough."

"I didn't think *I'd* be brave enough, Charley, when I was your tender age. But the time comes when you just have to do what's needful."

He stopped, coughing a little and thumping his chest with a fist. The pancakes had arrived. A tower of them, golden brown and crispy at the edges, with honey in a pot to drizzle over them. Charley started rolling them up one by one and cramming them into his mouth.

"Killing a Scriven isn't like killing a human being," Bagman explained. "They aren't made like us and they don't think like us, and if you let them live and breed there might come a time when it'll be *them* hunting *us*, and *our* kind hiding in the dark. You have to remember that. It's difficult sometimes. Take this one we're after. If we corner her, she's going to look almost like an ordinary girl. You've got to be ready for that. She might look pretty. She might say, *'Please don't harm me.'* She might say, *'Please have mercy.'* And you gotto be ready for that. You mustn't let pity creep in. You got to keep telling yourself, it ain't no different to killing rats."

He reached inside his coat with a quick, well-practised movement and suddenly there was a weapon in his hand. A long, ugly thing like the skeleton of a gun, with a big, oil-shiny spring inside it and a ratchet to wind the spring back. More notches than Charley could count had been cut into its worn plastic handgrip.

"This is a spring gun," said Bagman solemnly, holding it so the light slithered over its shining surfaces. "Those Scriven wouldn't let anyone but themselves own firearms, and we couldn't have afforded firearms anyway, but some of us worked in machine shops, so in our off hours we made these, in secret like. A spring gun will chuck a dart hard enough and far enough to cut a Scriven down, and when they were down we'd flay their skins off. Not to stop their spirit coming back, the way the foolish people tell it, but more by way of a trophy, to show the rest of London that Scriven died as easy as the rest of us."

Charley wanted to hold the gun. He wanted to aim it at imaginary Scriven and imagine himself back in those glorious days, slaughtering Patchskins and making London safe for ordinary Londoners again. But just then he became aware of a man edging up to the table. A big man, with the broad shoulders and over-muscled arms of a sedan chair bearer. He was looking sheepishly at Bagman Creech, and turning his cap around and around in his hands.

"Master Creech?" he asked. "I'm Bert @kinson, taxi bearer. I 'eard you want a word."

Bagman Creech took a slurp of porter and nodded as he gulped it down. "That's right, and thank you, Master @kinson. You know what this is about, I take it?"

The chairman twisted his cap in both fists, as if he were wringing it out. "They're saying that girl we took aboard down Stragglemarket was a Patchskin. I'd never have had 'er in my chair if I'd known."

"No one blames you, I'm sure, Bert," said the Skinner. "But what I'd like to know is, who was the fare you were carrying, the one who made you take the girl aboard?"

@kinson looked deeply thoughtful for a moment, and Charley started to fear that he had forgotten. Chairbearers doped themselves with powerful drugs to give themselves the strength to carry their burdens around the city. They weren't famous for quick thinking, or even thinking at all. But @kinson's face brightened and he said, "Picked him up at the tram terminus this morning. A gentleman, by the way 'e talked. 'E had two nippers with him, and 'e told us to follow the girl. Which was easy, on account of her big huge straw hat."

"And when you'd picked the girl up, where did he have you take her?"

"Why, to his home, sir. They all got out together. One of them old crumbledown Patchskin manses up on the 'eights. Ludgate 'ill Gardens, I think."

Creech nodded calmly. "Your help's highly 'preciated, Master @kinson. *Highly* 'preciated."

Charley was halfway down his pancake pile, honey running off his chin. "What now, Master Creech?" he asked stickily, as the chair bearer went away. "Do we go and talk to this bloke?"

Bagman Creech looked at him, or maybe through him, thinking. "Not yet," he said. "We want to go careful, like. If this bald-headed finch *is* Scriven, and he's a-sheltering of her, we don't want to put him on his guard. We'll ask around and work out who he is, and who she is, and what he wants with her. Hopefully it'll turn out poor old Lily Dismas was mistaken. But if not, we'll have to do what's needful."

He drained his mug and stood up, already scanning the passers-by as if one of them might have the answers that he needed. He picked up his stick and leaned on it while he waited for Charley to mop up the last of the honey. "Down these mean streets a man must go. . ." he said, and it sounded to Charley like the start of something, like a quotation or something, but he didn't say any more, just nodded and grunted and set off walking.

THE SCENT LANTERN

o Fever's relief there was no more talk of opening the Godshawk vault that day. She walked with Kit Solent among the mist and ruins on the hilltop, and then went back beneath the hill. Since they had no water with them she accepted a drink of cold, strong tea from Kit's pocket flask, and perhaps that was what made her feel giddy and slightly overexcited on the long walk back to Ludgate Hill.

Towards evening the sun peeped in under the quilt of cloud which had settled over London in the afternoon. It spilled gold light into the overgrown gardens of Kit Solent's house, and into his drawing room, where he sat with his daughter on his knee and his son at his feet and told a most unlikely story full of giants and heroes and light sabres and gingerbread houses. Fever watched him, and wondered how a rational man could waste so much time talking such nonsense to children. She tried not to listen to the story, and when she found that she was listening anyway and that she was quite eager to hear whether the hero rescued his princess, she made herself say goodnight and go upstairs to bed.

It was dangerous, this house. She felt that if she let down her guard she would find herself enjoying all its luxuries and irrational little pleasures, and who knew where that would lead? She had often heard Dr Crumb and the other Engineers talk about Thaniel Wormtimber, who had been a good Engineer himself before he left the Head and let himself be corrupted by the city. She did not want to end up like him; lost in London's maze of unreason.

Her bedroom was on the top floor of the house. It had sloping ceilings and when the wind blew the rafters creaked and the rooftiles rattled. There was a vase of cut flowers on the bedside table, which was irrational, and a potted plant on the window sill, which was not, because Fever knew that it would absorb some of the carbon dioxide she breathed out and help to replenish the air with oxygen. The bed was very large and soft, quite unlike the hard little cot which she was used to. On the wall above it hung another picture of Kit Solent's dead wife, looking much younger than she did in the picture downstairs, in a frame carved in the shapes of hearts and roses.

Fever carefully took the picture down, since it served no purpose. As she was propping it against the wall over in the room's far corner she noticed the little handwritten label on the back, which read, *Miss Katie Unthank*.

That must have been Katie Solent's name before Kit married her, Fever thought, remembering the irrational custom which made women take the name of their husbands. *Unthank*. She knew it at once. The digger whom Dr Crumb had gone to visit on the day he found her had been called Unthank. She thought for a moment, wondering if there was some link, then dismissed it as coincidence. For all she knew, Unthank was a common name.

61

She put on her night things and blew out the candle and lay on the big, soft bed, waiting for sleep. Downstairs she heard the voices of the children as their father tucked them in, and then, after a little more time, the sounds of Kit Solent making his own way to bed. After that there was only silence, the creaking of the old house, the distant noises of the city. But Fever could not sleep. However hard she tried to clear her mind of thoughts, they kept sneaking back in. She had had an eventful day – perhaps the most eventful day of her life – and it was hard to keep from thinking of it.

Katie Solent haunted her thoughts, too. That name, Unthank, could not help but recall to her the story that Dr Crumb used to tell her when she was little. Was it possible that Katie had had a child before she married Kit? One little girl whom she had abandoned in a basket on the marshes, near her father's dig? Was that why Kit had asked Fever into his house? Because he had found out somehow that she was Katie's daughter? And was *he* her father?

She had never wondered before about who her real parents were. Dr Crumb had told her when she was small that it did not matter, and she believed him. But remembering how cosy little Fern had looked upon her father's lap, she found herself wishing very much that she had grown up with a father like him, and a mother too.

"Don't be ridiculous," she told herself, sitting up in bed. She must have been lying there awake for hours. Wanting to clear her head, she got up and lit her candle and padded downstairs to find a glass of water. A faint, haunting musk hung in the air, making her wonder if Kit had left the scent lantern alight when he went up to bed, but when she looked into the drawing room the lantern was open and unlit. The portrait of Katie Solent smiled down at her from the wall, and she held up the candle for a while and stood there looking at the picture, and at her own reflection in the glass, trying to make out a resemblance. But there was none, and she could not really believe that she was Mistress Solent's daughter. In her memory, just out of reach, was the face of a quite different woman that matched her own much better. Who did she remind herself of?

Unsettled, she went to the kitchen for her drink and then hurried quietly back upstairs. On the first landing she noticed a door standing open. It had been shut earlier but Kit Solent must have been in there before he turned in. Fever's curiosity overcame her. She pushed the door wider, and stepped through into a library.

It was nothing like as large as the Order's library at Godshawk's Head, and many of the volumes looked worthless – novels and poems and fantasy quartets, no good for anything but pulping – yet it was impressive, all the same. Bookcases alternated with windows all the way round the room, and through the windows the moon shone, making silver-grey shapes of light on the floorboards. On a table in the centre, a book lay open beside a lit scent lantern, the source of that ghostly smell which still flavoured the air.

Fever breathed deeply, intrigued by the musty odour. It was the same scent that Ruan had put on downstairs, or one very like it. And it so *nearly* reminded Fever of something. She closed her eyes, and the scent seeded her mind with pleasant memories. Dew-wet evening lawns. Lilies in bloom on geometric pools. Fire balloons lofting into a lilac sky. . .

She shook her head, almost angry at herself. Those were not memories! The image was a fantasy, or a half-remembered dream, neither of which had any place in a well-ordered mind.

Feeling giddy, she leaned on the table, and looked down at the open book. It was a large, old-fashioned volume, with circular pages bound between two discs of leather in the Scriven style. On the open page was a drawing, or perhaps a diagram. Fever couldn't make it out at first. She set down her candle and placed her hands on the table on either side of the book and looked down at the page, and suddenly she was falling into the picture.

What was it? What did it show? She could not be sure. Looping lines of smudged pencil swept across the page, bisecting three big interlocking rings, and inside those rings were smaller rings, and other forms: small crosses, squares, shapes that reminded her of cogs and pistons. She wished that Dr Crumb were there with her. Together, she was sure, they would have been able to make sense of it. But even without him she started to understand that some of those pencil marks meant patterns of force, and she could see how some of those shapes might move inside each other, and around each other. And that egg-shaped thing marked *(d)* might act as a kind of regulator on the movement of the other pieces. . .

It was an engine, she realized, and with that realization came a blazing star of pain, somewhere at the back of her head.

She cried out, and the diagram seemed to jump up at her out of the creamy paper and close around her like a net. In the middle of it a red flower appeared, and she straightened up, looking in horror at the splash of blood which had fallen on the drawing.

Cupping one hand under her streaming nose she pulled out her handkerchief and set one corner of it to the bright little splat of blood. The white fabric soaked up most of it, and Fever dabbed carefully at the rest, but she could not get rid of the brown stain which it had left, like an extra cog wheel, in the heart of the diagram.

She was still trying when she heard footfalls behind her, and turned guiltily to find Kit Solent standing in the doorway, wearing a quilted nightgown, his long hair loose.

"Fever! You poor thing! Whatever's happened?"

"It's a nosebleed," said Fever. "I'm sorry, I've never had one before. I got blood on the book. . ."

Kit Solent strode over to her. He didn't seem to care about the book. He took her handkerchief from her and gave her his own, which seemed as big as a bedsheet, clean and fresh-smelling. "Sit down," he advised, guiding her to a chair. "Tip your head back. Ruan gets these sometimes. It is never as bad as it looks. Yes, the worst is over. I must have left the scent lantern burning when I went to bed. Foolish of me. Perhaps that's what made you feel faint. These old Scriven smells are not to everyone's taste."

The nosebleed seemed to have stopped. She said, "I'm sorry about the book. . ."

"Oh, don't worry about the book," said Kit, kneeling beside her. "I picked it up for a few quidd from a bookstall at Rag Fair, years ago. It's just one of Godshawk's old notebooks. Dozens of them were looted from the Barbican after the riots."

Fever nodded. "Dr Isbister has some at the Order's library."

"I bought it because it looked interesting. I don't really understand what it's about. Do those old drawings mean anything to you?"

He asked it casually, but Fever sensed a kind of eagerness under the words. Had he left the book out in the hope that she would come in and see it? She lowered her head cautiously, and looked at him, but she could see nothing in his face except kindness and honest concern for her.

Then she noticed something else. Behind him, the rugs of moonlight which had lain on the floor beneath each window were gone. Outside, above the rooftops, the sky was growing pale.

"What is the time?" she asked.

"Almost sunrise," said Kit Solent. "There's hardly any point going back to bed. Shall I sort out some breakfast?"

"But that can't be. . ." Fever went to the closest window and looked out. It was true. While she had sat staring at that diagram, the whole night had passed. Behind the Barbican, the sun was coming up.

10

SUMMERTOWN

it Solent did not take Fever back to Godshawk's secret vault that day. He had been troubled by her confusion when he stood her before the locked door the day before, and also by the events of the night. He had hoped that the scent lantern and the book would have some effect, but the blood and the girl's obvious distress had upset him. He was a kindly man, and for all her solemn, Engineerish ways Fever seemed a child to him, not so very much different from Fern or Ruan. It felt horrible to see her frightened, and to know that he was to blame. He thought a day of rest was in order before he tried again.

"No school today," he announced over breakfast that morning. "And no work neither. We'll go to Summertown instead!"

"Summertown!" shouted Fern and Ruan happily.

"Summertown?" said Fever, far from certain. She knew what it was; a great triangle of waste ground up in Clerkenwell where, every summer, the wandering land barges stopped to dazzle the citizens of London with sideshows and trade goods. She had often watched the barges rumbling along the Westerway and the Great South Road, and Dr Crumb had told her much about the engines that powered them, but as for Summertown itself. . .

"Is it not a rather irrational place?" she asked.

67

"If fun is irrational," said Kit Solent, through a mouthful of toast. "If colour and excitement and good things from far places are irrational, then yes. But I think you'll find it educational, Fever, and I'm sure the children will. Come; you can explain to us how all the engines work."

"Yes, sir," said Fever, lowering her head.

"You're still worried about what happened yesterday," said Kit kindly. "I'm not surprised. But Summertown is not the Stragglemarket, and you'll be with us, not on your own. Anyway, everyone will have forgotten you by now."

But Fever was not sure about that. As she left the house an hour later (for it took an extraordinarily long time for Kit Solent and his children to get ready) she noticed two figures standing on the opposite pavement. A ragged boy, and an old man in a long black coat and a black bowler hat. They did not do anything; they did not try to accost her; indeed, they drew back shyly into the shadows of an alley as Kit Solent let her out through the gates, and she knew that he had not seen them, but she could sense their eyes on her as she followed him along the street. It made her uneasy, and she did not know why.

From the far side of the street, Charley Shallow watched the girl go by. She strode along mannishly at the gentleman's side, with her hat in her hand and her bald head bared for all to see. She looked human enough to him, and pretty, almost. He glanced at Bagman, hoping for some clue as to how he should react.

"I can't see no speckles on her, Master Creech. . ."

"No, boy."

"So does that mean she's a human being after all?" Charley tried not to sound disappointed. He was half relieved that Bagman wouldn't have to kill the girl, but at the same time he found himself thinking that if Bagman had no prey to hunt he might not need a 'prentice any more.

"I'm not sure," said Bagman. "There were some Scriven who didn't have many markings. A few had no markings on their face at all. Blanks, we called 'em. I remember cornering a female like that once, and she held a baby that might have passed for human."

Charley waited for him to say more, but the old man fell silent. He started to realize what a terrible responsibility it was to be a Skinner.

Bagman had turned away, watching as the man and the children and the girl went on up the street, climbing towards Cripplegate. When they were out of sight he shook his head and gave a few soft, doubtful coughs. "Strangest thing," he said quietly, perhaps to himself. "Always before I could tell at a glance. Even if I couldn't see no markings I could always tell a Scriven by the way they held themselves, the way they moved. But this one. . . I ain't sure."

"So what do we do, Master Creech?"

"We follows her, boy, and we gets a closer look."

It was startling to come out of the quiet streets into the bustle of Cripplegate. Fever had expected Kit Solent to turn uphill towards the wind-tram terminus, but instead he simply stepped out into the mud of the roadway and raised one hand, and at once a sedan chair swerved towards him out of the passing scrum of drays, chairs and pedestrians.

He pulled the door open before it had even stopped, the children bundled inside, and as Fever scrambled after them she heard him call out to the bearers, "Summertown!"

The men did not reply; simply started trotting, turning off Cripplegate as soon as they could and cutting westward through the complicated little streets of Pimlicker and Chel's See. Several times, through gaps between the buildings, Fever caught a glimpse of Godshawk's Head, picked out from the clutter of rooftops and chimneys further north by stray beams of sunlight.

"Would you like to stop in at home on the way?" asked Kit Solent, noticing how she craned her head to keep it in sight.

"Godshawk's Head is not on the way to Clerkenwell."

"We could make a detour. I thought you might want to look in on Dr Crumb, and let him know that you are all right."

Fever wanted nothing more, but from across the city Godshawk's steel face seemed to be staring sternly at her, reminding her that she must be rational and not let down her Order. She said, "There would be no purpose in such a visit. I'm sure Dr Crumb knows that you would contact the Order if there were any problem."

Kit Solent started to say something, then changed his mind and sat in silence, smiling to himself, watching Fever strain for another glimpse of home. He liked her; her primness and her bravery. It was a shame, he thought, that those dry old tech-botherers at the Head had never let her have a proper childhood.

He did not think to look behind him, through the small window in the rear wall of the chair. If he had, he might have seen another taxi-chair following not far behind.

Ruan couldn't believe that Fever had never been to Summertown. "What, never?" he kept asking her, as if there was a chance that she had been but had forgotten – as if anyone could forget Summertown. To Ruan there was simply nothing in the world that mattered more than the land barges. Each Maytime, as the snows of winter melted, he would start to listen for the grumble of their engines on the Great South Road. He would lie in his bed in the quiet of early morning and strain his ears to catch that first distant whisper. Sometimes when a convoy had been sighted Daddy would take him down to 'Bankmentside and they would stand together and watch the great pachydermous vehicles passing, big as houses, big as castles, their tracks ingrained with the mud of Europe and their upperworks dusted by the sands of far-off Asia. There were big lumbering cargo hoys like herds of sauropods, but Ruan's favourites were the gaudy, speedy tinker barges and travelling fairs. Half the size of the sluggish hoys and twice as fast, they were painted in a million lurid shades, decked out with flags and chrome and mirrors and hung each night with strings of saffron lanterns. Dizzy op-art spirals whirled on their wheel hubs, and their exhaust stacks were striped like gypsies' stockings. And along their sides, in cut-out letters as high as house fronts, they wore their names. *Ma Gumbo's Travellin' Raree Show; The Dark Lantern; The Paradise Circus; A Dream of Fair Women.*

He did his best to explain all this to Fever while the

chair joggled them through the rookeries of Lemon Heel. He wasn't sure that she understood. She was a strange person, and he couldn't help wondering if she was a bit stupid, even though Daddy had told him she was clever. But she was very pretty – he thought she was the prettiest person he had ever seen – so he didn't want to think that she was stupid. Perhaps she was just shy, and that was why she didn't seem interested when he told her about the barge with the big dragon's head at the front, or the magician who made rabbits and ribbons appear out of his hat.

They crossed the Westerway and the chair slowed as it joined the flocks of chairs and people on foot all making for Summertown. Even Fever began to look interested as the breeze blew fairground noises in through the open windows – chingling music and bellowing, foghorn voices. She remembered Dr Crumb telling her how some of the land barges travelled all the way to Vishnoostan and Kerala. Even Zagwa, the crazy Christian empire which had conquered most of Africa and southern Europe and banned all technology there, still permitted land barges to visit the free-trade zones along its borders. . .

By the time they stepped out of the chair on to litter-strewn grass between the big barrel-shaped wheels and clay-clagged tracks of the barges, Fever was as wide-eyed as the children. Kit Solent paid the bearers, and took Fern's hand, while Ruan ran ahead, shouting back to draw Fever's attention to his favourite barges.

There was a boy who strode about on stilts, and a man who was juggling with shining knives ("You must not try that at home, Fern," Fever warned the little girl,

72

remembering her role as the rational member of their party.) There was a man who was busy sawing a woman in half. ("*Or* that," she added. "I expect it is all done with mirrors.") A barker on the deck of a barge shouted at them through a big tin trumpet, inviting them to climb the boarding plank and see for themselves the lizard girl and the three-headed goat. "Mutations, no doubt," said Fever, looking at the scary pictures painted on the barge's stern. "It would be unkind to go and stare at them." Ruan and Fern sighted a stall selling candyfloss, and their father bought three sticks. "It has no nutritional value whatsoever," said Fever, looking doubtfully at the pink cloud he handed her. She stretched her head forward, wary of getting the stuff on her coat. It tasted as it looked; scratchy and sticky and very pink. Not nice, not exactly, but fun.

Fern thrust Noodle Poodle into her father's hand and ran off after Ruan, both children gripping their candyfloss sticks like pink banners as they hurried to watch a fire-eater performing. Fever half wanted to go with them, but she told herself it was not dignified for an Engineer to gawp at vulgar entertainments. While Kit Solent strolled after the children, she hung behind, eating her candyfloss with awkward, bird-like movements of her head and an expression which was meant to signal to anyone watching her that she was not *enjoying* it, just tasting it in a spirit of scientific enquiry. And as she ate, she stopped to stare at the strange events on the open stage at the rear of a barge called *Persimmon's Ambulatory Lyceum*, where actors dressed in cardboard armour were talking too loudly to each other in front of a painted landscape. *It is all make-believe*, Fever thought. *The words, the clothes, the things – that's not a real sword, and I'm sure that man's beard is made of wool. Even the people are pretending to be other people. Why would anyone waste their time watching such stuff?* Yet people were; quite a crowd had gathered before the stage, and a pretty girl who seemed not to be needed in the play just then was strolling amongst them with a basket, into which they threw their offerings.

It was like a symbol for all the foolishness of the world outside the Head, and Fever was still staring at it when a hand came down on her shoulder from behind. It gripped her firmly, though not painfully, and turned her. She dropped the candyfloss and wiped pink stickiness from her mouth on the back of her hand. A gaunt white face stared down at her. Hard old eyes, pale as glass in the shadow of a tattered hat brim. A rough voice that said, "'Scuse me, Miss, I needs a word. . ." But it didn't seem to be a word the stranger wanted so much as a long, hard *look*. His pale eyes roved over Fever's face as if he were reading her.

He frowned. "What *are* you?" he muttered.

Fever gave a violent shrug, and the old man's hand fell from her shoulder. She turned away from him, almost knocking over the shabby boy who seemed to have sprung up behind her like a mushroom out of the littered grass. She scanned the crowds between the barges, and saw the fire-eater's burning breath flare up like a beacon, guiding her to where Kit Solent was. Hurrying towards him, she looked back and saw the old man and the boy standing watching her. They were the same pair who had been watching the house that

74

morning, she was sure.

"All right, Fever?" asked Kit, when she writhed through between the other spectators and arrived beside him.

She nodded, wiping at her mouth again. She did not want him to think that she could not be left alone for thirty seconds without trouble finding her. The old man had mistaken her for someone else, that was all. That was the rational explanation. She calmed herself, and looked sceptically at the fire-eater in his roped-off ring.

"I do not believe that he is really *eating* that at all. . ."

11

MASTER WORMTIMBER

hat afternoon, at the hour when the low sun shone flickering through the wheels of wind trams as they rumbled above the streets, Bagman Creech and Charley went down Cripplegate and turned right along 'Bankmentside. A wind huffed at them off the Brick Marsh, but it could not quite blow away the acrid smell of the big vats where scraps of plastic dug up from the fields around the city were being melted down and remoulded. They crossed one and then another of the slimy timber bridges which spanned the streams flowing into the marsh. People coming the other way stood aside for the Skinner, bobbing bows and curtseys, and he nodded back and rested one hand on Charley's shoulder, letting the town know the boy was with him.

Charley was getting used to his new life by then. He liked the way people called out to wish Bagman luck, and parents pointed him out to their children, and the children stared round-eyed at the old man stalking by, and stared at Charley too, because although he was no bigger or better dressed than most of them he was lit up by some of the Skinner's glory.

At last Bagman stopped at a tall, shabby warehouse with a painted sign above the door. *"Wormtimber's Historick Curios,"* he read out, for Charley's benefit.

"We'll have to teach you to read, son, if you're to be a Skinner's boy."

Inside the place was more like a cave than a shop. Stacked with old car parts and barrels of machine scraps, Ancient technology heaped up against the walls and dangling from the rafters. The owner popped out of a secret lair among the clutter and blinked at them. "Bagman. . ."

Charley knew the man, of course. Knew him by sight, at least, for Thaniel Wormtimber was one of Ted Swiney's cronies, and could be found most evenings propping up the Mott and Hoople's bar. He was small and walnut brown and dirty and he had large, watchful, yellow eyes.

"Charley," the Skinner said, "this here is Master Wormtimber. He's the New Council's Master of Devices, but I believe he won't be above lending us a helping hand."

"*Always* happy to help the Skinners' Guilds, Master Creech," replied Wormtimber, rubbing his little mittened hands over and over each other, like a cat washing its paws. His head twitched forward and those weaselish eyes looked hungrily at Charley. "Oh, *always* happy, Master Creech. Ted Swiney at the Mott and Hoople told me you were hunting again, but I didn't dare imagine that *I* might be of any use."

"You keep an eye on the digs around town, I believe? You keep the Council abreast of who's digging where and what they're finding?"

"Oh yes, indeed, Master Creech, that is one of my duties."

"What do you know about an archaeologist called Solent?"

77

Wormtimber blinked cautiously. "Kit Solent? He's nothing much. He married old Chigley Unthank's daughter. The daughter's dead too now, I believe. Solent's never found anything of much note. What makes him Skinner's business, Master Creech?"

Creech said nothing for a moment. Charley sensed that the old man was uneasy about sharing what he'd found with the Master of Devices. But he coughed, and then said, "Solent's hired a new Engineer. A girl."

Wormtimber nodded. "Crumb's foundling. I've heard of her."

"What do you mean, foundling?"

"Why, I mean what I say, Master Creech; that she was found. In a basket, on the Brick Marsh somewhere. Fever Crumb. . ." He stopped, and his eyes seemed to light with a pale fire. "I say, Master Creech – you don't suspect she's one of *them*?"

"It ain't proven neither way," said Creech. "I've had a look at her, but I can't be certain. I need to get in and check her over without *actually* getting in and checking her over, if you take my meaning. I heard you're the man to come to for the old machines."

"Oh yes, Master Creech, sir," said Wormtimber, nodding, rubbing, smiling so much that his eyes folded themselves away into deep creases. "I do have some *most* interesting devices at my disposal. Say what you will about the Patchskins, they left behind some lovely toys. Old-tech weapons, sir, and spyware. As Master of Devices it's my task to maintain such things for the New Council, but between ourselves, the post pays poorly, and so to make ends meet I do sometimes rent out or even sell the more useful pieces. Though of course I'd

78

not dream to expect a rental fee from you, Master Creech. I'm always pleased to help the Skinners. So this girl, you say, this girl who may be, or may *not* be. . .? We need a close look at her, do we? A sneaky peek, while she's asleep?" He gave a little slithery giggle. "Oh, yes, I think that can be done. Come back tonight, when it grows dark, and we shall see what we shall see. . ."

Some miles outside the inhabited city, where the sparse brown grasses blew on hummocks of brick and tarmac which had once been streets, the Orbital Moatway marked the borders of Greater London. An Ancient feature, built up and fortified in Scriven times, it curved through the heaths and fields like a thick green snake; a deep dyke and an embankment topped with a wall of salvage stone and a timber palisade. A stone guard tower stood sentry every mile, looking south towards the Channel Ports, east to the Minarchies of Upnor and Doggerland on the salt plains where the North Sea used to roll, west to the marches of Redding, and north towards – well, nothing much. North of the Moatway there were only more hummocks, more dun grass, the huts and fields of an occasional small settlement and sometimes, in clear weather, on the edge of sight, the blunt dirty snouts of far-off glaciers squatting in the haze that hung forever above the ice sheet.

Until that evening. That evening there was something new. In the afternoon some of the Moatway lookouts had noticed that a part of the northern sky was striped with dozens of grey lines which rose straight up and spread into a stain, like the bruise of smoke which might hang above a dense concentration of chimneys. As the sun went down and the shadows deepened they began to see lights beneath the smoke; dozens of lights, yellow and white like distant lighted windows, flickering red like far-off furnaces. It was as if a mirage of the city were forming itself out there; a mirror-London conjured from the tawny heaths and cold melt-water lakes.

The watchmen whose job it was to guard the Moatway against foreigners gathered on the palisades. They stood in worried clumps on the battlements of the mile castles, fingering the hafts of their pikes, the stocks of their clumsy muskets. Officers trained telescopes on the distant smoke. "Things are moving. . . Throwing up a lot of dust, but. . . Big things. . . Land barges. . . There's a whole city on the move out there!"

A moving city. That's how things were up in the wild and fridgy marches of the north. Up there, the tribes who had been set wandering by the plagues and firestorms of the Downsizing had never settled down again, the way sensible people had in warmer climates. They'd just kept going, century after century, millennium after millennium. They'd started out on foot, tramping after their herds. Then they had built wagons, and the wagons had become motorized, and the motors had grown more powerful, and the wagons had grown larger, turning into barges, land hoys, traction castles. And still they kept moving, too in love with their wandering life to ever settle now. And now, for the first time since the Scriven came, some of them had moved within sight of the borders of London.

The men on the Moatway could only look and wonder, taking turns with the most powerful telescopes.

Meanwhile, out of the scrublands and the scattered northern digger villages, the first grey-brown bundled processions of refugees were streaming, battering at the Moatway's gates to be let through. Women carrying children, children carrying babies. An old man wearing a cheap chest of drawers on his back like a rucksack. "Let us in!" Their thin, chilly voices scratched at the air like the voices of sheep. "Let us through! They are coming! The Movement are coming!"

12

THE FOLDABLE ASSASSIN

arkness settled over Ludgate Hill. The children went to bed, tired and contented. Ruan made a space on his bedside table for the toy land barge that his father had bought him at the fair, and fell asleep gazing at it. Fern snuggled against Noodle Poodle's blue fur and dreamed small, happy dreams. Upstairs, Fever recited logarithms to herself until she had cleared her head of all the dizzy memories of Summertown before she went to bed. After a little while longer Kit Solent turned in too. The house lay quiet for a long time. A clock ticked in the hallway, and another in the drawing room. A brown beetle hurried across the living room floor. Wands of moonlight reached slowly through the silent rooms.

Just before midnight, with a papery rasp, something was pushed through the letter flap of the street door and fell with a soft thump on the mat. It lay there for a silent while among the children's kicked-off shoes; a dim block of white in the gloom of the hall, like a tightly folded newspaper.

Then, if you had been watching, you might have seen a shy, sly movement. A corner curled. It settled again, cautious, as if waiting to make sure no one had noticed. Then, very swiftly, with quick crinkling, crisping noises that were almost too faint to hear, the paper boy unfolded itself and stood upright, balancing on the edges of its flat white feet. Its blank face swung to and fro, scanning the emptiness of the hall.

Outside, Charley Shallow hurried away from the house, afraid that some passer-by would have spotted him cramming the folded paper through Solent's door. But no one challenged him. He ran across the empty street, ducked into an alleyway, and pounded on the door of a big sedan chair that waited there, its four bearers dozing between the shafts. After a moment the door opened and he was pulled inside.

One of the chair's seats was taken up by a strange machine; all copper wire and twisty brass tubes and complicated little lead boxes, with a tiny screen glowing in the middle of it all. Thaniel Wormtimber had clipped a magnifying lens in front of the screen, and he sat on the opposite seat, his feet working the pedals which powered the contraption, his hands gripping a set of brass levers, his eyes peering fiercely at the flickering picture. Beside him, statue still, sat Bagman Creech.

"We're in," said Wormtimber, in an excited sort of whisper which kept threatening to turn into a giggle. "That's Solent's hallway."

"It's hard to see much," said Bagman, unimpressed. "All blurs and splodges. Can't you make it clearer?"

"Make it clearer?" snapped Wormtimber. "This is old, old technology, from the Black Centuries, Master Creech. We're lucky it works at all. If anyone knew how to improve it, they'd have done so. Paper boys' eyes sense heat, not light. Those dark grey bits are cold, the light grey are warmer. Warmest of all will be living things, like this girl of yours. Let's see if we can find

83

her. . ." He pedalled a little harder, and the tiny picture flickered brighter, like a grey moth trapped behind the magnifying lens.

The paper boy went rustling across the hall and started upstairs. It walked jerkily, leaning forward like a man walking into a gale. As it passed the landing windows moonlight shone through it. If you'd been watching you might have seen the wafer mechanisms pressed between its paper layers; the wires of its bones, thin as horse hairs; the shadows of its electric eyes in the blank page of its face. It moved along the landing to a bedroom, hesitated a moment, then folded itself to the floor and posted itself under the door like a note.

In the chair outside, Bagman Creech leaned closer to the tiny screen, and made out the fuzzy white shapes of the Solent children sleeping in their beds.

"That's not her. Move on."

The paper boy went crisping and crinkling on its way. It climbed more stairs, and crept towards the door at the end of the landing. It spilled through the crack beneath it like a paper flood.

Fever was sleeping on her back, as always, her hands by her sides. The paper boy circled the bed like her own bleached shadow, sprung to life. It studied the neat piles of her clothes, and the picture she had taken down, propped up carefully against the wall. It came close to the bed and leaned over her, its flat, dead face above her sleeping one. It raised one hand and flexed it, with a sound like someone smoothing out a screwn-up

84

banknote. It stretched its forefinger and with a ripping sound no louder than Fever's breathing, a curved needle tore out through the paper. It was a sharp little hypodermic claw, and it glinted in the moonlight spilling round the edges of the curtain.

Out in the sedan chair Wormtimber moistened his lips with the tip of his pink tongue and wiped the palms of his hands against his robes. He was giggling softly, and when he giggled he actually said *Tee hee hee*. . . "A little needle, Bagman. That's how the Patchskins used paper boys to kill off their enemies and rivals. Foldaway assassins. A fingertip-needle connected to a sac of venom. . . Now, just a jab in her pretty neck. . . Just a little prick. . . Tee hee hee!"

"You'll respect that girl, Wormtimber. For all we know she's as human as you or I. I ain't ever killed a human being yet and I don't mean to start now."

"I know, Master Creech, I know. You don't want her dead; you just want *proof*. . ."

Fever frowned and stirred as the needle pierced her skin. After a moment the paper boy stepped back. There was a bead of blood on Fever's neck. She turned on her side, murmuring something. She opened her eyes, and half lifted her head from the pillow, but the paper boy turned sideways on to her, and stood motionless, almost invisible.

When she had settled it went back across the room and slid itself out under the door again. It walked back down the stairs. It stopped on the front doormat and started to crumple. It screwed itself up small and bundled itself out through the letter flap. Outside, it went bounding and tumbling away along the street, and if you'd been watching then you might have thought it just a bit of wind-blown litter, except that there was no wind, and it moved too purposefully, rounding the corner and rustling into an alley, where it fetched up against the door of Wormtimber's sedan chair.

Charley scrambled out, picked up the bundle of dirty paper and passed it inside. Then he set about waking the drowsing bearers.

Inside the chair, Wormtimber uncrumpled the paper boy. He found its hand and lifted it into the light of the now blank screen. There was a tiny, rust-brown smudge on the forefinger. Beneath the paper a small sac bulged, filled with the blood of Fever Crumb.

13

MORNING AFTER THE NIGHT BEFORE

n her dreams that night Fever returned to Nonesuch House. Not by the tunnel this time, but across Godshawk's old causeway and up a gravelled path to where the fine, unruined house stood waiting for her. There were lights in the windows, music and perfume on the evening air, and the lamps of London twinkling across the marshes in the twilight. She walked on the lawns, watching servants light big paper float lanterns and set them free to rise into the sky, their glow reflecting in the ponds. The sedan chairs of the party guests stood on the drive like wardrobes lined up at an outdoor furniture sale. Doctor Crumb was there, and Fever felt proud that she would be able to show him her house, and her vault beneath it, filled with wonders. . .

She woke with a gasp, her mouth still full of the taste of the wine which she had been drinking in her dream. The scent of some pricey, bespoke perfume hung in her memory like fog. Her neck hurt, and when she touched the place she felt a tender, raised lump. *Cimex lectularius*, she thought. It was hardly surprising that an irrational old house like Kit Solent's should be infested by the common bedbug.

She threw off the covers and went down to the bathroom to dash water at her face. It was light outside. She looked in the mirror and felt slightly disappointed to see her own bald, big-eyed self staring out at her, as if she had been expecting someone better. A peach-fuzz of sandy down furred her scalp. She reached for her razor, then changed her mind. Why should she not have hair? She was not in Godshawk's Head any more.

Downstairs, to the clatter and chatter of the conservatory. The smells of coffee, fresh-baked bread, fried bacon, fishy dishes Fever didn't know the names of. The children falling quiet as she walked in, still shy of her, although she did her best to smile encouragingly at them. Kit Solent was reading the *London Alarmist*, holding it up in front of him with one hand while he buttered toast with the other.

"Sleep well, Miss Crumb?" he asked.

"Yes," said Fever, and then, seeing no cause to lie, "No. I had irrational dreams. About Nonesuch House."

"You didn't happen to dream the code to get us through that door, I suppose?" He waved the newspaper at her as he put it down. "We must find our way into Godshawk's treasure chest soon, I think. It looks as if London may have visitors before long."

"You mean the Movement?" asked Fever, taking her place at the table.

"Are the nomads coming here?" asked Fern, looking half excited and half scared. "Is there going to be fighting?"

"No, no, no, nothing like that," Kit Solent said hurriedly. "The Movement's hoys and wagons have been sighted north of the Moatway, that's all. Even Gilpin Wheen has finally admitted that it's time to do something. The Trained Bands are mustering."

"The Movement have a traction castle," announced Ruan. "They have armies of Stalkers too. They're hairy savages, and they think only of fighting and conquering!"

"That's not really true, Ru," his father said patiently. "Northerners aren't so bad. In many ways they're more civilized than a lot of people in London. But if they do plan to capture the city, I'd like to have the contents of Godshawk's vault in my possession by the time they arrive. They'd pay me well for it."

"How do you know?" asked Fever.

"Why do you think they're coming here? They've never shown any interest in this place before."

"You think they've learned of the vault somehow? But you said no one knew of it. . ."

"I said no other *human being* knew of it," Kit corrected her. "There were always stories that a few Scriven had escaped and sought refuge with the nomads in the north. And what if one of them knew something about Godshawk and his secrets? If you feel up to it, I'd like to take you back through the tunnel."

"But I can't open the door, Master Solent!" Fever couldn't understand why he had such faith in her. "I can't just pull the right combination of numbers out of thin air. . ."

Kit reached out and touched her, gripping her shoulder with a firm, fatherly hand. "Not out of thin air, Fever. Out of that remarkable brain of yours. You can do it. I'm sure you can."

For the second morning running, Charley Shallow came awake to the noise of Bagman Creech's helpless, chesty coughing. He lay for a moment wondering where he was, letting the memories of the day before assemble themselves around him in the dark.

He was lying in the spare room of Creech's lodgings on Ketch Causeway, on a bed he had made for himself out of old sacks and his bundled-up coat. Brown paper was pasted on the windows to keep the room shady, but that wasn't for Charley's benefit; it was to protect all the books. The books rose all around him, crammed on to shelves which covered every wall. Not just books, but rolled-up documents and sheafs of yellowed paper done up with hairy string. All of them were about the Scriven. Creech called them his archive.

Charley thought back to the night before. That paper boy folded up and twitching in his hands as he tiptoed up to Solent's house. Later, back at Wormtimber's place, he had watched as the former Engineer carefully snipped open the paper boy's finger and took out a little rubber sac. He had let two ruby droplets fall from it on to a glass slide, and then carried it to another of his weird old machines. This one he called a 'Lectric Microscope. It was powered by a treadmill, and since Wormtimber's slaves and servants were all in bed and this was Skinner's business, it was Charley's job to walk the treadmill while the two old men peered into the machine's viewing window.

"Is that Scriven blood?" Wormtimber had asked.

"I don't know." Bagman Creech sounded unsure of himself, the same way he had at Summertown when he was staring at the Crumb girl's face.

"Well, it ain't human, is it?" insisted Wormtimber.

"There's *something* wrong with it. . . . What are all them little whirligig things?"

"I don't know, Master Wormtimber. A disease, perhaps. Maybe the girl's sick and that's what makes her look not quite right. . ."

"No one's *this* sick, Master Creech!" insisted Wormtimber, bearing his sharp little dog teeth. "When I view human blood through this device, or that of any decent animal, I see little red spots; corpuscles and such. Not this."

They moved away, still talking, and Charley stepped off the treadmill. In the second or so while the microscope still had power he put his face to the viewing window and gazed deep into the ocean of Fever Crumb's blood. Strange things were swimming there all right. They left their after-image on his eyes long after the light of the screen had died. Little square shapes, dithering this way and that as if surprised to find themselves no longer in Fever's veins, each one propelled by a tiny, twirling tail.

He kicked his way out from under the sacks, pulled on his coat and crept down a passage walled with stacked bundles of old newspapers to Bagman's room. That room was book-lined too; there was also a desk, and a lamp, and the old man sitting up in his narrow bed, coughing and coughing to rid his lungs of the snots and slurries that had puddled in them while he slept. He nodded his good morning to Charley, wet eyed, too breathless to talk.

Charley stood and watched him from the doorway. He felt helpless in the face of Bagman's gales of coughing. You didn't grow up in Ditch Street without learning that a cough like that usually ended in a coffin, but he couldn't quite bring himself to frame the awful thought, *Master Creech is dying.*

"What about some breakfast?" he asked nervously, feeling that he had to do something. "I could do some eggs and stuff."

Bagman nodded, and gave him a thumbs up. Inside his chest his lungs rustled like two brown paper bags being blown up. Charley didn't wait for the next fit of coughing, but fled down the stairs to the street door and out on to Ketch Causeway, buttoning his coat as he went.

Bagman hadn't given him any money, but he guessed the Skinner's name was good for credit at any shop in the low city. He crossed Ditch Street and ran round to the market on St Kylie Hill. The stallholders there knew him, and to his surprise they already knew about his change of luck. "You're with Master Creech now, ain't you, Charley? Give him my compliments, son. Any luck finding that Patchskin girl yet?"

"We're working on it," Charley promised. He picked out six eggs and a slab of butter and they waved away any talk of payment. "Bagman Creech don't need to pay. Specially not in troubled times like these. . ."

Charley wasn't certain what that last bit meant. Then, walking home, he started noticing the clumps of people stood gossiping on the street corners. Curious, he followed a gang of 'prentices into Celebrity Square, which he found to be full of men in the uniforms of the Trained Bands; thick coats of russet felt with white facings, and black leather helmets. Two quartermasters

92

stood in the back of a wagon, handing down arquebuses and pouches of powder and shot.

A big red fist seized him by his coat collar and spun him around. There stood Ted Swiney, his breath smoking in the chilly morning air. He'd come through from the Mott and Hoople to see the muster, and spotted Charley Shallow instead.

"Well?" he said.

"Well what, Ted?"

Ted shook him briefly. "I told you to keep me informed, din't I? So what have you been playing at?"

"I couldn't get away, Ted, honest. . ."

Ted noticed that people were watching and let go his grip on Charley's coat. He smoothed the crumpled fabric and grinned, as if he'd only been teasing. "So what's old Bagman turned up? Anything more about that Patchskin girl?"

Charley was shaking so badly that he dropped one of his eggs. It broke on the cobbles between his feet with a sound like a tiny clap. "Master Creech ain't even sure she *is* a Patchskin. He's still investigating."

Ted growled, looking past Charley at the militia men. A drum had started to rattle, and there was a lot of shouting and confusion as the part-time soldiers tried to form up in battalions. Some heavy horses, commandeered from a dairy in St Kylie, trotted past pulling a cannon. "Well, you tell Bagman he'd better hurry up," Ted said. "Our boys are off to guard the Moatway, in case those Movement numpties try breaking through. They don't want to think there's a Patchskin on the loose at home, menacing their womenfolk and nippers. They want to see it sorted."

"But if she ain't a Scriven, Ted. . ."

"Who gives a blog? Kill her anyway. You can always paint some speckles on her afterwards. It'll cheer people up. Tell you what, once you've offed her, I'll have the skin. Look good on the wall behind the bar, a Scriven skin would."

"I don't think Master Creech would like that, Ted."

"Who cares what Master Creech thinks? I'm running this show, Charley. You bring me the skin. Think what a boost it'll be for our brave lads." And he sent Charley on his way with a friendly pat on the head and called out to some passers-by, "My boy. We're helping Creechey out. Don't worry, we'll soon have that Patchskin caught and butchered."

Charley ran all the way back to Ketch Causeway. He didn't tell Bagman about his meeting with Ted, but he thought he ought to hear about the Trained Bands mustering. The sound of drum and fife came faintly from the streets outside while he breathlessly explained the news.

Bagman Creech just shrugged. He had news of his own. "I been thinkin', Charley. . ."

The desk, the bed, the floor of Bagman's bedroom were covered with open books and spread out papers. There was a big, yellowed map with red crosses marking all the places where Scriven had been found and killed in the years since the riot. Bagman stabbed his finger down on to a little cluster of crosses out in the Brick Marsh, south-east of the city.

"I checked the records, the notes the old Skinners made. There's things that don't add up; Scriven we had cornered at the Barbican during the riot who vanished and turned up weeks later, holed up in Godshawk's old gaff out on the marshes. I never caught on at the time, but there must be a passage, a tunnel of some sort. Linking Ludgate Hill with his old house. I reckon that's where Solent's doing his real digging. We need to get down there, see what he's found, and how the girl's involved."

Charley looked down at the bag in his hands. The five eggs and the butter. "What about breakfast, Master Creech?"

"No time, Charley. A bite of toast, maybe; a mug of tea to set us up. We'll save your eggs for later. For a victory feast."

14

SKINNERS IN THE BRICK MARSH

hat day, although the long walk through the tunnels was the same, the chamber and the vault door seemed changed. They felt too familiar to be places which Fever had seen only once. She remembered a cracked flagstone three paces from the door, and held her lantern up to look for it, and there it was, although she was sure she had not noticed it the day before, because it lay in the shadow cast by the toolbox.

So how had she known?

She was starting to feel scared. She wished Dr Crumb was there. She missed his calm, careful way of getting to the bottom of mysteries. Without him she felt panicky and very young.

"Are you sure it would not be better to send word to Godshawk's Head?" she asked meekly. "Perhaps a more experienced Engineer. . ."

"Try the door," said Kit, and held his lantern up to light the lock.

Weird feelings of *déjà visité* flooded through Fever. Memories of yesterday mingled with memories of other yesterdays which could not possibly be her own. Pain was beating again at the base of her skull. She began to wonder if she were still inside her dream. If she climbed the stairs again and went outside would there be lights in the unbroken windows of Nonesuch House? Would

96

the float lanterns be rising still above the ornamental ponds, pink as blushes, gold as harvest moons?

She forced her eyes to turn towards the line of keys set in the door frame, and suddenly, as if one of those gods in whom Engineers did not believe had just whispered it in her ear, she knew the code.

They were pushing through the marshes south of 'Bankmentside, following one of the old causeways through the birch woods and diggers' heaps and the ruins of drowned boroughs. Bagman had commandeered a coracle, a marshman's little wicker and tarcloth boat, and Charley carried it up-ended on his shoulders, blundering along behind his master like a black beetle.

"Where is this place we're going?" he asked.

"Godshawk's gaff," said Bagman Creech, scanning the drifting mist ahead for hints of trouble. "His summer palace in the Marsh."

"I heard of Godshawk. He was King of the Patchskins, weren't he?"

"He was at the end. He didn't want to be. The Scriven elected him King thinking he'd save them, but they were past saving by then. Godshawk was an inventor, mostly. Forever tinkering and fiddle-arsing with the old technology, the way some Scriven did. They said there was a laboratory under that summer place of his where he did experiments on dead people and stuff. Though I never saw it for myself."

"You were there?"

Bagman Creech nodded. "The place got overlooked in the Riots, but a couple of weeks later we got word that some escaped Scriven had holed up there. Me and some of the lads got together and came out here. We followed this very path you're walking now, boy."

Charley tried to feel suitably awed, and told himself that he was walking on history, but mostly it still felt as if he was walking on porridge. The wood of the causeway was rotted and slimy, and the coracle on his back made him clumsy. Several times he almost fell, and at last Bagman called a halt. They left the path and squatted in the angle between two old walls, eating a bath bun and wiping the sugar and crumbs from their mouths on the sleeves of their coats. Bagman lit his pipe, and the smoke went up to mingle with the mist, and his memory went homing back to that day on this same path, long ago.

"When we got to Godshawk's gaff we found they'd cut the causeway and we had to wade the last bit. A slough of water, shoulder deep, with Godshawk's gardens rising up out of it ahead. Croquet hoops still stuck in the lawns. I was in the lead, halfway across, when all of a sudden these things started jumping up out of the water all around us. Wet and shiny they was, like black snakes, jumping straight up. I didn't know what was happening till the bloke on my right got hit, and then the bloke on my left, and I realized there were bullets coming down all around us. There were Scriven hiding in Godshawk's gardens, shooting at us with hunting guns."

"What did you do, Master Creech?"

"I ducked, didn't I?" Bagman fingered a half-moon nick in the brim of his bowler where a bullet had taken a bite. "It was all I could do. Went down quick, like I'd been shot. Ducked right under the water so that only my hat was left, floating on the surface. At least, that's how it would have looked to the Scriven. Only what they couldn't see was that I'd got my face poking up inside the hat so's I could breathe. I stayed like that for hours."

"And the other men?"

"All dead, son. There was one just wounded – Billy Kite, from B@ersea – I could hear him yelling out for help. But the Scriven kept banging their guns at him and after a while they must have hit him again, 'cos he shut up. And there I stood, up to my nose in marsh mud, hiding in my own hat till sundown. And then I pushed on."

"Didn't you want to go back? Run away?"

"Course I did. I was half frozen and two-thirds drowned. But I had work to do, didn't I? So I pressed on till I reached Godshawk's garden, and I reckon the Scriven weren't expecting me, because they hadn't set much of a guard. I climbed out of the marsh looking like a part of the marsh, and I went creeping through them gardens and up to that house and I did what was needful. That's the good thing about a spring gun. There's no powder to get wet, so a soaking won't harm it much."

"You killed them?"

Bagman Creech nodded. "I was pretty sick of killing Scriven by then, mind. It didn't feel like a big victory. It weren't rock'n'roll, the way the Riots was. It was just this nasty job I had to do. And when it was done I lit the place on fire, and the flames went way up high because it was full of smart furnishings and tapestries and stuff. And the light of all that burning was enough for me to find my way back home to London by."

"And was Godshawk there?" asked Charley. "Was he one of the ones you killed?"

"No, he was dead by then. Killed in the Barbican, third day of the riots. Gnasher Modbury's crew caught him. 'You can't kill me,' that's what he told them. Stood and laughed at them. He wasn't short of courage. But they killed him all right. Later there were stories that he'd tricked them somehow and escaped, but I saw his speckled hide with me own eyes. He's dead all right."

They moved on, and soon the need for the coracle became clear. The causeway they were following stopped short, as if it had been bitten off. A stretch of glassy water spread itself before them, filled with clumps of reeds and drifting litter and the reflection of a strange, stepped hill which rose up ahead, with overgrown gardens around its feet and a crown of old walls. Charley scrambled through the thick mud at the water's edge and set the coracle afloat. As he helped Bagman in, the vessel wobbled, and beads of water swelled along a badly sealed join, but it floated, and Charley scrambled in as well and unshipped the paddle that was lashed under the seat.

Ahead, the hill was silent. The ruins blanched and faded as the mist blew past them. It was hard to imagine that there was anyone there, let alone Kit Solent and his tame Scriven, or whatever she was. Charley wondered what would happen if they found nothing.

He didn't know if he'd be disappointed or relieved.

And she knew the code. She stood there frozen, her fingers raised in front of the lock's keys, and just as surely as she knew that she was Fever Crumb, she knew that if she pressed the numbers 2519364085 in sequence the door would slide up into the roof, and the door behind it would slide to the right, and the door behind *that* would slide to the left. The counterweights that moved the heavy doors would rattle, and the gears would make a noise like big dogs growling.

"Go on," said Kit, softly and kindly, but with something steely hard beneath the kindness, an eagerness she had not heard before. "You know it, Fever, don't you? Open the door!"

Outlandish visions burst in Fever's brain. Battles and balls and ships at sea and Dr Crumb kneeling before her on a tiled floor and a woman she knew but didn't know laughing in sunlight and the pools and lanterns and—

"Open it!" shouted Kit Solent.

Fever fled. She stumbled sideways, kicking the lantern over so that it went out, but she found her way easily through the darkness and her hand closed on the familiar ivory handle of the door that led outside. *Outside*, she thought. *Fresh air*. She could hear Kit behind her, calling out "Fever!" Up the stairs she went, and out through the door in the hillside, into mist.

"Fever!" Kit Solent was calling, down inside the hollow hill. "Fever, come back! It's all right! I didn't mean to shout!"

Fever still felt groggy, but she forced herself to move away from the door and climb the hill, going up from terrace to terrace the way she had the day before. She wanted to find somewhere where she could sit quietly alone for a while, and *think*.

What was happening to her? Was she ill? Was she going mad?

On the top of the hill the mist moved among old, burned timbers, between the fallen walls. Something splashed in the marshes – a bird, Fever guessed. She walked through the roofless, ruined rooms and found she knew them. This one had been carpeted; this one had been tiled. In this corner had stood a fine teak bookcase, glass-fronted, whose silver handles she uncovered with a bit of scrabbling, little dirty blobs of pooled metal buried in grass and clinker underfoot.

I must have been here before, she reasoned. *I must have been here when I was a tiny child.* But she knew that she could not have been more than a few months old when Nonesuch House burned. Surely a child that tiny would not know what a bookcase was, let alone remember it?

Along the hall she walked, through the arch where the grand front door had been, out on to the gravel drive, gone all to moss and nettles now, where the guests used to leave their sedan chairs. She hummed a dance tune from twenty years before, and it stirred up fresh memories. The ghosts of Scriven dancers moved around her, shadowy, the great dresses of the women rustling and sighing. But they were not real. They were in her head. *It's not the house that's haunted*, she thought. *It's me. . .*

There, across the lawn, was the dear old summer house, its roof fallen in now, its walls thick-grown with ivy. . . She walked towards it, and remembered walking towards it one warm evening, with music spilling from the house behind her and ahead of her in the night a soft laugh, a sigh. . .

She stopped short, clutching her head, wincing at the

pain that hammered there. When she opened her eyes again a boat had drawn up at the foot of the hill, and a man and a boy were climbing the overgrown lawns. For a moment, confused, Fever thought they were guests arriving late for the party. She started downhill to greet them, then realized her mistake. She would never have invited such a shabby pair to one of *her* parties. . .

It was the old man from Summertown and his ragged boy.

"Master Creech!" the boy shouted, looking up and seeing her standing there.

The old man came straight for her, and his pale eyes were shining, fixed upon her face. He stopped ten feet from her, facing her across one of the ponds. "What *are* you?" he asked again, in a hoarse voice. "*Who* are you?"

"I'm not sure," said Fever.

The boy came panting up the hill behind him, and stopped, and they stood side by side, staring at Fever.

"Lily Dismas was right," said the old man, more to himself than the boy. "Whatever she is, she ain't proper human."

Something hot touched Fever's lips. She tasted redness, put up a hand to her mouth, and took it away smeared with blood. Her nose was bleeding again. "Sorry," she mumbled, reaching for her handkerchief. When she looked at the old man again he had taken out a spindly gun and he was pointing it at her.

"This ain't personal," he said. "It's my reckoning that you must be some kind of Scriven half breed, so I'm doing what's needful for the good of London and the human race. . ."

But the cough which had been building up inside

Bagman Creech's chest while he was speaking burst out of him as he pulled the spring gun's trigger. He doubled over, blue-faced, hacking. The bolt whirred past Fever's cheek like a May bug and the sound seemed to jar something loose in her. She turned, and started running.

15

HUNTING FEVER

"aster Creech!" shouted Charley, as the girl spun about and set off into the mist. The old man was folded over, choking. He held one hand out, waggling the gun at Charley. "Get her, lad!" he managed to gasp, before another fit of coughing started.

Charley snatched the gun and hared after the girl. She was a white blob in the mist, turning a corner of the ruined house. He ran after her, and saw her bounding away from him down the steep terraces of the hillside, her arms outstretched for balance. As he started down his feet went from under him on the wet grass and he fell and slid, but he kept hold of Bagman's gun.

Halfway down the hill Fever stopped, lost, looking for the door. Mist hung in the bushes. The door was nowhere. Maybe she had come down the wrong side of the hill. "Help!" she shouted. But she doubted Kit could hear her. The boy was already scrambling down behind her, crashing through wet branches.

She ran on, plunging into the thick growth of scrub and alders which broke along the hill's foot like green surf.

And Charley followed her. He was Bagman's boy, and he wasn't going to lose sight of her. In among those trees the mist was thick and the light was dim, but the girl's white coat still showed, bobbing ahead of him. He was faster than her. He got closer, and saw that she was crossing a patch of green moss beyond some tall reeds up ahead. She glanced back at him, and she looked young and pretty and human. He wasn't sure he had it in him to shoot her with the spring gun, even if she was what Bagman had said she was. But he couldn't let the old man down.

He looked behind him, but there was no sign of the Skinner. He plunged through the reeds. The girl was on the far side of the moss, where birches in their ragged silver wrappers stood in the mist like wands. Following her, he slithered down a short, steep stair of tree roots and plunged into cold mud. That was why the girl had taken her time crossing; she had picked her way along the top of an old drowned wall which Charley in his hurry hadn't even seen. The moss he had stepped out on to was just a green rug laid over a pit brimful of watery stuff like cold black soup.

It didn't suck him down like quicksand in a story; he simply sank, his mouth and nostrils filling with mud as he went under. His hands alone stayed above the surface, clutching the precious gun. He thought of Bagman, nose-deep in the lagoons, hiding under his hat.

And Fever, on the far bank, unsnagging her coat skirts from the brambles there and readying herself to run, stopped short, startled by his choked-off scream. Crossing the moss she had fully hoped that the boy would miss his footing and plunge in. It had been a stratagem, and she'd been proud of it: he had a gun, but she had reason. Now, as she listened to him blurt and

106

founder, she could think only of the chill black water forcing its way into his lungs.

She turned. A hand rose from the water, holding aloft the dripping gun, which glimmered green and silver in the light that came through the leaves above. Somehow the boy got his head above the surface. She thought for a moment that he was going to point the gun at her, but he was sinking again, and he turned and threw the weapon on to the bank behind him as he went down. "Help!" he gasped.

What harm could he do her, unarmed and half drowned? He was a pasty little thing, younger even than her. She grabbed up a fallen branch and held it out towards him.

"Take this!" she shouted.

Charley went under again, drinking more mud. When he came up the girl was still holding the branch out.

He grabbed it like she'd told him. He clung to it, and scrabbled along it, gasping and choking and whimpering. Struggling towards the girl, he met her eyes. They were odd colours, which scared him, but the thought of drowning scared him more. Was her helping him just a trick? Was she going to let him get almost to dry land and then let him sink while she looked on, giggling? He felt a hot, furious anger at her for playing with him. Like a cat with a mouse!

But all the time he went on scrabbling his way towards her, and she didn't let go, and when he was close enough she reached out and her hot hands caught hold of his and dragged him to firmer ground. He lay there gasping.

Fever backed away from him, but she didn't think he would still want to hurt her, not now that she had helped him. She said, "Why are you doing this? Why did you chase me?"

Charley's ears were still clogged with moss and mud. He looked up at the girl and he saw her mouth was moving, but all he could hear was his own heart pounding and whooshing. He thought how like a normal girl she was. Then she looked past him, scared, and he sat up so quick his ears popped and he could hear Bagman's voice shouting out his name.

Fever had forgotten the other man, the old one. She'd thought him too ill to follow her down the hill. But here he was, coming quick through the trees on the far side of the mud pool, long and black like an idea for a new punctuation mark. She started to move, and the brambles between the birch boles snagged her coat again.

And Bagman Creech was stooping to pick up the gun, then striding on across the moss like he was walking on water, his feet finding the hidden footholds under the surface without his even needing to look for them. His face was white and his pale eyes were the colour of sunlight through fog. It was as if the sight of Fever had stripped twenty years off him and made him young and fit again. As he reached Charley's side of the moss he lifted the spring gun.

Fever saw it, and struggled harder, but it was rooty and brambly the way she was going, and she moved with nightmare slowness, her white coat catching on thorns and low branches.

Bagman grinned. He pushed his jaw forward, and the

set of his long yellow teeth gave him the look of one of those dogs that, once it bites you, can't let go. He strode past Charley, and the skirts of his coat brushed Charley's face. The girl was trapped in the trees, struggling. She let out a moaning noise, and Charley wanted to shout out and tell Master Creech how she'd saved him from the mire, but he knew that wouldn't make any difference, 'cos she was still Scriven. She was looking at him with a white, woeful face as the Skinner moved sideways along the moss-edge, seeking for a clean shot between the trees. And now something else was moving, away to the left, behind the mist.

Charley thought for a moment he must be wrong. It was just an old tree, surely, an old willow that had grown twisted, and the mist drifting past it made it look like it had moved. But then it stepped out of the mist, and it was a man and he was holding a pocket pistol, aimed at Bagman Creech.

"Stop!" shouted Kit Solent.

Creech hesitated. In the silence, Kit made his way through the foliage until he was between Fever and the Skinner.

Bagman's long face twitched angrily. "Don't you go protecting her!" he warned. "Them as protects Scriven is worse than the Scriven themselves. . ."

"You don't understand a thing, old man," said Kit, his voice trembling slightly. "You don't know what she is. Put down your gun."

Creech scowled, ignoring him, and Fever saw his fingers whiten as he started to squeeze the trigger of his strange old weapon. "No!" shouted Kit again, warningly, and then, in a sort of angry grief, "No!"

There was a single sharp, high-pitched clap. Kit's pistol spewed sparks and smoke. Bagman Creech seemed to jump at the sound, and for a moment there was a look of absolute amazement on his face. His gun went off, punching its dart into the undergrowth ten feet away. He coughed quietly and fell over backwards. The air was filled with tiny flakes of goose down lining blasted out of his quilted coat. It looked like snow.

"Oh, Poskitt," Kit kept saying. "I didn't mean to— I was aiming at his *arm*. . ." He had lowered his pistol. His face was nearly as white as the old man's.

Charley scrambled across the mud, shouting, "Master Creech!"

Bagman's white face flopped towards him. There was pink froth in the old man's mouth and it spilled out down his chin when he spoke. "Go! You are the last of us! Save yourself, so you can finish this!"

His head dropped back. Charley hesitated only a moment. Just long enough to snatch Bagman's hat out of the mire where it had fallen. Then he was off, finding his way along the wall-top easy this time and running away between the trees.

16

THE LONG WALK HOME

 or a while the birds which had been scared into the sky by the gunshots kept circling and calling, but gradually they settled again, and it grew very quiet. Fever crouched among the birches, picturing cubes and pyramids and cones and making herself recite their different properties. She had wrapped her arms tight round herself, and her breathing was quick and shallow and she was trying not to move.

Kit Solent dropped his pistol and stooped over the Skinner, feeling for a pulse amid the white stubble on his throat, as if there was a chance he might still be alive. Blood flowed steadily and sadly from him, looking almost purple as it curled into the green water.

"I think this is Creech," he said. He tried to laugh. "I think I've killed Bagman Creech. . ."

"Who?" said Fever.

"Old Skinner general from the riots. I thought he'd died years ago. Well, he's dead now all right. Oh, Poskitt. . . I've never shot anyone before. I carry the gun in case of thieves, but I never expected. . . Why didn't he listen to me? The stupid old fool! I told him to drop his gun, but he didn't listen! He was just going to go ahead and. . . The gods alone know what he was thinking!"

"What did he want with me?" asked Fever, edging closer to look at the dead man. It seemed to her that you did not need to be an imaginary deity to understand why Creech had acted as he did. It was simply that he thought Fever's death was more important than his own life, and he had thought he would be able to kill her before Kit killed him. What she still didn't understand was what it was that had made him hate her so.

"He said . . . he said I wasn't human. . ."

"He was mad," said Kit firmly. With trembling hands he picked his pistol up and stuffed it back into his pocket. "Fever, I'm so sorry. It's my fault. I should never have brought you here. You're not ready. . ."

Fever looked up at him. "He said I was a Scriven. A half-breed Scriven. . . but there's no such thing, is there?"

"He was a mad old man. He didn't know what you are."

"But you do?"

Kit looked away, scanning the marsh for signs of movement. There were none. He left Fever alone and went to look for the Skinner's boy, but soon gave up. What could he do if he did find him? Shoot him too? The kid hadn't looked much older than Ruan. He gave up and returned to where Fever waited. "He's run off. If he goes back to London and tells what happened here you'll be in danger. . . We both will. . . People still look up to the Skinners in the cheap boroughs." He reached down and pulled her to her feet. "Fever, can you open the vault?"

The door code was as clear in Fever's mind as it had been before she met the Skinner. Her fingers knew the precise movements that they would have to make to type the right sequence on the ivory keys. But she was too scared and confused to trust Kit Solent any more. What would happen if she did open the door for him? What would become of her when she was no more use to him?

"No," she said. "I don't know the code. I never did."

Kit stood staring at her. He was more than half sure that she was lying. When she said, "No," her voice dipped in the middle. When she said, "I don't know the code," a blush spread right across her face and her ears turned red. He wanted to drag her back inside the hill; force her back to the lock and make her open it. . .

But he was not that sort of man. Ruthlessness had never been his style. All his life he'd been kind; the sort of boy who came home bloody nosed from school after standing up for smaller boys against the bullies. The sort of man who could never bring himself to smack his children when they misbehaved, or even to stay cross with them for long. He looked at Fever as she stood in front of him all trembly and mud stained yet still trying to look poised and rational, and it was impossible to even imagine himself making her keep working at the lock. She needed help; she needed his protection; she needed, like any lost and frightened child, to be home.

And so did he. Killing Creech had shocked him. He felt sick of Nonesuch House and its secrets. They weren't worth a life; not even the life of a crazy old man. Let the Movement have them. He wanted to go home.

"Come on," he said, taking Fever's hand, and she numbly let him hold it and lead her uphill to the hidden entrance. "We'll get you back to Godshawk's Head. You'll be safe there, if that boy makes trouble."

113

Kit shut the secret door behind them and they went downstairs to where their lanterns waited. Fever's had gone out, but she found a box of matches among his tools and re-lit it and stuffed the matches in her pocket as she followed him back into the tunnel. Kit did not even look at the vault door and the lock as they passed it. Fever dimly understood how much he was giving up. Half of her, the still-rational half, wanted to turn back and find out if her hand still knew the dance it had longed to do on Godshawk's keypad. But she was afraid. Something deep and strange had stirred inside her when she stood there before. She had been overwhelmed by something, and the most frightening thing about it was that she could not find any rational explanation; it had felt as if she was possessed by some malevolent spirit.

"I'm sorry," she managed to mumble, trailing Kit back along the tunnel.

"No, Fever," he said. "I'm sorry. I should never have brought you here."

They walked on in silence and thought of the Skinner's boy haring home across the marshes, somewhere above their heads.

"Why did you?" asked Fever. "Bring me here, I mean? Why did you think I could help?"

Kit stopped and looked at her again in the lantern light. "I don't know."

"But you must have had a reason for choosing me."

He turned and walked on, so fast that Fever had to run to keep up. They splashed through a flooded section of the tunnel, sloshing shadows and wet echoes ahead of them. After another fifty yards or so Kit stopped again, turned back to her, and seemed to come to some decision. "Fever, I haven't told you the truth. Not everything."

Fever waited while he looked at the floor, the tunnel walls, the lantern, anywhere but at her, working out in his head what he had to confess to her.

"It all began when I found that notebook of Godshawk's at Rag Fair," he said. "I didn't know what those strange designs were for, and I still don't, but it got me interested in the old man. I'd heard a lot about Godshawk the king, but nothing about Godshawk the scientist. So I started asking questions, and after a while my questions led me to a girl named Katie Unthank. Her late father had been an archaeologist who'd worked sometimes with Godshawk, and she had heard things from him. She had heard about the existence of the vault, the workshop where Godshawk was supposed to have devised his most secret inventions. And she had heard about you."

"Me?"

"Katie didn't know much. Only that the Order of Engineers were bringing up a child called Fever Crumb, and that you were important. There had been some kind of experiment when you were newborn. Unthank believed that some of Godshawk's knowledge had been transferred into your brain."

"That's impossible," said Fever, Engineerishly.

"Maybe, but that's what Katie told me. Her father used to say, 'When that girl grows up, she'll be the key that unlocks Godshawk's secrets.' He claimed that whatever Godshawk had done to your brain, its effects wouldn't be apparent until you were an adult.

"It was Katie who told me the story of the old tunnel

which was supposed to link Nonesuch with the Barbican. We spent months looking for it. We didn't find it, but while we were trying, we fell in love. After that we were so happy, and so busy with each other and the children, that we let ourselves forget Godshawk and his secrets. Then, last year, I heard about that cave-in and guessed the tunnel's course. I thought Katie would have wanted me to explore it, and use whatever treasures I found in Godshawk's vault to provide for Fern and Ruan. When I came up against his lock I remembered that strange tale she'd told me about the child who'd gone to live with the Engineers. I knew you wouldn't be old enough yet for Godshawk's memories to have surfaced, but I thought that if I took you to Nonesuch House, and exposed to you to the old man's favourite scents and tastes, it might jog something. . .

"I shouldn't have done it. I knew all along that it was unfair to use you like that. But lately, with this news from the north. . . I thought it was worth trying anything that would get me into that vault before the Movement arrived. I was wrong. I'm sorry."

"I don't believe it's possible," said Fever again, after they had walked on a few hundred yards in silence. "I don't believe Godshawk could have put thoughts into my brain. That's just voodoo science, the kind of foolish story that the newspapers like to print, to make people think that the Ancients were capable of miracles. . ."

But she was trying to convince herself as well as Kit. Because the Ancients *had* been capable of miracles, or at least of science so advanced that it *seemed* miraculous, even to an Engineer. And did Kit's story not offer an explanation, at last, for the memories that had been gathering in her head like fog ever since she first came to Nonesuch House?

"I'm sorry, Fever," said Kit again, after another half mile. "You should not have had to hear all this from me. I don't understand it and I can't explain it very well. You need to talk to Dr Crumb."

"Why?"

"He must know something. It isn't usual for the Engineers to take in a baby girl. They must have known about you from the start."

"No!" said Fever. "Dr Crumb *found* me. In a basket. And he thought it would be irrational to leave me. He told me so, and he wouldn't lie. He doesn't believe in telling lies. . ."

But as she spoke she was touching the back of her head, tracing the silvery scar which had been there since the day she was found. Could she really believe all Dr Crumb had told her? Was that not a little too much like blind faith? And even if she trusted him, could she trust Dr Stayling and all the other members of the Order? Katie Solent's father, who had worked for Godshawk, had been the same Master Unthank whom Dr Crumb had gone to visit on the day he found Fever. . .

Had her discovery been carefully arranged? Perhaps Dr Stayling and the other senior Engineers had taken her into the Head in the same spirit that they gave space to white rats and fruitflies and cultures of bacteria on Petri dishes; merely as an experiment to be observed.

17

STORM COMING

t seemed a long, long way, that walk back through the tunnel. But they emerged at last into the antechamber behind the bookcase, and stood staring at each other for a moment, like conspirators, listening to the faint sound of the children's laughter from upstairs.

"That's strange," said Kit, looking relieved that he had something else to talk about besides the contents of Fever's brain. "They should be at school. . ."

The laughter grew louder as they emerged through the bookcase. They found Ruan in the hall, lumbering along on all fours, while Fern clung giggling to his back. "Ruan's a horse!" she shouted, when she saw them. "Fever, look, Ruan's a horse!"

"No, Ruan is a bipedal primate," said Fever helpfully. (She had still not got the hang of make believe.)

"Children," said their father, stooping to hug the little girl as she tumbled laughing off her brother's back, "why aren't you at school?"

"School's shut!" said Ruan, looking very happy about it. "Miss Wernicke's run away for fear of the nomads attacking. . ."

"It's true, sir," announced Mistress Gloomstove, who appeared just then from the kitchen, dusting her hands on her apron. "We found a notice on Miss Wernicke's door this morning saying as how she's gone to stay with her sister in Slugg's Pottage on account of the nomad horde, sir, and school's closed indefinitely. She apologized for the inconvenience, as if that made it any better. Why, I'd give her inconvenience if I had her here. Have you ever tried dusting and tidying this place, sir, with these two young savages rampaging around and getting under foot? I'm glad to see you home to deal with them, sir, I do say. . ."

Kit Solent gave the housekeeper his most charming smile. "I'm deeply sorry, Mistress G; you know that I'd not have left them with you if I'd had the least inkling that school was off. But I'm afraid I can't relieve you of them just yet. I have to take Fever back to Godshawk's Head, you see. It will take only ten minutes. . . Half an hour at most. . ."

Mistress Gloomstove's face took on a cold, faraway look. "I don't know about that, sir. I'm employed to keep house, sir. If it's a nursemaid or a governess you're wanting. . ."

"Naturally, I'll make it up to you," said Kit hastily, and hurried upstairs to his office.

Fern, Ruan and Mistress Gloomstove all stood and looked at Fever.

"You're all muddy," said Fern at last.

"Yes. Yes I am," admitted Fever, looking down at herself. Her neat white coat was splashed and scribbled with dark sprays of Brick Marsh mud and greenish stains of moss and grass. For all she knew there was blood there too. "I fell over," she said, rather lamely. "In some mud."

She was glad of the clatter of Kit's boots coming back down the stairs. He had Fever's cardboard suitcase

119

under his arm, and he was rummaging in a leather purse. "Here," he said, handing a shiny coin to Mistress Gloomstove, "I hope that will be some small token of my thanks – sorry it can't be more, but I must save some for the chair fare. I shall be back as soon as I can. Don't open the door to anyone while I am gone."

He kissed the children, and suddenly Fever found herself making her quick goodbyes and stepping outside after him into the sullen stormy light, and it occurred to her that she would probably never see the house or the children again.

There was rain in the air. They didn't go towards Cripplegate but turned downhill instead, walking quickly through quiet and half-deserted streets and empty courts until they reached the edges of Limehouse, where Kit hailed a passing chair. The chief bearer asked, "Where to, mate?" and Kit told him, "Godshawk's Head."

Fever climbed inside, and Kit got in with her and shut the door. As the chair set off she heard a sound, and she thought that it was thunder, but it went on and on, coming from the lower end of the city; a shifting, snarling sound, which made her think of some vast and dangerous animal stirring in its sleep. All down the street the shopkeepers were putting up their shutters, and knots of working men stood talking, turning to stare as the chair went past.

The day was dark by the time Charley Shallow got back to London; still not noon, but the sky gone black as a winter's evening, as if the clouds themselves were putting on mourning for old Bagman Creech.

He hadn't dared to go skirting back round Nonesuch Hill to find the coracle, but had run blindly through the marshes till he stumbled on a plankway, a path built by scavengers or hunters, which he followed till it brought him to the southern edge of the city. He was mud-caked, leech-nibbled; dirty water spewed from his boot tops at every step. A wind tram was passing and he leaped on board, ignoring the old-fashioned looks which the other passengers gave him when they got a whiff of his marsh-steeped clothes. The tram was moving slow, with the whole crew busy poling it along, and Charley thought that with a bit of luck he might get several stops nearer home before anyone bothered asking him to pay. When they did, he'd have to jump off quick, 'cos he was skint.

But when the conductor finally appeared in front of him, he changed his mind. He wasn't just the pot boy from the Mott and Hoople no more. He was Bagman Creech's 'prentice. And now Bagman was gone, that made Charley his heir, didn't it? *You're the last of us*, Bagman had said. The last of the Skinners. Charley pulled himself up stiff and straightened the old bowler hat on his head and said, "Sorry, mate, I've got no money. I'm on Skinners' business."

"Skinners?" said the conductor, checking his natural urge to throw this filthy, smelly urchin off his tram.

"Bagman Creech is dead," said Charley. "We was hunting a Scriven and she had a friend and he shot Bagman down. I've got to. . ." Here he hesitated, for he wasn't quite sure what he had to do. "I've got to sort it."

The conductor still looked uncertain, till one of Charley's fellow passengers, a woman, said, "That boy's all right. I saw him with old Bagman up in town yesterday."

"Bagman's dead!" said someone else, passing on what Charley had said to their neighbour. The news was spreading down the tram. Even the crew were looking at Charley now.

The conductor took an oyster shell from his satchel and looped its string over Charley's head. "Good luck, boy. Anything you need, you just ask."

Charley looked at him, and at the faces of the other passengers. He wasn't used to this. To power. He wondered what Bagman would have told them. He said, "Just keep a look out, that's all. She was in the marshes, but she could be back in town by now. She looks like a girl and she dresses like one of them Engineers what live in that old head. She's got a human gent protecting her; an archaeologist name of Solent."

The track swung east towards the distant terminus, and the sails flapped and then tautened, filling with a sudden breeze. The sky astern, over the marshes, was smeared with rain. Charley sat down again, and no one complained now about the smell of marsh that rose from him or the stain he'd leave upon the seat slats. He'd not been sure where he was going, but he knew now. Back to Bagman's house to clean himself up and find himself a new weapon. And then he'd finish the job. Find that Patchskin, and kill her.

Charley hadn't reckoned on the power of rumours, though. The story he'd told had a life of its own, and it moved faster than he could. At every stop the tram made, passengers got off and told the news of Bagman Creech's death in pubs and street markets. Diggers told it to their wives, and their children overheard it and went shouting it through the shabby streets. Along 'Bankmentside and up Cripplegate and through all the rookeries of St Kylie the story spread and grew. Drinkers carried it from pub to pub. In the Crate of Codlings and the Rose Reviv'd, wild rumours got hammered into hard fact. There was a Patchskin loose. Maybe more than one. They were in league with the Movement, and hoping to seize power and have all London for their own again. Bagman Creech had found this out, and one of the 'Skins had killed him for it. And worst of all, the murderess had human help. . .

A ripple of anger moved through the cheap parts of town. By the time Charley hopped off the tram at Celebrity Square people were yelling about it in the streets and smashing the windows of any old-tech shop that had ever done business with the traitor Solent.

Charley went past them, wondering what the fuss was all about. He was halfway down Stragglemarket on his way to Bagman's house when a big hand grabbed him from behind and heaved him hard against a wall. He hung there, pinned, kicking at empty air and staring up once more into the large, red face of Tedward Swiney.

"Crice, you stink of the bog," exclaimed the pub keeper. "I been looking for you all over. Is it true what they're saying? Bagman's croaked?"

Charley couldn't answer. It was all he could do to breathe, with Ted's big fist clumping his coat collar in a tight knot against his windpipe. Ted was wearing his old oil-cloth outdoor coat, which stank like a wet dog. The wind flapped it open and in an inside pocket Charley glimpsed the handle of the blunderbuss which usually lived under the counter at the Mott and Hoople in case anyone tried to rob the place or complained about the quality of Ted's beer.

"What about this Patchskin girl?" Ted growled. "Still live an' large, is she? Well?"

Charley managed a nod, and Ted gave another growl and let him drop. He knelt on the cobbles, hacking and gasping.

"You sound worse than the old man did," said Ted. "Where is she then? 'Ow do we find her? Pity to waste all this community spirit you've roused up. I ain't seen the commons look this lively for years. So how do we get hold of her? Out in the marshes, you say?"

"Kit Solent," choked Charley.

"An' who the blog is Kit Solent?"

"He's an archaeologist. He's helping her. He murdered Bagman. Maybe he's a Scriven too. I didn't see no speckles on him, but then the girl ain't got none neither. This Solent lives up on the hill. I can't remember the street. I can take you there."

Ted Swiney cursed viciously under his breath, which helped him to think. Then he reached down and grabbed Charley by both shoulders, lifting him to his feet. He patted the dust off him with both big hands, trying to look friendly, even fatherly, for the benefit of the gang of onlookers which had gathered to watch. He could sense the anger of the mob building. They needed a leader, but with Bagman gone who could they turn to? Ted meant to make sure that it was him.

Charley stood there uneasily while Ted set his hat straight. Rain was falling heavily now. A chair passed, its bearers tramping along like dray horses with their heads down and the rain slicking their hair. Charley watched it going by so that he didn't have to look at Ted Swiney's attempt at a cheery smile. He saw a girl's white face framed in the window space; the familiar curve of a shaved head.

"Ted! Look! *It's her!*"

18

CHAIR VS CHAIR

he chair slowed a little as the rain came on, the bearers growing mistrustful of the greasy cobbles. Rain rattled on the roof and speckled the window glass as Fever peered out to see where they were. She saw the sign outside a tram stop, CELEBRITY SQUARE. She saw more groups of men, sheltering under shop awnings as the downpour increased. She saw a barrel-shaped man lurch forward out of one of the groups. He had his finger pointed straight at Fever, and he was shouting something.

"Damn that bald pate of yours," said Kit Solent. "You stand out like a beacon." He thrust Fever back against her seat, out of the sight of anyone outside, but the damage had been done, and Fever could hear the roar of angry voices spreading. Her breath came in little shallow gasps, and she was afraid that she was going to be sick. Kit Solent leaned past her. He had his pistol in his hand, and he used the handle to pound on the woodwork behind her head, shouting to the lead bearer, "Faster! Faster!"

The chair started to lurch as the bearers broke into a heavy trot. Fever craned her neck, looking out through the small glass pane in the back wall. She saw the barrel-shaped man flagging down a passing taxi chair. She saw his mouth move, and knew that he was shouting, "Follow that chair!"

"They're coming after us!" she said.

"They won't catch us. . ." Kit Solent twisted round to look, and for a moment his head and shoulders obscured Fever's view. "Damn! That's Swiney!"

"Who's he?"

"Landlord of the Mott on Ditch Street. A real troublemaker. A big man in the bad parts of town. . ." He turned back to hammer on the wall behind Fever's head again, shouting, "Faster, man! Faster! I'll make it worth your while!"

A moment later the chair was racing up Cransbeigh Notch and crossing Cripplegate. The bearers were fit and fresh and too heavily dosed with lifting drugs to question Kit's order. People who saw them coming just had to dive aside to let the chair go past.

But the chair Ted Swiney had commandeered was fast, too. Fever could see it twenty feet behind; a lean red chair with go-faster stripes and three bearers, one at the front and two behind. The publican's angry face could be seen shouting from a side window. After a few hundred yards he wriggled one hand out too, clutching something silvery which he pointed towards Fever's chair. Fever couldn't make out what it was until his hand jerked and a flare of orange sparks and white smoke hid him. Something struck the corner of the chair above her with a startling crack.

"He's shooting at us!" she said stupidly.

"Two can play at that," said Kit Solent, tugging a window open. He leaned his whole body out into the rain and Fever heard his gun go off and saw the pale puff of smoke whipped sideways on the wind. He must have missed, though, for a moment later Ted Swiney's gun fired again and a hole the size of a two-quidd coin appeared in the woodwork of the chair's back.

Kit Solent twisted himself round and threw his empty pistol into Fever's lap, followed by the ammunition pouch and powder horn. "Reload that!" he shouted, drawing out a second, identical gun. He had been half expecting this sort of trouble, she realized; he had armed himself for a battle while he had been upstairs fetching her things and Mistress Gloomstove's money. She felt hopelessly, helplessly grateful to him for daring to come with her, and she hurried to do as he said, gripping the pistol with trembling fingers, terrified she'd drop it. "A charge of powder, wadding, then the ball, ram it all home with the rod," Kit told her, shouting to make himself heard over the roar of the rain on the roof. Coarse-grained powder, black as pepper, sprinkled down her coat. Kit fired his second pistol as she pushed the ball home, and she was still busy with the ramrod when he reached back in, dropping his empty gun on her and groping for the other.

The rain grew suddenly heavier. Gutters gurgled, and the bearers' boots skidded as the chair turned another corner. Ted Swiney's three-man rig was still close behind. Other chairs were joining the chase now, as word got round of who it was that the publican was pursuing. One of them slammed into a fruit and veg stall at the side of the street, scattering apples and cabbages into the path of another, whose bearers stumbled and went down, the thin boardings of their chair splintering as it hit the cobbles.

*

Crouched in Ted's chair, Charley Shallow watched the juddering view, rain-spattered, gun-lit. He flinched each time a panicked pedestrian dived out of the chair's path, ducked whenever Solent's pistol fired from the chair ahead. Once a ball came through the boarding beside his head, making a big, splintery hole that the rain gusted in through. It couldn't be worth all this, could it, he kept thinking. They were all going to end up as dead as Bagman. . .

But there was no telling that to Ted. The publican was cursing steadily, happy and fierce in the excitement of the chase, pulling his thick body back inside the chair to reload his old blunderbuss and then cramming himself out into the rain again to shoot, bellowing abuse at the straining bearers; "Faster, you bloggers! Faster, you useless cloots!" The gun going off again, smoke blowing through the chair with a sharp, scorched smell. "Got him! I got the blogger!"

Fever finally managed to get a pistol filled before Kit asked for it, and then realized that she'd only managed it because one of Swiney's shots had hit him. He groaned as she pulled him back inside. He had dropped his pistol and there was a scorched hole in the front of his coat, near the shoulder. He looked dazed and white and disbelieving. She let him sink to the floor, thinking he'd be safer there, and looked down and saw that she was still holding the loaded pistol.

The chair went pounding along a tight, brick-paved street, past pubs and eel bars and dodgy archaeopharmacies. Fever leaned out and saw that Ted

Swiney's chair was still behind, though the others had missed the turning and were bunched up at the street's end, bickering about who should go first. Swiney had ducked back inside his chair to reload.

What had he and Kit been thinking of, she wondered, shooting at each other? If you wanted to stop a chair it was not at the *passengers* you should be shooting. . . She pushed herself out further, until her hips wedged in the window space. Rain battered at her face. She held on grimly to the pistol and tried to aim at the legs of Ted Swiney's forward bearer. She was about to pull the trigger when her own chair plunged suddenly into the rookeries of Kitesbridge, a tangle of grim little streets barely wide enough for it to fit through. A jutting window ledge smacked the gun from her hand and she threw herself back inside as mossy brickwork scraped against both doors. She had a hopeless after-image of the lost pistol glinting as it bounced on the cobbles. Maybe Ted's bearers would trip on it. . .

But when the street widened enough for her to look out again, the pursuing chairs were close behind, moving in a pack, clattering after hers through the shadow of an archway where fires burned in food-sellers' braziers. Swiney popped out of his window again, gun in hand, struggling for a clear shot. Other chairs swerved to let the chase go past, crashing against one another or into the metal pillars of a wind-tram viaduct which were flicking past on either side.

The blare of a klaxon rebounded suddenly from the wet house fronts. Twisting round, Fever saw a huge shape slide across an intersection just ahead. A house-high mass of painted upperworks and dim-lit windows,

130

tall smokestacks striped like gypsies stockings. . . It was a land barge heading out of town along the Westerway. The barge traders must have heard the uproar, and decided to quit London before the rioting spread. Fever's chair shot through the space between two of the barge's many wheels; the rattle of rain on the roof stopped for a dark, breathless moment, then began again as it shot out on the far side. Behind, one of the pursuing chairs, choosing a bad moment to try and overtake Ted Swiney's, was smashed under the barge wheels with a crunch that Fever heard even above the drumbeat of her bearers' boots. The rest stopped, bunching up behind the wreck. The barge went by, but there was another behind it, and then another, following each other like overdressed elephants. *We're saved,* thought Fever.

But Ted Swiney's chair dove through a gap between two of the vehicles and kept coming after her. It was probably moving too fast to stop or slow down, Fever reasoned. For all its streamlining, it looked bigger than her chair; heavier; more massive. She thought, *Momentum = Mass x Velocity. . . They can go as fast as us, but they can't stop or turn as quickly. . .* It was time for some applied physics. She shouted to her bearers, "Turn left here! Left!"

Because she knew where she was now. These were the streets around the Head, where she had often walked with Dr Crumb. The chair swung on to Gritpipe Lane, heading steeply downhill towards a corner where the street made a sharp right angle. Another shot from Ted Swiney's gun tore past her, rattling against a pub sign. Ahead, where the street turned, she could see a scent shop on the corner. She remembered passing it with Dr Crumb; how he had always complained at the irrationality of it. The chair slowed as its straining bearers wrenched it round that ninety-degree bend, canting steeply to one side, finials screeching along wet brickwork.

A few feet behind, Ted Swiney's men tried to do the same, but their chair would not obey them; their momentum kept driving them towards the scent shop. Charley Shallow, feeling them lose control, kicked open a door and flung himself clear, and Bagman's bowler saved him as his head glanced off a wall.

The window of the scent shop came apart in bright icefalls of glass as Ted's chair went through it sideways on. A belch of perfume from a thousand shattered phials and bottles broke across the street. Charley stood up carefully, checking himself to make sure that he was still all there. That bang on the head had wrenched his neck and jarred his teeth; he'd bitten down painfully on the corners of his tongue. The chair bearers scrambled past him and scattered, bruised and bleeding, frightened of what they'd done to Ted.

Charley went to the smashed window and peered in. The wrecked chair lay on its side in the shop. Ted Swiney was scrambling out through the hole where a door had been. He saw Charley watching, and shook his fist. "I'm going to get that girl," he growled.

The curious old-tech lamp inside the *For Hire* sign on the chair's roof exploded with a wallop of flame, singeing off both his eyebrows.

Fever was two streets away by then. Her chair was

slowing, juddering as her winded bearers began to weaken. She crouched on the floor and tried to help Kit Solent, shocked by the amount of blood which had soaked his clothes and the way he howled when she started to lift him. Then, without warning, the whole chair leaned sideways and she was howling too, shrieking in helpless fright as it crashed down and slid on its side across the cobbles.

"The children," Kit was saying. "I must get back to the children. . ."

Fever reached up and heaved the door open and clambered out. One of the bearers lay in the road, gasping for breath, his legs jerking fitfully as if he was still trying to run. The other, too drugged to notice what had happened, stood patiently between his splintered shafts.

Fever reached down into the chair and did her best to help Kit Solent out. "I'm sorry," she kept saying, uselessly, as he cried out at the pain. His anguish made her angry. *He* was supposed to be helping *her*, not the other way about. . . Curious Londoners had emerged from shops and houses to see the crash. She could feel their eyes on her scalp, and although she could not hear what they were muttering to one another, she could guess.

"Come on." She told Kit. "It's not far to Godshawk's Head. . ."

"I must get back to Ludgate Hill," he said, swaying as he pushed himself away from the wrecked chair. "The children. . ."

Fever caught him, drew his arm across her shoulders and did her best to take his weight. "You can't. Not now. Those other chairs. . ." She could already hear the weary thud of running feet behind them. "Come on, Master Solent, please," she begged. And slowly, slowly, slowly they went on along the street.

19

DR CRUMB

long the street and up another, and there in front of them was Godshawk's Head, huge and craggy in that leaden light, with the rain making waterfalls down its face and spraying off its chin.

Kit Solent leaned heavily on Fever as they climbed the wooden stairs to the tram platform and went through the gate in the wire fence, which she locked behind them, and then up more stairs to the door in Godshawk's nostril. Fever pounded on the glass with the flat of her hand and left a smeared red handprint there. A shocked face appeared behind the glass and stared at it, and then at her. It was Dr Isbister, looking like something in an aquarium. "Go away!" he shouted. But other Engineers were appearing behind him, and soon Dr Stayling was there, ordering Isbister aside and undoing the heavy bolts.

"Thank the gods," said Kit Solent as the doors opened. And if Fever had had gods she would have thanked them too, for there at Dr Stayling's side was Dr Crumb.

She wanted to run to him. She wanted to hug him. She contented herself with saying, "Greetings Dr Crumb, Dr Stayling. The commons are rioting, and Master Solent has kindly brought me home. He is hurt. . ."

"He needs a doctor," said Dr Isbister, looking warily at the spreading stain of blood on their visitor's coat.

135

"I'm fine," Kit insisted. "What I need is to get back to my children. My gods, what if the rioters work out who I am, and go to my house?" He turned back towards the door, but stumbled, and would have fallen if several Engineers had not reached out to steady him.

"He must have a doctor," said Dr Isbister.

"There are no doctors of that sort here," said Dr Whyre.

"We must send to the Guild of Physicians in Clerkenwell," Dr Stayling said.

"There is no time!" Fever shouted. "Don't you understand? If the men who did this follow us here. . ."

The Engineers flinched at her outburst. "Your time outside the Head has left you somewhat unreasonable, Miss Crumb," said Dr Isbister tartly. But the others seemed to understand her. Sometimes, she thought, it might be allowable to be angry or emotional, in order to make people see the urgency of things. She leaned against the stair rail and watched while the Engineers barred the doors and helped Kit Solent away, saying, "We must at least clean and bandage that wound before you go." Soon she was left alone with Dr Crumb.

She hadn't noticed until then how hard her heart was pounding, how raggedly she was breathing, how her body still trembled as the terror of the chase shook its way out of her muscles. She looked at Dr Crumb and said, "Kit took me to Nonesuch House, Godshawk's old house on the marshes. And I *remembered* it."

Dr Crumb tried to keep looking as calm as ever, but the corner of his mouth twitched, and his fingers twined themselves together. "That is impossible," he said. "You were only a few months old when I found you, you could not possibly remember. . ."

"Remember *what*?" asked Fever. She knew that she sounded edgy and emotional, but she could not help it; she *was* edgy and emotional. She said, "I have some connection with that place, don't I? With Godshawk?"

"Oh. . ." he said, when he heard that. (Another man, less rational, might have said, "Oh gods!", "Oh, Poskitt!", "Oh, great Lud!") He hid his eyes for a moment with one hand, then looked at Fever. "Come," he said.

Outside people were moving in small groups on to the stretch of waste ground around Godshawk's Head. More and more of them, gathering in the dim and rainy light like crows.

Fever followed Dr Crumb up the stairs. Up and up to Dr Crumb's quarters. She saw as she went in how it had changed. Her things had vanished from the little alcove which had been her bed space, and there was another workbench there instead. Of course it was only reasonable that Dr Crumb should make full use of the space while she was away. So why did the sight of it make her want to cry?

Dr Crumb poured boiled water for them both from a jug which he kept beside the stove, the water faintly warm as always, and in her own old mug. She clasped her hands around it and drank. She sat on the new workbench and Dr Crumb stood facing her. He said, "There are some things which I did not tell you, and some things I told you which were not quite true."

"About me? About who I am? What I am?"

"Partly. More about *me*, and what I am."

137

"But I thought you didn't believe in telling lies?" said Fever. "Not even white lies? Not even to little girls?"

Dr Crumb looked at the floor, as if he had suddenly become very interested in floors. He took a sip of his boiled water, and began.

When Gideon Crumb first came to London the city was still ruled by the Scriven. There was already talk about rebel outfits called the Skinners' Guilds, and a few anti-Scriven graffitoes had been scrawled up on walls in the lower parts of town, but Auric Godshawk still sat on his throne in the Barbican, and Scriven still owned half the city's businesses and all its better property.

Gideon grew used to having to stop in his tracks and drop to his knees in the street mud when the chair of some Scriven nobleman was carried past, or risk being beaten by the servants who walked behind it. He grew used too to the gales of brutal cheering and jeering that gusted from Pickled Eel Circus, where handsome gladiators like Ted Swiney and "Slow" Loris Dimbelow did battle with each other, and with the weird killing machines which the Scriven pieced together with infinite skill and with no purpose beyond their own cruel amusement.

But at least the Scriven's *penchant* for machines meant that they needed a steady supply of machine-builders and machine-tenders. That was why they had founded the Order of Engineers. But the Order of Engineers had become more than just machine-builders and machine-tenders. They had started out by trying to understand ancient devices, and ended up by trying to understand *everything*. They looked carefully and clearly at the workings of the world. They gathered evidence, and made experiments, and developed brilliant theories which they were always ready to abandon if new evidence proved them wrong. They were more than engineers; they had become scientists, and every year they welcomed twenty young men into the Engineerium and started training them to be scientists too.

Gideon was one of them, escaping from a childhood in the outlying borough of Lesser Wintermire, with its plashy farms and midge-bite fens, its sputtering tallow candles, its vague religious spasms of hope and terror. He did not care who London's rulers were. All his attention was focused on its future, which would be lit by gas and 'lectric and the hard white light of reason.

During his first three years at the Engineerium he was an apprentice, and lived with other apprentices in a honeycomb of small chambers behind the main building. Their life was simple, but comfortable enough. A few of the senior Engineers, men like Dr Stayling, shaved their heads and avoided all pleasure, saying that it interfered with the ability to reason, but there were others, like Dr Wormtimber, who argued that good food, a little drink of an evening and a comfortable bed helped to relax a man, and made it easier for him to think. That attitude appealed to Gideon Crumb, who did not want to shave off his curly, nut-brown hair, or stop eating the oat biscuits and apple-and-bramble pies which reminded him of the nicer bits of his childhood. (Of course he would not go so far as Wormtimber, who had recently moved out of the Engineerium and married an archaeologist's widow. Gideon had always been shy around girls, and had long since decided that romance and marriage and parenthood were things best left to other, less reasonable men.)

Then, in his fourth year at the Engineerium, everything changed.

It was a blue, bitter day, way down in the cheerless deeps of winter, with thick snow heaped along the street sides and weighing down the roofs and long months to go until Spring Festival. Gideon, out scouring the dig markets for interesting relics, took a wrong turning down a street he did not recognize, and found himself in the middle of a strange disturbance. An elaborately carved sedan chair had halted in the middle of the street, but although it was so expensive looking that it could only have belonged to a Scriven, none of the pedestrians around it was kneeling down. When Gideon started to kneel, a man nearby said half angrily, "Don't you bend your knee to *her*, mate!"

He hesitated, knees already awkwardly bent, and looked again at the chair. It was not a true sedan chair at all, but a type of rickshaw, with tyred wheels at the back where the rear bearer usually walked. In front of it, between its shafts, stood a Jaeger, or "Stalker", as Londoners called them. The Scriven had brought several hundred of these reanimated warriors with them when they arrived in the city, but over the years most had gone mad and destroyed themselves, or simply stopped working. The one which had been pulling this chair seemed to have malfunctioned in some critical way. It stood rigidly to attention, but its bulky head twitched restlessly about, and from the mouth slot of its face shield poured a stream of meaningless words. "I

AM I WAS I WHAT SEVERAL TOO LONG TOO LATE LONELY LONELY. . ."

"It's gone off its trolley!" yelled a barrow boy, and shied a half brick, which bounced off the Stalker's armour with a clang.

The occupant of the chair wound down a tinted window and leaned out, shouting at the Stalker to walk on. Glimpsing her dappled face, Gideon dropped to his knees in the dirty snow. Several of the other onlookers followed suit. If the Stalker came to its senses the Scriven woman would have it kill anyone who had been disrespectful enough to remain standing in her presence.

But the Stalker was too far gone for that. A veteran of the nomad empires' long wars, it had finally worn out. "SLEEPY NOW," it bellowed, and reaching up, caught hold of its own head with both steel hands and wrenched it off in a shower of yellowish sparks and a gurgling of thick fluids. The green light in its eyes faded, and, still holding its head, it toppled over like the statue of a fallen tyrant and lay on the cobbles, trailing thin strings of smoke.

For a moment there was silence. It was so quiet that Gideon could hear the north wind sighing between the icicles which trailed from the eaves above him. For years hostility to the Scriven had been growing, but this situation was new to everyone; a Scriven alone and defenceless in a St Kylie street. The Londoners looked at each other, wondering whether they dared take their revenge.

Before they could decide, the chair door opened and the Scriven stepped out. She wore a tortoiseshell cat-fur cape with the collar turned up so that all you could see of her was her face. A beautiful face, large-eyed and porcelain pale, the cheeks and forehead darkly dappled with the Scriven markings.

"Move this out of the road," she commanded, pointing one gloved finger at the Stalker's wreck. "And take me to the Barbican."

None of the watching Londoners moved. How they hated her! You could feel it in the air, like a rising mist. That cape she wore cost more than all their houses. The price of those gloves would have fed and clothed their children for a year. And she'd been so sure of herself, with her resurrected heavy to protect her, that she hadn't even brought the Scriven's usual honour guard of thugs and soldiers with her when she ventured through St Kylie.

Someone threw a stone. It wasn't thrown hard, but it struck the Scriven on the side of her perfect face and she put up a hand to the place where it had hit, and her eyes widened a little, and she seemed at last to understand what danger she was in.

"You wouldn't dare!" she said, but she didn't sound at all certain about it.

"No!" said Gideon. (Was it really him speaking? It had to be; he could feel his mouth shaping the words, and see the breath smouldering in front of his face as he spoke them into the cold, still air.) "No! Come along, this isn't reasonable. You have nothing to gain by assaulting this person. Do you think the Scriven won't send their mercenaries down here to take revenge, if you go any further in this foolishness?"

"Who's he?" asked a woman.

"No idea," said another.

"Engineer, by the look of him."

"Blog off, Scriven lover!" yelled a man in the stiff blue overalls of a plasticsmith, hefting a cobblestone ready to hurl at the Scriven. But he sounded half-hearted, as if even he could see the sense in what Gideon had said. The stone stayed in his hand, unthrown. Gideon walked past him towards the Scriven.

"Thank you," she said thinly, as he drew near to her. Some of the onlookers gasped and murmured. They had never heard a Scriven thank anyone before. She was trembling slightly. How old was she? She didn't look much more than twenty, but it was hard to tell with her kind. The joke in London was that if you wanted to know how old a Dapplejack was you had to cut them in half and count the rings.

She reached out and took Gideon by the arm before he could object. "You will lead me to the Barbican, Engineer," she said. She didn't have any idea where she was, he realized. Conveyed around London all her life by chair, she knew nothing of the layout of its streets. Whereas he, who had never been able to afford to travel except on foot, could easily get his bearings by glancing up at the temples and buildings whose spires he could see poking up behind the snowy rooftops.

A stone flew past him and smashed one of the chair windows. He felt the Scriven woman flinch at the sound of the glass shattering. He flinched too, but he calmed himself by reciting pi and telling himself that he was doing the only reasonable thing. And, arm in arm with the Scriven, he walked up that street and back on to streets he knew, while behind them her would-be

143

murderers contented themselves by making a bonfire of her abandoned chair and smashing the fallen Stalker up for spare parts.

It was starting to snow again, or perhaps it was just the winter wind lifting flurries of powder snow from the roofs and chimney stacks. The small flakes settled like sequins in the tortoiseshell fur of the Scriven's cape as she and Gideon walked past the lighted windows of exclusive restaurants and high-class scent shops and boutiques until they reached the square in front of the Barbican. Despite the masonry which filled its wheel arches and the new spires and turrets which spoiled its timber upperworks, the old fortress clearly showed its origins as a huge vehicle; a high-prowed ship of the steppes in which the Scriven had been dragged halfway across the world by their armies of slaves. Gideon thought his companion might be interested to hear the latest news from the nomad empires, whose technomancers were now fitting engines to their traction fortresses, but just as he was about to mention it she let go his arm and turned to look at him.

Her eyes were the rich brown of expensive chocolate, with some unguessable emotion in them, and suddenly she laughed, and Gideon saw that she wore a metal brace on her teeth. It glittered in the light from the windows of the shops like a tiny railway track. So she wasn't perfect after all, or at least she must not *think* that she was perfect, if she had paid some dentist to attach all that careful engineering to her smile.

That was when he fell in love with her.

She asked his name before she left him and went up into the Barbican. He told her, but he was too startled by his own feelings to ask hers, or ask her what she had been doing in the backstreets of St Kylie all alone. Not until the next morning, when he read the front-page story in the *Alarmist*, did he learn that Wavey Godshawk, daughter of Auric Godshawk, had been waylaid in the low city when her malfunctioning Jaeger servant took a wrong turning, and that the Scriven's mercenaries had executed twenty Londoners by way of punishment.

20

AT NONESUCH HOUSE

hat brief confrontation in St Kylie, and the Patchwork king's spiteful response, would change the history of London for ever. By the summer of that year few Scriven dared venture far beyond the expensive, well-lit streets which surrounded the Barbican. Those who did were slaughtered by the Skinners' Guilds. Brutish reprisals by Godshawk's Suomi mercenaries seemed to have no effect beyond making the commons hate him even more.

But Gideon Crumb, safe in the Engineerium, barely noticed any of it. He had never taken an interest in politics and, except for that one morning after he walked Wavey Godshawk home, he avoided newspapers, which everyone knew were unreasonable things, filled with scaremongering and the wildest rumours. He was busy with the study of ancient engines which he hoped would win him his place as a fully fledged Engineer, and he had no more time for wandering the streets of London.

The only trouble was, he could not forget Wavey Godshawk. At night in his bunk while he waited for sleep, when he should have been turning over ideas about torque and fuel efficiency in his mind, he kept being distracted by the image of her face, her smile, her way of speaking. Her voice had been soft but rather deep, he recalled. She had had very small hands. Her hair, or at least those strands of it which had escaped the hood of her cape, was tawny blonde. . .

He told himself not to be so foolish, and forced himself to consider power-weight ratios until he fell asleep, but Wavey Godshawk waited for him in his dreams. It was all most distracting, and almost enough to make him wonder if Dr Stayling didn't have it right when he said that a good Engineer must purge himself of all emotions.

And then, on a September afternoon, when he was puzzling over books in the library, the sounds of uproar and disorder reached him, coming not from distant quarters of the city, as they had all summer, but from somewhere inside the Engineerium itself.

He closed the book he was reading and hurried out of the library. In the corridor which led to the Engineerium's main entrance men in the gaudy jackets of Godshawk's private militia were striding about with muskets among a lot of white-coated, kneeling Engineers. "Kneel!" one bellowed, seeing Gideon standing there staring, and Gideon knelt.

In through the main doors, as if she were solidifying out of a blaze of sunshine, came Wavey Godshawk. The gown she wore was the most unreasonable thing ever seen in the Engineerium. Its skirts whispered along either wall as she passed. Even Dr Stayling, who had often declared that it was irrational and unreasonable to kneel before a Scriven, went down on his knees at the sight of her. Gideon, too embarrassed to look at her face, looked at the floor instead. He heard her dress come whispering and sighing and hissing towards him, and then the creak of the huge wicker frame beneath her skirts as she stopped just a few inches away.

"I am here on behalf of His Excellency the Civic Commander Auric Godshawk," she said, in that well-remembered voice. "He has sent me here to find an Engineer to be his assistant." She paused, and Gideon pictured her looking about at all the kneeling Engineers like a lady shopping for new gloves, until he felt her hand touch the back of his bowed head, light as a butterfly.

"I think I'd like this one. Have him sent to Nonesuch House this afternoon."

There were a lot of men in the Order far better qualified than Gideon Crumb to serve as an assistant to the great Scriven inventor. Later, there would be all sorts of spiteful rumours about him. The unemotional Dr Whyre grew quite angry that *he* had not been offered a chance to explore the mysteries of Godshawk's laboratories, and stubbed his toe rather badly when he kicked his workbench in a fit of pique. But Gideon was never aware of that. He must have spent the next few hours gathering his books and belongings, packing clean shirts and underwear and travelling somehow to 'Bankmentside and out along the causeway. But when he thought back on it in after years it seemed to him that he had gone straight from kneeling before Wavey Godshawk in the Engineerium to kneeling before her father in the hallway of Nonesuch House, watching Godshawk's slippers and the hems of Godshawk's robes as the tyrant-inventor paced towards him.

"Get up."

Gideon climbed to his feet, still too nervous to look

148

directly at his new employer. He glimpsed peacock-coloured robes, a speckled hand gripping the handle of a steel cane, a lot of rings, a crisp white cuff. The voice said, "Why should you kneel to me, Londoner? There are thousands of your kind in this city, and barely two hundred of mine. The time of the Scriven will soon be over."

Gideon couldn't help but look up at that. Except for a strange, half-mocking smile, Godshawk's face was the same face that Gideon remembered from a thousand wall posters, and from the immense statue which was being built in the west of the city. A long, angular face, leopard-speckled, white-bearded, white-maned. The large, watchful eyes of a big and dangerous cat.

"I've shocked you, eh?" he said. "You've never heard one of the Scrivener's chosen people speak the truth about ourselves that way? Well, I'll go further. There *is* no Scrivener. There is no real difference between us and any other race of human beings. Our longevity, and these attractive marks of which we are so proud, are just minor genetic quirks. Fate has blessed us with robust constitutions and an interesting skin complaint, and in every other way we are as human as you. We managed to grow powerful for a while, but we have not done much with that power. We played games, like children, imagining that the real business of our kind all lay ahead. Now playtime is nearly over, and we see that there is nothing more to come. That's why I must work fast, if I am to leave the world anything to remember us by. So I need an assistant. My daughter tells me that you did her a service once, and those fools at the Engineerium assure me you are clever."

"What would you have me do, sir?" asked Dr Crumb, excited at the thought of working on one of the old Scriven's inventions.

But by way of answer, Godshawk merely led him to a side room and flung the door open. It was a big room, and it was filled from side to side and floor to ceiling with old-tech. There were big pieces and small, well-preserved ones along with a few that were no more than hunks of rust.

"I need money, Crumb. I have a project in mind, and it must be funded, so I have decided to sell off my collection. This lot has been acquired over a lifetime, and I've had a long life. I can't remember what's in here myself, so I want you to catalogue it, and assess it as you go. Sort the trash from the treasures. Make notes. If you need anything, ask my daughter. I'll pop in from time to time and see how you're doing."

"I'll do my best, sir," said Gideon. But Godshawk had already gone striding on his way.

Days went by. Weeks went by. Slowly, Gideon worked his way through the mountains of machinery, studying, describing, puzzling. Had this battered plastic frame been part of a TV set, or only a window? Could this crushed orange rubber ball really have hopped into space, as its name suggested? He made drawings and notes in a circular ledger. He grew bored. He thought often of asking Godshawk to release him from this work, which any half-trained scavenger could have done, and let him return to the Engineerium. But he never did. At the Engineerium he would not be near Wavey Godshawk.

Wavey worked as her father's assistant. When she was in that role she wore her hair tied back and put on a white coat, tailored to spread over the wide bell of her skirts. Each afternoon she would come in and listen carefully while Gideon explained the more interesting pieces he had found and catalogued. She dropped in questions and suggestions, always perfectly timed. She set him thinking. She challenged his assumptions. The Order had taught him that women were weak, unreasonable creatures, but Wavey was neither. The Scriven dapplings on her face and neck made chains of little V shapes, like wild geese flying. He imagined mathematical formulae which might describe the angle of her cheekbones.

21

NOCTURNE IN BLUE

n the summertime, some of the objects which Gideon had studied were shipped north to the city to be sold at auction in the Tech Exchange, and the rest were cleared into a smaller room, for Nonesuch House was to host a party. As Lord of London Godshawk was expected to be hospitable. His Suomi mercenaries went to and fro along the causeway, checking for booby traps and clearing stands of trees where Skinner terrorists might lurk. Canopies and marquees flowered on Godshawk's lawns, and famous scent artists like Eldritch Hooter and Odourita arrived to load the scent lanterns with their specially composed perfumes.

Gideon's work languished as the day of the party drew near. Godshawk seemed to have forgotten all about the remainder of his collection, and even Wavey stopped visiting, spending her afternoons instead trying on dresses with the help of a new slave girl her father had bought for her in the city. Gideon sat in his room, thinking about her, listlessly trying to concentrate on his notes and drawings, distracted by the tuning-up of power shawms and pneumatic sackbuts in the bandstand below his window.

He wasn't invited to the party, of course. But nor was he forbidden from attending, and when the whole of Nonesuch House was filled with revellers and rowdy as a St Kylie boozer there was not much else that he could do. He wandered through the crowded rooms, listening to the music and sniffing the rich odours which unfurled from the scent lanterns. Wavey had told him that her people could see scents, and had spoken passionately about the great perfume symphonies of Hooter, Klopstock and DeFries, which to her were not just smells but shimmering, luminous fields of subtle colour. Gideon tried to imagine what that would be like, but he couldn't; the scents just made him sneeze. He swiped a glass from a passing waiter's tray and wandered on, ignored by the Scriven, who shouted small talk at each other over his head.

"Hooter's in good form! What does he call this scent?"

"I think it's *Nocturne in Blue*."

"Did you hear about Stefan Destrier? The Skinners got him, laid in wait for him by his own gate."

"Disgraceful! Godshawk must do something to discipline these monkeys. . ."

The Scriven men wore stack-heeled boots and pearl-studded evening coats; the ladies in their vast skirts looked like mythical creatures, half woman, half sofa. Wavey Godshawk glided by, heading to the dance floor, arm in arm with some old Scriven lord. Her face was lifted towards her partner's, and her eyes were smiling, but she kept her mouth closed, and Gideon knew that it was because she felt self-conscious about the brace on her teeth. She was the most beautiful thing he had ever seen.

"There goes Odo Bolventor with the Godshawk girl," said a Scriven, leaning over Gideon's shoulder to point out the couple to his friend.

"I hear Godshawk's been trying to arrange a marriage. He needs an heir."

"And Bolventor needs her dowry. He calls himself Margrave of Thurrock, but he's as poor as a gnat!"

They moved on, still gossiping, never realizing that they had just squashed Gideon's dreams. He pushed his way out of the room. He did not want to watch Wavey dancing with her Margrave. He went out into the gardens, glad to be away from the heat and noise of the party and the cloying odours of the scent lanterns. He walked past the ghostly marquees, past the gangs of servants who were busy lighting float lamps and setting them adrift upon the evening air. The sounds of music and chit-chat faded as he went downhill towards the still lagoons.

"Having fun, Doctor Crumb?"

There were statues among the shrubbery. As Gideon turned to see who'd spoken one of them seemed to come to life. Auric Godshawk strolled towards him, the night wind flipping the skirts of his printed silk evening gown. There was a glass of brandy in his hand. It slopped and glittered as he gestured uphill towards the house. "They make a racket, don't they? Parties are meant for the young, not old men like me."

"Yes, sir."

He came closer, peering at Gideon's face in the light of the moon which hung low and yellowish above the hill.

"You look crushed, Crumb. Like a well-trodden biscuit. What's wrong?"

"Nothing, sir," said Gideon. He wondered if the old Scriven understood what he felt for Wavey. He said,

154

"Sir, do you think that some of my fellow Engineers are right when they say that emotion should be avoided? That we must suppress all feelings if we are to be truly rational?"

Godshawk looked surprised, the way that people generally do when you ask them philosophical questions in shrubberies in the middle of the night. He snorted, and took another sip of his brandy. "I don't know about that, Crumb. We Scriven have always been very keen on emotions. Sensations, feelings, that sort of thing. We live only once, and we might as well enjoy all the pleasures that the old world has to offer us on our journey through it."

"But emotions are so painful," said Gideon. He felt as if he were confessing, *I am in love with your daughter*. He felt sure the old Scriven must understand him.

Godshawk nodded, looking out over the lagoons. Lanterns drifted above the water, and beyond the marshes the lights of London twinkled in the mist.

"Yes, pain's a part of it," he said. "When we see something beautiful we want to possess it. But we know we can't, don't we? And that hurts. Beauty fades, things change, time moves us on." He drained his glass and raised it to Gideon before throwing it aside. Then, reaching inside his robes, he took out a small silver case. "Look at this," he said. He flipped it open. Inside, on the crumpled silk lining, lay a shining thing of polished steel, or maybe some other alloy that no one any longer knew a name for. Something from the Ancient world. Godshawk took it out, holding it carefully between the tips of his forefinger and thumb. Just a wee thing it was,

155

the shape of a walnut, the size of an almond. "Look at this, Crumb. In theory, a man's whole life could be recorded in a seed like this, all his hopes and loves and fears and all his knowledge."

Gideon looked at the object, and wondered what Godshawk expected him to say. "I see," he murmured at last, trying to sound impressed, but fearing he sounded merely foolish.

Godshawk chuckled, for no reason that Gideon could understand. He snapped the case shut and put it back in whatever inner pocket it had come from. The moon had risen higher, and shone ghostly in the garden's mysterious pools. "It's a pretty world," he said. "What a pity we Scriven won't inherit it. And now I must return to my guests. They'll probably expect a speech or some such nonsense. Don't stay out here in the cold too long, Dr Crumb! Back to bed with you, and get some sleep."

But Gideon knew that sleep would be impossible. The party was set to go on all night. He walked along the water's edge, all the way around the hill. Long after midnight he started to climb back up the terraces. Glass broke somewhere near by; a small prickling sound. He looked towards the summer house and saw a movement there. Went closer, and heard the sound of soft sobs. Someone weeping.

"Wavey?" He recognized her dress, in the summer house dark. She stood with her back to him, a hand raised to her face. The shards of a glass glittered on the floor nearby. She held a little jar in her hand. As he watched she upended it, tipping out some of its contents on to a lint pad. Then she went on rubbing her face.

156

"Miss Godshawk?" he said.

She turned with a little gasp. "What are you doing here?" she asked. Her words wobbled in the middle and blurred at the edges. She was a little drunk, and he thought she had been crying. And then, as he went towards her, he saw that the markings on her face had gone. He thought at first that it must be a trick of that dim light, but it was not. Those Scriven stains which had showed so strikingly on her forehead and high cheekbones and along the curve of her jaw had been washed away.

"You are not really a Scriven!" he said.

"Of course I'm a Scriven, you fool," replied Wavey Godshawk. The soft, consoling scent of the cream she'd used to clean her face came wafting towards him. She threw the wet lint pad on the floor. "I am as much a Scriven as he is. Look!" And she came closer to Gideon and twisted her head and lifted her hair to show him a sepia patch on the side of her neck. "Look. . ." She tore open her lace collar and undid the top two buttons of her bodice and pulled it open to show him another speckle, black in the moonlight, which lay in the hollow above her collarbone like a pool of ink. "Not good enough for Odo Bolventor!" she said nastily. "Odo Bolventor, Margrave of Thurrock. Margrave of Puke! I'm better without him. To think I would have married him!"

Gideon took a nervous step away from her, alarmed by the unsettling impulses which were telling him to go closer. Wavey had always seemed to him so haughty and so self-assured. He would never have imagined that she would behave in such an emotional, undignified way,

157

and in front of a mere human like him. He said awkwardly, "I don't understand. . ."

"Of course you don't. How could you understand? You're just a dull old *Homo sapiens*, and I am Scriven!" She lifted her head, tilting her pale chin proudly at him. Her dress rustled; beneath the silk, stays and corsets and the stiff wicker frame that gave her skirt its shape creaked softly in time to her hurried breathing. Then, turning away, she said weepily, "I was born like this. Some Scriven are nowadays. Our race is failing. I have a few markings, but not many, and none on my face. When I was little the other girls used to say that the Scrivener ran out of ink when he came to write on me.

"So I used make-up. Wendigo's Patent Body Ink. I spray it on through a stencil mask, so my marks look always the same. But Scriven society is such a small world, and there is so much gossip, that of course the Margrave came to hear of it. Tonight, while we were dancing, he asked me if it were true, and when I said it was he said he would not be made a fool of, and would not marry a freak, and risk having his sons born blank like me. He said I was as ugly as boiled fish."

Gideon wanted to say, "You aren't ugly." He wanted to tell her how beautiful she was. But instead he said, "Your father says that the time of the Scriven is over. Perhaps it will be an advantage to have no speckles, which would show what you are to the commons. . ."

"The commons," said Wavey, dismissively, and then looked up at him as if she had remembered something. "It was you who saved me from them. That day in the city. . ." She laughed, a soft, wondering laugh. "Why *did* you do that?"

"I don't know," said Gideon truthfully.

A floating lantern drifted past, and its light came through the glass roof and brushed Wavey's face. She smiled, sudden and bewitching. "I don't believe I ever thanked you," she said. "We can be so thoughtless, can't we, we *Homo superiors*?" She took his hands and drew him close to her. She smelled of wine and cosmetics. Her breath felt hot against his face. "Why are you shaking like that?" she asked. "What *is* your name, anyway? I can't just call you Doctor Crumb."

"I'm G-gideon," he managed to say.

"Then thank you, G-gideon," she said, and at last she kissed him, and her lips were parted, and the wires of the brace on her teeth gently grazed his mouth.

22

THE FIFTH WORD

t had not lasted, of course. A love affair between a Londoner and a Scriven? It had not lasted out the month.

But for a while the whole balance of Gideon's life had shifted. Instead of reason he was guided by the unfathomable feelings which Wavey aroused in him. He neglected his work and sat waiting for her brief, stolen visits. He once or twice considered writing poems. He didn't know if she loved him as much as he loved her or if he was just a distraction for her. At night sometimes, while the rest of the house slept, he would go quietly out into the gardens, and she would be waiting for him in their summer house. "Godshawk must never know of this," she said, holding him in her strong, speckled arms.

But Godshawk knew almost everything that went on in his house. He had been suspicious of his daughter's reasons for choosing Gideon ever since the young Engineer arrived. That new slave girl he had bought her was his spy. One afternoon, in the middle of a hissing storm of cold grey rain, Gideon was called before him.

The great man was waiting for him in the vault beneath the house, a place which Gideon had never visited before. It seemed devoted to the study of Stalkers. Dozens stood or lay about like charmless statues with their heads prized open. In the vats which lined the walls floated dead people – or at least, Gideon *hoped* they were dead. Severed heads in jars lined a shelf behind Godshawk's desk, and the glare which the inventor shot at him as he came in made Gideon fear for a moment that his own would shortly join them.

"Do you take me for a fool, Crumb?" the inventor asked.

"No, sir. . ."

Gideon looked for help. In a corner of the room stood Wavey Godshawk. Her face was stencilled with its familiar markings, that flock of wild geese on her brow and cheeks. He remembered how closely and solemnly she had watched him as they lay together in the summer house amid the shipwreck of her dress. Now she would not even look at him, just stared haughtily at the ceiling.

"Did you think I wouldn't find out about your little romance?" asked Godshawk.

"No, sir," said Gideon. "I thought. . ."

"Thought what? That I'd *approve*? Great Scrivener, women of child-bearing age are in short enough supply among my people as it is, without I go marrying one off to *you*."

"But—"

"You wretch, Crumb! If I weren't kinder than most of my breed you'd be dead by now, or on your way to meet the death machines at Pickled Eel Circus! As it is, I want you gone. What, do you think I won't be able to find another little scribbler like you to aid me in my work? You're nothing. If you come near Nonesuch House again I'll set the dogs on you. Now go."

Gideon looked again at Wavey, but Wavey was still not looking at him. She seemed bored.

The next thing he remembered was the huge front door of Nonesuch House slamming shut behind him, leaving him alone on the drive in the pounding rain. Twilight was coming on. He was already soaked. He looked at the windows above him, hoping to see Wavey look out. Godshawk would have ordered her not to, but she would take no notice of Godshawk, would she?

He waited while rain trickled down the back of his neck and crept in through the seams of his sleeves and plastered his wet hair across his face and filled up his boots. But he never saw her again.

Six months later he would stand once more in Godshawk's garden. It was a few weeks after the Skinners' Riots, and a story had been doing the rounds about how a band of Scriven had been found holed up at Nonesuch House, and how the Skinners had gone there and slaughtered them.

Gideon had not let himself think about Wavey Godshawk since he returned to London the previous summer. He had gone back to the Engineerium, and Dr Stayling had allowed him to pick up his studies. When thoughts of Wavey came into his mind he forced them away, and made himself concentrate on his work instead. He had worked hard all winter at forgetting her, and he had grown good at it. But when the riots started, he could think of nothing but Wavey.

On the evening when it began he was outside the Engineerium, assaying circuit boards for a digger in Womblesden. Hurrying home, he stopped to watch the Skinners running down Cripplegate in the summer twilight. The smack of their shoes on the cobbles sounded like applause. Some stopped just long enough to hurl burning brands in through the windows of shops and banking houses. They carried things he thought were banners, until one passed close by and he saw that it was the flayed skin of a Scriven. From Ludgate Hill came the crackling, brush-fire sound of muskets.

In some ways it was almost a relief. The anger of London had been building for so long, it had been like living on the flanks of a volcano. Now that the eruption had finally come there was no time to worry about it, no time to think. Crumb hid among some bins near the tram terminus to avoid another gang of Skinners, and was then almost shot down as a Skinner himself when he rounded a corner near the Engineerium and came upon a battalion of the Scriven's mercenaries, their crisp white uniforms smudged with soot and powder. Luckily the Scriven officer in charge of them recognized him from his Nonesuch House days and ordered them not to shoot.

"What is happening?" Gideon asked him, as he was bundled through the lines. "Where is Godshawk?"

"Safe in the Barbican, doctor, waiting for us to finish off this London rabble."

"What about his daughter?"

"Scrivener alone knows! These mobs are everywhere! Get back to your Engineerium, man; you'll be safe there. . ."

But next morning the mobs broke into the Engineerium itself, smashing and looting, shouting that the Engineers were Scriven lackeys and no better than their masters. The frightened and bewildered Engineers were herded out into the courtyard, and there they might all have been killed, except that a second, larger band of Skinners happened by. They were led by a man named Creech, who scrambled up on an overturned sedan chair and fired his spring gun in the air to call for quiet. He wore a leather apron smeared with brown and crimson stains, and stuck through his belt was a long curved blade like a shard of the moon. But it turned out that, in this mob, he was the voice of reason.

"These men are our kind," he shouted, pointing at the captive Engineers. "We got no argument with them. This place of theirs will make good homes for human widows and human orphlings. You want to do some killing, you better come with me; Godshawk himself is still holding out in the Barbican!"

The Skinners went roaring off, leaving the Engineers to pick up the pieces of their smashed experiments and try to salvage their scattered and damaged books. Pickled Eel Circus was blazing like a colossal brazier, sending thick swathes of smoke across the Engineerium compound. More rioters passed, and this time many of them wore once-white uniforms; the Scriven's mercenary soldiers had decided that the fight could not be won, and were changing sides. A few hours later the Engineers heard the cheering spread from the Barbican all through the city as word came that Auric Godshawk had been killed.

But surely Wavey's blank, unspeckled skin would have saved her? Gideon kept thinking about her all through the confused days which followed the riots, while he helped the Order to move to their new home in the abandoned head of Godshawk's giant statue. As he wheeled the Engineer's belongings on handcarts down the Westerway he was watched by severed Scriven heads which the Skinners had stuck on the railings outside the houses there. None of them was Wavey's. But how could he know that hers was not among the flayed bodies which lay in the gutters, attracting the attentions of rats and ravens and stray dogs? Oh, surely, he thought, when she heard the rioters coming, she would have had the sense to wipe her false markings off and mingle with the mobs?

But Wavey wasn't logical; she had her prickly Scriven pride, and he could well imagine her stencilling darker markings on just to taunt the Skinners. . .

When he neared Nonesuch Hill that morning he saw that the house he had known so well was scorched and tumbled. Charred grass crumbled into ash as he climbed the terraces. A film of soot lay on the surface of the pools. The blackened roof beams ticked softly, embers glowing red as the breeze fanned them. Metal had melted and flowed in silvery puddles and lacings over the blackened tiles underfoot.

"Wavey?" called Gideon, over the cawing of the carrion birds.

He started looking for her among the crumpled outbuildings, hoping that she might have hidden somehow, but all he found were the dead. Whether Wavey was among them or not, it was impossible to know; they all looked like heather roots scorched by a brush fire.

It was on his way back to London that day that Gideon decided to turn off his feelings. He had seen for himself now how dangerous emotions were. Tenderness and anger, love and hate, they all led to nothing but trouble; he blamed them for his own broken heart, as well as the feverish violence of the Skinners' Guilds. He was not an animal. From now on, he decided, he would live without feelings.

Looking carefully at himself in the speckled mirror which hung from a nail on his workspace wall, Gideon shaved his head, and gathered up the pile of chestnut curls and carried them to the stove and threw them in and watched them burn.

It was a few weeks later that a note arrived in the careful, childish writing of Chigley Unthank, asking him to come and assess a new dig far out on the marshes. Dr Crumb remembered Unthank, an archaeologist who had worked for Godshawk, and been a frequent visitor to Nonesuch House. Now he was an outcast, scratching a living for himself and his daughter in the Brick Marsh. His note claimed he had unearthed the fragments of an Ancient computer brain, but when Gideon reached the place, Unthank could only show him a few scraps of ruined circuit board lashed together with wire and strung with animal bones; a common tribal totem from the time of the Downsizing. When Doctor Crumb explained patiently that such things could be dug up almost anywhere, and were of no use except as an illustration of how far mankind had sunk into savagery and superstition after the fall of the Ancient world, Master Unthank had grown embarrassed, and even Gideon could tell that the tale of the computer brain had been just a ruse to bring him there.

Nervously, almost shyly, Unthank beckoned him into the miserable little smoke-filled, scrap-plastic hut which was his home. His daughter Katie, a scruffy-looking teenager, was scrubbing circuit shards in a tub of muddy water. Beside the fire a basket lay, and in the basket was a child, kicking its legs, jerking its tiny fists about. It stared up at Gideon with odd-coloured eyes.

"Woman brought it here soon after the riots," said Unthank, from the doorway. "She kept her face hid, wouldn't give her name. Said she had to go a journey, and couldn't take the kid. Said I was to send word for you."

"Why me?" asked Gideon.

Unthank did not reply. His daughter had stopped scrubbing and was watching Gideon curiously, as if waiting to see what he would do. Gingerly he reached into the basket and lifted the luggage label which was tied around the child's wrist.

He knew the handwriting at once. Wavey Godshawk had been her father's assistant for a long time; each drawer and library shelf at Nonesuch House had been labelled in the same careful script that he saw on that brown paper tag, in the smoky light of Unthank's hut. There were just five words.

HER NAME IS FEVER CRUMB.

23

UNDER SIEGE

hen you are my father?" asked Fever, when he had told her everything. She was shocked, of course; terribly shocked and disappointed that Dr Crumb had ever given in to such fervid and unreasonable emotions. (And there was another feeling in her too, a quivering, fluttering feeling which arose at the thought that he really was her father. But feelings did not matter; they were a distraction; all that mattered now was finding out the truth.)

"That's what she meant, isn't it? *Her name is Fever Crumb.* Wavey Godshawk was my mother, and she was saying that you were my father."

Dr Crumb looked away, towards the rain-wet windows and the city outside them. He set down the cup he had been holding, and the sound made Fever start. "You are her child, of that I'm sure. It has always been thought that *Homo sapiens* and *Homo superior* could not have children together. . ."

"But perhaps Wavey was not like other Scriven," suggested Fever. "She had hardly any markings. Or perhaps Godshawk was telling you the truth, and there was never as much difference between us and them as they liked to claim. . ."

"Both those things are possible," admitted Dr Crumb. "But we have no evidence. All I know is that the label was in Wavey's handwriting, and that it said *Her name is Fever Crumb.* At the time I thought she had just written that to make me think that you were mine, hoping that would make me take care of you. I didn't mind. I would have taken care of you anyway. It was the only reasonable thing to do. But later, as you grew, you seemed so like me in so many ways that I began to wonder if you might be mine after all."

Fever went to the mirror on the wall, which she had stood before so often to shave her head. She could see herself reflected there, and Dr Crumb behind her. She saw now that they had the same narrow faces, the same sticky-out ears. But she hadn't inherited his small mouth or long nose. Her mouth and nose were echoes of another face; the face of Wavey Godshawk.

"Didn't you try to find her?" she asked. "After you'd found me, I mean. After you knew she must still be alive?"

Dr Crumb shook his head. "It was impossible, Fever. I had no way of knowing which way she had fled. North, south, east or west? I had no contacts outside London whom I could ask about a fugitive Scriven. And if I did ask, and they had seen her, I might only have caused her to be recognized, and killed. For all I know she died in the Marshes somewhere, after she left you at Unthank's hut. The Skinners still had patrols and watchers out there. She vanished, Fever. She was swallowed up by history, and we shall probably never know what became of her. I am just glad that at least I have you."

"The other Engineers? Dr Stayling? Do they know all this?"

Dr Crumb shook his head. "I have always told them

169

what I told you. That I found you in a basket on the marsh. . ."

Fever kept looking at herself. Half Scriven, she thought. Wavey's daughter. Godshawk's granddaughter. She said, "There's more. I *remember* things. Things that happened before I was born; things that only Godshawk could have seen. . ."

Dr Crumb frowned. "Some sort of inherited memory? It does not sound likely. . ."

Something slammed against Godshawk's Head with a sound like a huge bell ringing.

Dr Crumb went to the window. "There is a mob out there!" he said.

Fever joined him, looking down. The rain had slackened, but an ominous, end-of-the-world gloom still hung over the abandoned factories. A tide of people was flooding on to the wasteland that surrounded Godshawk's Head. Sedan chairs bobbed upon it, and burning torches made bright points of saffron light behind the rain. Those at the front of the crowd were throwing things, and a few of them threw hard enough to hit the Head. Tiles and half bricks clanged and sang against the metal, and from some neighbouring room came the clash of a smashed window.

Fever and Dr Crumb ran from his quarters and down the stairs. Down on the library level they met Dr Stayling and some others coming up. "The commons have surrounded us," said Stayling. "It is like the Skinners' Riots come again. But there is no call for alarm, gentlemen, or, ah, Fever. I have switched on the intrud-o-cuter; that should hold the troublemakers at bay."

From outside came cries and curses, accompanied by

flutterings of hard, blue light. The Engineers had not forgotten the attack on their old premises, and they had taken measures to defend their new home. The high fence which ringed the Head was wired to a 'lectric pile in the basement, and at the first sign of the rioters attacking Dr Stayling had turned it on. Once a few of the roughs outside had been blasted by the powerful current the rest drew back, scared of the Order's magic and content to hurl stones and insults up at Godshawk's impassive face.

"Scriven lovers!"

"Send out the Patchskin maid!"

"Throw her out, or we'll climb up and get her!"

Their words came thinly into the Head. Fever listened, and tried not to tremble. "I should go out there," she said. "That would be the most logical thing. If I give myself up, they might leave the Head alone. The survival of the Order is more important than the survival of . . . of me."

"Nonsense!" said Master Isbister hotly.

"Give you up to those unreasoning brutes?" said Dr Stayling. "Never!"

A movement on the stairs behind her made Fever start and turn, but it was only Kit Solent, still pale and weak looking, with Dr Pither hurrying behind him saying, "You should not try to move, Solent. You will open the wound again. You should rest until we can find you a physician. . ."

Kit waved him away. "Fever. . . You're all right?"

Fever nodded, but could not take her eyes off his bloodstained coat.

"Don't worry about me," he told her. "I can look after

171

myself. I'm going to try and get back to Ludgate Hill. . ."

"Impossible," said Dr Stayling. "The Head is surrounded, and if we switch off the intrud-o-cutor that rabble will be over it in a jiffy."

"But Doctor, I must try! My son and daughter. . ."

"Oh, be reasonable, man! You will be no use to your children dead. Even if you did get out, that rabble would tear you to pieces. They've seen you with Fever, remember, or their leaders have. You would never make it to Ludgate Hill."

A fresh surge of shouting and cheering came from outside. A barrage of stones rattled like hail against Godshawk's face. Even if Kit had tried to argue with the old Engineer, he would never have made himself heard. Dr Stayling waited patiently for the din to subside, then went on.

"There is only one thing to do. We must get you and Fever to safety. Once they see that you are gone, the mob will lose interest in this place. There is little loot in it apart from books, and they do not look like bookish types. I shall send someone to fetch those children of yours, Solent, and you can return as soon as these riots are over."

"But when will that be?" demanded Kit. "And where shall we hide in the meantime?"

"I believe Dr Collihole's balloon is airworthy," said Stayling. "The wind is from the south-west today. It will carry you north, where help will be waiting for you."

"What help?" asked Dr Crumb.

"The Movement," said Dr Stayling, glancing about fiercely to quell the startled murmuring of his Engineers. "Yes, gentlemen, I have been in contact with agents of the Movement."

"You're in *league* with those nomadic ruffians?" cried Griffin Whyre, aghast.

"I have talked with their agents," said Stayling calmly. "And I do not believe they are ruffians. They respect knowledge far more than most Londoners; their entire society is based upon the application of technology. I have received overtures of friendship from their leader, Land Admiral Quercus, who has given me to understand that once he controls London we Engineers shall be given the status of a Guild. We shall be consulted by our new rulers, and allowed a seat on council alongside the Guilds of Surgeons and Wig Makers and Perfumiers. . ."

The Engineers started to brighten at that, but the boom of some heavy object crashing against the outside of the Head reminded them of their predicament.

"How long before these friends of yours arrive?" asked Kit Solent.

Dr Stayling shook his head thoughtfully. "They are coming to London because of the technology we possess. They have been waiting beyond the Moatway while their agents make contact with various important persons such as myself in the hope that they might achieve a peaceful takeover. But their patience has its limits, and once they learn that riots have broken out, I should imagine they will move fast to secure the city. I would expect them in a day or so, no more. Until then, you and Fever will be safe in their convoy. They will have surgeons there who can attend to your injury."

"And the children?" asked Kit.

"I shall send Dr Crumb to make sure that they are safe," the chief Engineer promised.

"Why me?" asked Dr Crumb.

"You are our childcare expert, Crumb."

"But I must go with Fever. . ."

"Impossible!" cried Dr Collihole, who had been fluttering nervously behind Dr Stayling all through his talk. "My balloon will not lift more than two persons. Indeed, we do not know for certain that it will lift anyone at all. I had planned to make the first ascent myself; I would not feel easy in myself entrusting the lives of Fever and Master Solent to such an untested device. . ."

"It seems we have no choice, Doctor," said Kit Solent, smiling weakly at him. "I do not think that your 'lectrified fence will hold off that mob outside for long. Those people out there don't think like Engineers. They are barely thinking at all. Once they've worked themselves up into enough of a rage they'll find a way in here, even if they have to bridge the fence with their own dead. I don't like Dr Stayling's plan much, but I can't think of another."

Dr Stayling nodded, pleased that Kit had given in to reason. "As soon as this mob disperses," he promised, "I shall go straight to the Movement's chief agent, a woman named Madame Lakshmi who has a tower in the Astrologer's Quarter. She is in possession of a remarkable piece of old technology which enables her to communicate with our friends in the north. I shall ask her to warn them that you are on your way. Well, gentlemen?"

The Engineers stood gazing at him. They were men of thought, not action.

"Come on!" urged Dr Stayling, starting to lead them up the stairs. "Come on! We have a balloon to fill!"

They started after him, up towards Collihole's attic. Soon Fever and Dr Crumb were left alone, except for Dr Isbister, who had never placed any credence in either the intrud-o-cutor or old Collihole's dreams of flight, and intended to stand guard over his precious library.

Fever knew she should be concerned at Dr Stayling's scheme – she could already see a dozen flaws in it – but her mind was too numb. She had come through so much madness that day that a little more seemed to make no difference. Why not take Dr Collihole's air balloon, if that was the only way to leave? Why not seek shelter with the Movement, if there was none to be found in London? But there were things she needed to do before she left. She pointed towards the library doors.

"Dr Isbister, don't we have some of Godshawk's notebooks in the collection?"

"We do," admitted the librarian, "but this seems hardly the moment. . ."

Fever turned to Dr Crumb. "Perhaps one of them contains something about what he did to me. . ."

"But Fever," he said, "we have so little time!"

"It will take at least an hour to fill Dr Collihole's balloon," Fever reasoned. "I would rather spend that time in the search for knowledge than sit listening to *them*."

The sound of the crowd outside rose to a bullish roar as she spoke. Then it died away. A single voice bellowed angry words that Fever could not make out. Some tub-thumper, she guessed, rousing them for another onslaught on the fence.

"Please, Dr Crumb!" she begged. "I remember such strange things. I thought I was going mad, but now I think. . . Now I don't know *what* to think."

"As long as you *are* thinking, Fever," said Dr Crumb warningly. "As long as you are not giving in to emotion." But she could tell he was wavering. "I am sure Dr Isbister will not approve of us rummaging through his collection," he said.

"Oh, nobody takes any notice of Dr Isbister, it seems," said the librarian peevishly, and waved them towards the library's tall doors.

24

THE LIBRARY

hrough the crowds outside, an old-fashioned sedan chair came creeping. It was heavy and richly ornamented, and needed four bearers to carry it along. Ted Swiney, who was standing up on the roof of another chair with Charley at his side, shouted, "Let them through! Make way there! Let him through!"

The crowd eddied, jostling Swiney's chair and making Charley fearful that he'd fall from it and end up trampled. But the mob were just obeying Ted's orders, pushing aside to let the big chair through. Its bearers set it down, and Thaniel Wormtimber stepped out of it, blinking in the glare of the torches which men held up all round him.

"Is all this trouble your doing, Master Swiney?" the Master of London's Devices grumbled, squinting upwards through the rain.

"I didn't rouse this lot up," said Ted. "But now they're roused, I mean to make sure they keep on seeing me as their mate, and you'll do the same, if you're wise." He shouted to the crowd, "Here we go, mates! This here is Master Wormtimber, our Master of Devices. One of the few men on the New Council who still cares how us commoners feel. That's why I sent for him. He's brought us what we need to winkle the Patchskin maid and her cronies out of that Head!"

Wormtimber slipped a satchel from his shoulder and passed it up to Ted, who held it high.

"This is old tech!" bellowed Ted. "With what's in 'ere, our new Skinner can finish his work." He pushed the satchel at Charley. His face, with its eyebrows scorched off, looked more furious than ever.

"Go on then! Take it!"

Charley took the satchel from him and peeked inside. Folded paper, thick and white. The bag was stuffed with paper boys.

"What do you want me to do, Ted?" asked Charley, feeling scared of Ted, of the crowd, of the magic fence that ringed the Head, scared of everything.

"Use it!" said Ted, sounding fierce, but smiling as he spoke, because he wouldn't want to let the crowd see him treating Bagman Creech's heir as if he was a common pot boy. He looped the satchel's strap over Charley's head and seized him under both arms, swinging him down off the chair roof. Charley never quite reached the ground. Other hands took hold of him, lifting him high. He was passed from man to man across the crowd's heads until he reached its edge, where they set him down, cheering him, thumping him between the shoulder blades.

Ahead, a few score yards of sodden mud and rubble lay between him and the Engineers' fence. The weeds which had grown there had been tramped flat by the crowd earlier, and the air was filled with the salady scent of their crushed stalks.

"Three cheers for the Skinner!" shouted a voice behind him – Ted's – and three great waves of sound rolled and broke against the giant metal face that towered above him. Charley looked up at it. He thought of the girl with odd eyes, and imagined her crouching inside, terrified and doomed. *Well, serve her right,* he told himself. *Best get it over with.* He undid the fastenings of the satchel. Then he ran at the fence and, just before he reached it, flung the satchel as hard and as high as he could. He almost overbalanced as he let it go; almost reached out and grabbed those deadly wires, but he saved himself just in time. The bag landed with a dull flump among the weeds and rubbish between the timber props which supported Godshawk's massive chin.

A half-dozen white shapes spilled out, like dropped sandwiches. They lay there for a moment. Then, with furtive, papery motions, they started to unfold.

The Engineers had dragged Dr Collihole's great paper balloon up out of his attic workspace and spread it on the Head's tarpaper roof. It looked like a giant's eiderdown, and it was growing plumper and cosier-looking by the minute as hot air, pumped through special tubes from modified braziers, started to fill the envelope.

"Careful!" shouted Dr Collihole, bustling about like a rheumatic hen. For years he had been studying the possibility of flight, inspired by the discovery of the great complex at Eefrow, to the west of London, from whose broad runways he believed Ancient machines had once sped into the air. His own scrap-paper invention looked hopelessly small and childish now, compared to the great rusted bird-shapes which archaeologists had uncovered there. He had only ever meant it to be a beginning; a first, tentative step on the ladder which would carry men back into the sky. Now everything was suddenly rush and hurry, and Fever's life depended on him. He wished that he had time to go below and check his calculations one last time. "Don't let the braziers burn too hot!" he insisted. "We must not let the whole thing catch ablaze!"

Godshawk's surviving notebooks were kept in a locked case deep in the stacks, as if even the Order of Engineers considered them dangerous. Dr Isbister brought the key and kept watch over Fever and Dr Crumb as Fever pulled out the notebooks one by one. The books were circular, like the one she had seen at Kit Solent's house, and with typical Scriven perversity their titles were written only on their front covers, not their spines. At last she found one which looked promising. *On Stalkers*, Godshawk had scrawled across its binding. Isbister had labelled it neatly "Vol 86".

She pulled it down from the shelf and sat on the floor and opened the book on her lap, while Dr Isbister fussily rearranged the other volumes she had upset in her search and Dr Crumb stood over her holding a 'lectric torch. Its light fell upon page after page of intricate diagrams and Godshawk's tiny, crabbed handwriting.

"He knew so much," whispered Fever, turning and turning the pages. Careful drawings traced what happened when a Stalker brain was inserted in a corpse's skull; weird wiry tendrils unfurling to colonize the dead man's nervous system, wrapping like bindweed round the spinal cord. . . "No wonder Godshawk wanted immortality. He could not just let all this knowledge vanish. He had to *do* something. . ."

She lost patience and began flicking through the packed pages, past images which jogged a cascade of memories, until she reached blank, empty leaves at the end. She flicked back and found the last picture in the book. A tiny object, drawn life size in a corner and again, much larger, in the middle of the page. The shape of a walnut. The size of an almond.

"That is the thing he showed me in the garden!" said Dr Crumb.

Fever flicked back through the final pages, but they were as blank as before. "He lost interest in Stalkers after he found that. It set him off on a new course, in a new notebook. . ."

Dr Crumb went back to the shelf, almost shoving Dr Isbister aside in his eagerness to grab the next volume. He came back empty handed. "It's not there. Lost in the riots, I expect."

"Shhhhh!" said Isbister abruptly.

They fell silent, listening.

From somewhere nearby came odd sounds. Crinklings. Scratchings. Tiny, papery creaks. Mouse noises, not out of place among so many books and papers, but too deliberate, somehow. The sound of someone or something keeping much too quiet.

"Have the rioters broken in?" asked Fever, and the puzzle which had been coming together in her mind fell apart again. How could she think about her past when her future looked set to be so brief and violent?

"Who's there?" called Dr Crumb.

"Keep your voice down, Crumb, you're in a library!" hissed Dr Isbister.

In the sudden silence, the sound of dust settling.

"We should leave," said Dr Crumb.

"After first replacing the books," Isbister reminded him in a whisper.

Behind the librarian a white figure stepped out of an impossibly narrow gap between two bookcases. It was exactly the same size and shape as Fever.

"Dr Isbister!" she shouted.

"Shhh!" said the librarian, pointing upwards at the SILENCE sign which hung above them. The paper boy lunged forward and drew a needle claw across his neck. "Ow!" he shouted. "I mean, ow!" he whispered. He turned, but the paper boy's venom was already taking effect; stumbling drunkenly, he crashed sideways into the shelves which held Godshawk's books. Glass starred and shattered, dropping with him in long blades as he slid to the floor, shuddering, choking, dead.

The paper boy, with a tiny ripping sound, stuck out a second claw. Fever stared at it. She was remembering how it had felt to glue its two halves together and carry it out on to the roof to dry. She remembered how it had felt to lie on that paper while Dr Crumb drew her outline around her. It was like being menaced by her own shadow.

Dr Crumb, more practised than her in the art of keeping calm, just snatched a heavy book and threw it. The near-weightless paper boy was carried backwards and trapped beneath the book as it thudded to the floor. Its arms and legs flapped helplessly. It rattled like a paper bag caught on a branch in a gale.

"Come on, Fever!"

"But Dr Isbister. . ."

"He's dead. And if the rioters have access to the New Council's store of paper boys there may be many more of them in here with us. . ."

Fever started to follow him between the stacks, and as she went she heard the awful sound of paper footsteps keeping pace with hers along a neighbouring aisle.

"How many do you think there are?"

"There were seven in that last batch we made. . ."

They rounded a corner in Ancient History and a paper boy rose up in front of them and stood there swaying like a cobra. It's claw lashed out at them, missed, and snagged in the leather binding of an old grimoire. Before it could free itself Dr Crumb grabbed it by its head and one shoulder and pulled as hard as he could. Paper ripped. The torn boy freed its claw and raked it across his coat, but it did not pierce the fabric. Dribbles of venom shone for a moment in the weave of the cloth. In another moment he had wrenched its head off.

Fever watched, surprised. She had never imagined Dr Crumb doing such things. She would have to revise her whole picture of him.

"Fever!" he shouted.

She snatched up a big book to use as a shield. Two more paper boys were rustling along the aisle. Fever turned, and two more blocked the way behind her. They crouched and came creeping slyly forward while their flat white faces wove from side to side.

"Oh, Dr Crumb. . ."

*

"They have her!" screeched Thaniel Wormtimber, crouched in his chair, eyes on his screens and fingers on the paper boys' controls. Ted Swiney, standing just outside, bellowed, "They've got her!", and Charley, who stood next to him, heard the news spread outwards through the crowd; "They've got her!" "She's cornered!" "She's dead meat now!"

None of them noticed the balloon inflating on top of Godshawk's Head.

Fever shoved a line of books from a shelf beside her and the paper boys drew back, wary now of being trapped or torn. Dr Crumb toppled a stack into the path of the two confronting him and they went whispering away, circling round among the high bookshelves, looking for an easier way to reach their prey.

Father and daughter stood breathing hard, listening to the rustlings and flutterings that the paper boys made as they crept along neighbouring aisles. Fever stuffed away her feelings and groped in her pockets, looking for something that might be of use. Usually she carried a small penknife, but she had left home that day in such a hurry that she had not thought to bring it. Instead her hand closed on the box of matches that she taken with her when she left Godshawk's vault.

She took the box out. Dr Crumb said, "Fever, it would be most unwise to use fire against them, here among all this dry paper and other flammable materials. . ."

"Better unwise than dead," said Fever. She stopped and ripped a page out of one of the books she had thrown down, screwed it into a spill and held it between her teeth while she lit a match.

Behind some nearby books, a rasp, a rustle. The dry slither of paper being slipped through a crack in the back of a bookcase.

The match would not strike. Fever discarded it and tried another. Twice it scraped uselessly over the rough strip on the matchbox side, but on the third attempt it lit, and she put down the box and held one end of her paper taper into the match flame. It flashed into fire at once, and just in time. Out from between some large, leather-bound volumes of journals on a nearby shelf, a paper boy's hand came groping. Fever scrambled away from it, holding the burning paper out in front of her. The paper boy slid his whole body out into the aisle and rose up quivering.

Fever thrust the burning paper at him, and he drew back a little. She made another lunge, and again he fell back. "It works!" she told Dr Crumb. But just then the flames reached her fingers and she squeaked and dropped the page. The paper boy started towards them again, but as it stepped over the fallen paper a lemon-yellow flame stood up wavering among the books on the floor. The paper boy looked down as the flame spilled up its leg. It patted at the fire with its hands, but they caught fire too. Its legs crumpled into ash and it curled backwards and flopped to the floor, spreading flames to other fallen books.

Fever raised a hand to shield her face from the brightness and the startling surge of heat. "Fever!" Dr Crumb was shouting. She turned and he grabbed hold of her and dragged her along the aisle, stumbling over the spilled books there, the rising flames stretching their shadows ahead of them.

What had she done? All those books! Those thousands of pages, those millions of words, stacked up like tinder in the Head. . .

Sparks jetted into the shadows above the shelves; flags of burning paper floated like gaudy jellyfish from aisle to aisle, spreading the fire. Another paper boy, his blazing arms windmilling, struggled towards the fugitives, leaving trails of flame behind him. He crumpled into drifting ash before he reached them, and his charred brain disc came rolling past Fever's feet like a spent Catherine wheel.

They reached Isbister's desk, and Fever snatched from behind it a long pole with an S shaped metal hook on the end which Dr Isbister sometimes used for opening the library windows in fine weather. She used it to flail aside a paper boy who had stationed himself between the desk and the door. He scrumpled, turned, and charged at her again, but she stuck the iron S through him, hoicked him over her head and held him up like a marshmallow before the flames which now filled the library. He struggled for a moment on the pole's end, but then Dr Crumb pulled the door open, and the inrush of air made the fire roar up fiercer and brighter than ever. Flames rushed across the ceiling, lapping over one another like waves of golden water. The paper boy charred and ignited, and Fever dropped the pole and ran.

25

HEADS WILL ROLL

here was fire on the roof, too, but it was controlled, directed fire. The balloon stood upright now. The Engineers had attached a basket to the ropes which dangled from its sides. A brazier was bolted above the basket on a metal tripod and the glow of the burning charcoal came softly through the paper, reminding Dr Collihole of the floating lanterns which used to drift across the city from the Godshawk place out in the Marshes, and which had first led him to ponder the lifting properties of hot air, all those years ago. Well, his project was ready now. It shifted and shivered. It took all the strength of his fellow Engineers to hold it down.

"We're ready!" Dr Stayling shouted. "Where are Crumb and the girl?"

Kit Solent had fallen into a chilly half sleep, crouched at the roof's edge in the wind. He was wandering in his memories of Katie and the children, and he felt desperately sad when Dr Stayling's voice roused him and he found himself back in the present, cold and stiff and in pain and trapped on a giant head. Smelling smoke, he glanced down over Godshawk's brow.

"What in the name of—? Dr Stayling! *Fire!*"

Godshawk's Head blew a plume of white smoke out of either nostril. A jack-o'-lantern glow came from its eyes and lesser windows, lighting up the rioters below.

When Fever and Dr Crumb reached the roof a minute later the tarpaper was already beginning to grow tacky in the heat. The Head let out weird metallic booms and groans, snorting dragonish showers of sparks which drifted across the crowds in front of it.

"Crumb! We cannot remain here much longer!" shouted Dr Stayling, clinging to one of the ropes of the restless balloon.

"What will the rest of you do?" Fever asked, as Dr Crumb helped her into the balloon basket, where Kit Solent already waited, reaching out to help her. Dr Collihole fussed about, muttering about lift-weight ratios and checking the bags of ballast which were tied around the edges of the basket.

"We shall go down the fire escape and seek safety on the ground," said Stayling. "People laughed when I installed a fire escape in this Head. They will not laugh when they see what an eminently rational precaution it was. . ."

Fever rolled over the side of the basket and dropped in next to Kit. Instantly the basket slumped down on to the roof, where Fever felt it sink stickily into the liquefying tar. Smoke started to come up through the wicker floor.

"Dr Collihole, what is wrong?" asked Dr Crumb.

Dr Collihole shook his head nervously. "I must have miscalculated! We must shed some ballast. . ."

Hurriedly, Engineers fumbled with the knots which tethered the big, gravel-filled sacks of ballast. One splodged down on to the melting roof, then another, and the balloon shifted and reluctantly began to rise, tethered to the roof only by a few thick strands of tar

188

which stretched like scorched toffee and at last gave way. Fever gripped the edge of the basket with both hands and leaned out, shouting Dr Crumb's name.

He turned and waved. "Good luck!"

"Steady on, Crumb," warned Dr Whyre. "This is no time for emotionalism!"

"When you get there tell them where you come from!" shouted Dr Stayling. "Tell them you're an envoy from Stayling and the Engineers!"

The balloon rose unsteadily into the sky, and the crowd below saw it, and greeted it with a hoarse, raw-throated roar. Bricks and stones were flung up at it, and a few guns went off, but the wind caught it and wafted it beyond their range. Looking down, Fever saw people streaming like insects through the narrow streets. She looked ahead, and saw rows of tall tenements on the slopes of Clerkenwell Hill. The balloon was headed towards them, on a level with the chimney pots, and already the insect mob was swarming darkly up on to their rooftops, waiting with pikes and gaffs and guns for the wind to bring it to them.

"Kit!" she shrieked. "We have to go higher!" She leaned over the edge of the basket and started to claw at the tight, wet knot which held the nearest bag of ballast in place. Kit did the same on the other side; she heard him shout with pain as his bag came free and he took its weight for an instant, wrenching his wounded shoulder. Then his was falling, down, down, down, and Fever's close behind it, smashing tiles from a roof down there, and the balloon lurched upwards.

At the back of the Head, unnoticed, the Engineers hurried down their spindly fire escape to safety, jumping sections where the steps had collapsed, scorching their fingers on the hot handrails, but stumbling out at last on to the rubbly ground. No one tried to stop or harass them as they opened a gate in the fence and scattered into the crowd. All eyes were raised skyward, watching the balloon, and most of the mob was streaming north, as if hoping to catch it when it fell.

Once he was a good distance from the Head, Dr Crumb turned to watch it, too. He was feeling rather irrational that afternoon, and it seemed to him that Godshawk's Head looked wonderful, lit from within by the glow of the fire, with firelight shafting out of every vent and window and the balloon rising palely from its crown like a thought bubble, one last idea wafting free in the updraught from that mighty brain.

Someone seized him by the arm. He turned with a start to see Dr Stayling thrusting a filthy, flattened hat at him, cramming it on to his head. Behind him the others of the Order were almost unrecognizable under the hats and scarves and shawls of sacking which they had picked up from the littered ground and used to hide their bald, distinctive heads.

"Come on, Crumb. This is no place for men of reason. . ."

Just then, with an enormous noise, the timber props under Godshawk's chin gave way. There was a long groan, and the ground lurched. The remaining crowds scattered backwards, barging and trampling each other.

Wormtimber's chair, its bearers fled, was left alone on the stretch of ground in front of the tilting head. Ted Swiney stood beside it, his angry little eyes still fixed on the balloon. Charley pulled at his sleeve. "Ted! The Head! It's coming down!"

Ted looked up at Godshawk's enormous face, which glared back at him with flame-filled eyes. The timbers of the tram platform groaned as they took the whole of the Head's huge weight. *"Cheesers Crice!"* Ted shouted (it was the name of some obscure cockney god) and knocked Charley sprawling in his hurry to get away. Charley got up, yelled a warning to Master Wormtimber and ran after him.

The Master of Devices opened his chair door and jumped out, just as the tram platform gave way and the Head started to topple. He squealed, started to run, then realized that there was not time, and darted back inside the chair, slamming the door behind him.

The Head fell forward, slowly at first and then very fast. It smashed the chair and all its contents flat with one colossal head-butt, and hammered the splinters deep into London clay. Charley dropped to the ground, overshadowed but not quite crushed by the curve of the statue's brow. The air was crammed with dizzy sparks and streaked by embers, thick with flung divots of earth and gobs of molten tar.

Above it all, like panicked birds, the singed pages of a thousand books danced on a tower of heat. And northwards, all but forgotten, Dr Collihole's experiment faded into the pigeon-coloured clouds.

PART TWO

26

THE FLIGHT NORTH

or a long time, Fever was terrified. Terrified of that gulf of air below her, and of the sparks and glowing scraps which gusted all around her, sometimes settling for a moment on the wicker of the basket or on the surface of the envelope itself. Terrified that lightning would leap from the ink-blot clouds above her and strike the wet balloon. Terrified that, even if she survived the fall, she would come down among Londoners ready to tear her to pieces.

But slowly, as the balloon passed over the low, scruffy streets of Finnsbry and out above Hampster's Heath, she was able to bring her feelings back under control. *Hot air rises*, she told herself. The paper bag above her was filled with hot air and it would bear her up until the fuel in the brazier was exhausted and the last of its heat given up to the cooler air outside, then set her gently down. Those were not thunderclouds above her. With luck, the fortunate wind would carry her and Kit Solent to the Movement. She was safe. The balloon worked. One day, perhaps, people would sail the skies of the world in machines like this. . .

Kit had slumped down against the basket side, and she busied herself with him for a while. His struggle with the ballast sack had tugged his wound open again, and she ripped a strip from the skirts of her coat and did her best to staunch the bleeding. Kit, barely conscious, groaned with pain when she moved him. She laid him on the floor of the basket and bundled the remains of her coat beneath his head for a pillow.

"We must go back," he kept saying. "The children. . ."

"Dr Crumb will take care of them," Fever promised. "They will be waiting to greet you when you return." She didn't think that was necessarily true, because she was not sure how Dr Crumb was supposed to get halfway across London to find Fern and Ruan in the middle of a riot, but she could think of no other way to comfort Kit. "The Movement will have doctors," she said, "and when you are better we shall go back to London. Think how happy Fern and Ruan will be to see you. . ."

"Katie," said Kit, finding her hand and holding tight to it.

"Katie is not here," said Fever. "I am Fever Crumb."

She wasn't sure that he had heard her. He kept holding her hand. "You'll look after Fern and Ruan, won't you?"

"Of course," she told him, embarrassed.

She was glad when he fell asleep. She hoped he would be more rational when he woke. She sat beside him and rested her head against the scratchy, creaking side of the basket. It was cold up there in the sky without her coat. She closed her eyes, wondering what had befallen Dr Crumb and the other Engineers. She wondered if he had made it safely to Ludgate Hill, and if Fern and Ruan were all right. Images of her terrible, unreasonable day kept flaring behind her shut eyelids. She felt exhausted. All her muscles ached. She thought, *I must not fall asleep. Dr Collihole will want to hear my observations of this flight.*

But she slept, and memories came to her like the shards of something broken falling through her dreams.

She was wearing a thick fur coat and standing on the heaving, creaking deck of a sea hoy as it plunged through grey waves under a snow-scoured sky.

She was at an island in that same cold sea, standing before a savage, stately, fur-robed woman, surrounded by guards with spears and knobkerries. She was fetching out of her pack a metal tube, and out of the tube a precious sheet of Ancient tinfoil which she laid on the ground before the queen's sealskin shod feet as a gift and token of friendship.

She was at home, in her own workroom, and Wavey Godshawk was fastening thick leather straps across her wrists, binding her to the arms of a heavy wooden chair. She could hear a steady thumping noise. Something was clamped tightly around her head, metal screws digging into the flesh of her brow and tugging at her hair. *Hair?* she thought. *I don't have hair.* She looked down at her trapped hands and they were not her hands but the hands of an old man, weathered and speckled.

And she woke. It was the balloon, not a ship, which creaked and heaved. It was only a headache which pressed against her temples. She had been asleep, huddled on the basket's floor with her head on Kit Solent's shoulder. The fire in the brazier had gone out and the balloon seemed to have shrunk a little, its sides dimpled and crumply. The thumping noise was still going on, interspersed with a lot of shriller crackles and bangs.

Stiff, wet, chilled, she stirred herself, reached out and took hold of the basket's brim and levered herself up until she was peering over it.

The rain had stopped, and the clouds were breaking up, allowing the evening sun to shine redly through. It lit up the ground, not far below her now; not much further than it would have been if she had still been on top of Godshawk's Head. Flat, gorse-scabbed commons where the sheep scattered as the shadow of the balloon went sliding over them. Drainage ditches glistened in complicated patterns, like the mazes of silvery wire on Ancient printed circuits. The city was far behind her. Ahead, a thick blanket of white smoke was curling over the Orbital Moatway like a slow-breaking wave. Darts of orange flame showed in the heart of it, and all around its edges there was movement; men running and men on horses galloping, hurrying towards the smoke and away from it so that the Moatway seemed to seethe with secret motion like an ants' nest.

Fever stared, her head still stuffed with dreams, trying to understand what she was seeing. And then, over the crest of the Moatway, punching out of the smoke, a square shape came lumbering, scattering splintered stockade logs ahead of it, spraying up fans of mud as it slithered down the southern face of the embankment. Flame stabbed out of ports along its flanks. It was an armed and armoured land barge, and seeing it, Fever knew what was happening.

The Movement had made their move at last. They

had attacked the Orbital Moatway, and they were breaking through.

"Master Solent!" she said urgently. "Kit!"

He did not answer her. She twisted round to look at him, and saw that he was dead.

"Master Solent!" she said again, not wanting to believe it. She stared down at him, and she had no idea what to do. She knew that she must not give in to grief. Death was a natural occurrence. People who were sick or injured often died. It was a simple process of cause and effect, like the slow loss of heat which was making the balloon sink. But in this case it was a process that had begun with Kit Solent trying to protect her, and now he lay here white and still and uncomplaining and Fever felt as though some veil had been torn aside and she was seeing the world as it really was, without illusion or comfort or consolation. He was dead.

With a sound like a sharp sigh a bullet hole appeared in the side of the basket close to Fever's face. She looked at it, and wondered what to do. She did not even know who was shooting at her. Was it the Moatway's defenders, taking her balloon for another of the Movement's devices? Or was it the Movement, assuming her to be a London spy? She crouched down, though she knew that would not save her; the bullets were just as likely to come through the floor of the basket as through its sides.

She felt more strike, chunking against the wicker like flung pebbles. *If this many are hitting the basket*, she thought, *how many have hit the balloon?* And she looked up and saw the paper envelope starting to sag and lose its shape.

The bullets stopped. Whoever had been firing them had given up, or fled. Fever crouched low and put her nose to the floor of the basket and peered through its weave. The ground was just a few yards below; lumpy, desolate ground, covered with long, pale grass, which soon began to brush against the underside of the basket. A few moments more and the basket touched down, striking against the top of a low ridge and dragging through the grass for several yards before lifting again.

Fever clung on hard, shaken like a dice in a cup. Kit Solent's body rolled against her knees and she felt how cold and stiff he was.

The basket touched down again. It landed harder this time, juddering violently as the balloon dragged it through stands of thistles and low clumps of furze. At last it tipped over and spilled Fever out. She landed hard in the coarse grass, rolling over and over. When she looked up she saw the balloon billowing away from her, Kit's arm trailing from the basket.

"Master Solent!" she shouted, as if he were still alive. She stumbled after the balloon. The crumpled envelope was itself touching the ground now, hissing over the furze tops with the basket trailing after it like a drag anchor. Fever caught up with it, grabbed the cuff of Kit's coat and pulled him out. Freed of his weight the balloon lifted a little, drifted away from her like a lazy ghost and came to rest entangled in a line of trees a half mile away.

Fever stood up and looked around. A riderless horse came galloping past, stirrups trailing. Far off to her right a group of men in russet coats were struggling along a raised bank between the meadows, but they showed no interest in Fever or the crashed balloon. The long line of the Moatway stretched across the land to the north. Smoke still hung thickly over the place where the battle had been, but she could no longer hear gunfire. She squinted at the smoke, making out the smashed outlines of the Moatway defences and the shapes of men moving about among them. Movement men, presumably. The balloon had set her down among London's enemies.

There was no time to ponder it, for the fall of the balloon had been noted. She had not stood staring long before she saw a small vehicle coming towards her out of the smoke. It was a mono; a single fat wheel with a cabin mounted on gimbals in its centre. She had heard of such things but never seen one, since the powerful Guild of Sedan Chair Bearers forbade motorized passenger vehicles in London. It bowled quickly across the heath, smoke squirting from its exhaust flutes, the evening light blinking from the windows of its hub-cabin. It circled the wrecked balloon and then rolled towards Fever, stopping quite close to her. Two men jumped down from it and came towards her. They wore armour and marched with a heavy, merciless stride. When they drew closer she saw that they weren't men at all, not any more. She swallowed, and fought off an urge to run. She had forgotten that some of the nomad empires still had Stalkers in their armies; dead warriors resurrected as armoured battle engines.

The Stalkers' mechanized armour grated as it bore them towards her. From the eye slits of their faceless metal heads there seeped a thin green light. A wheeled tower, the symbol of the Movement, was painted on their breastplates, and their names were stencilled in neat white lettering across their armoured brows:

201

Lammergeier and Corvus. Their hands sprouted blades. The one called Lammergeier pointed at Fever and said in a grinding iron voice, "DON'T MOVE! PUT YOUR HANDS UP!"

Fever hesitated, knowing that she could not obey both instructions. Put her hands up without moving? Dr Crumb would have expected her to point out to the Stalker his faulty logic. But Dr Crumb was not facing those ugly-looking steel claws. She cautiously raised both hands and stood there, feeling foolish, watching the machines approach. They went past her and stopped, looking down at the body which lay in the grass.

"He's dead," said Fever helpfully. Then, remembering what Dr Stayling had told her as she left London, she added, "I am from Godshawk's Head. I am an envoy from the Order of Engineers."

The Stalkers stared greenly at her. They lowered their hands, but did not sheath their claws. The one called Corvus said, "ARE YOU DAMAGED?"

Fever shook her head.

The second Stalker pointed towards the waiting mono. "YOU WILL COME WITH US. THE LAND ADMIRAL WILL QUESTION YOU."

The other Stalker lifted Kit Solent's body and carried it to the waiting mono as if it were a sack filled with something not very heavy. They strapped him into a seat, and motioned for Fever to get in beside him. She could not understand why they wanted him, but she was glad they were not leaving him out on the heath for crows to snack on. His head lolled against her as the mono set off. He smelled of blood and smoke and damp clothing, and Fever supposed that she must smell as bad. The odours seemed strong and out of place among the clean, metal and leather smells of the mono cabin. But the Stalkers did not seem to notice.

27

PUBLIC DISORDER

uan had never liked Mistress Gloomstove. He was only seven, but he'd always seen somehow what his father had failed to: that there was no real feeling behind the smiles and pats and pet names that she gave the children; that they were just a show she put on because she thought that was how plump housekeepers were supposed to treat children; that she didn't really care for Fern or Ruan at all.

In the middle of that noisy afternoon, when the mob came milling along the street, demanding justice and Kit Solent's blood, she proved him right. A housekeeper in a story would have stationed herself at the street door with a rolling pin, or perhaps a carpet beater, and told the rioters to clear off. Mistress Gloomstove simply said, "The master may think I'm your nursemaid but he don't pay me enough to be your bodyguard as well." And she bundled up a lot of Father's silverware in the best damask tablecloth and hurried out by the back door.

"But what are we to do?" asked Ruan, catching at her apron as she went.

"How would I know?" the housekeeper snapped back. "Wait for your father to come home and deal with these people. It seems he cares more for that baldy-headed Engineer girl than he does for either of you."

"That isn't true," Ruan told his sister, who stood

close behind him, clutching tight to Noodle Poodle and looking ready to cry.

Ruan felt ready to cry himself, though he knew he mustn't. The air outside was full of strange, frightening noises; smashing glass and angry shouts. The sky had gone a funny colour, and it was full of smoke and the smell of burning. Ruan closed his eyes and held Fern's hand tightly and prayed to Poskitt, Lud and Mama Cellulite that his father would come home. But when he led his sister back through the house to see if the prayer had worked they found no trace of Daddy.

Outside, the growl of the crowd echoed off the Barbican walls, gruff as a fairytale troll. Ruan wiped his sleeve across his eyes and took Fern's hand again – the little girl was saying, "But what do they *want*, Ruan? What do those people *want*?"

Ruan didn't answer her. He wasn't quite sure. All he knew was that he and Fern had to hide, before the growling troll outside came in and got them. The linen closet or the living room curtains sprang to mind – they were both favourite hidey-holes when he and Fern were playing hide-and-seek with Daddy. Then he had a better idea.

He dragged Fern after him into the kitchen, where she watched him gather the provisions they would need. Some bread and jam, a big double handful of biscuits, half a fruit cake. He told her to wait there while he ran upstairs, but she came with him, following him like a shadow through the suddenly scary house. A brick punched through the landing window while he was busy gathering up his best toys, and some of Fern's, and their favourite red storybook. He bundled it all up, together

205

with the food, in his bedspread (so Mistress Gloomstove had taught him something about making bundles, at least) and slung it over his shoulder. It was heavy, but not too heavy, and he liked the feeling of it bouncing against his back as he went quickly back downstairs, holding Fern's hand.

He knew the way to the secret basement well. He'd often spied on Daddy when he went through the bookcase, and he climbed its shelves and found the little hidden button that opened it quite easily. But once he and Fern were on the other side and the bookcase had slid shut behind them it occurred to him that if *he* had found it, then so might someone else.

There was a huge bang, still frightening despite being muffled by the bookcase. Ruan didn't know that it was the sound of the front door being kicked in, but he knew that it meant something bad, and he understood the next sound he heard: the voices of rowdy, drunken Londoners rushing in to his house.

"Ruan?" said Fern. "Noodle Poodle's frightinged."

"Hush, Fern," he told her, in a whisper. "We've got to be quiet. Like playing hide-and-seek. Quiet as mouses, all right?"

"Shhhh!" said Fern.

They stood in silence, listening.

As the balloon carrying Fever away from him faded into the haze of smoke and rain above the north boroughs, Dr Crumb parted from his fellow Engineers in an alley near Ox-Fart Circus where they had hidden from the crowds. Dr Stayling was intending to strike through Clerkenwell to the Astrologer's Quarter, and the others were inclined to go with him, intrigued by what he had told them about the old-tech machine with which Madame Lakshmi kept in contact with the Movement. But Dr Crumb had a mission of his own which could not wait; he left them there, and set off to fetch the Solent children.

Scurrying through the riot-torn city towards Ludgate Hill, he felt as if he were running through his own memories. The sky above the rooftops was smudged with inky thumbprints of smoke again, and dead bodies lay in the road, well-to-do Londoners who had been dragged from their chairs and kicked to death by the rioters. The terrible roar of the mob, which he remembered too well from the time of the Skinners' Riots, came rolling at him down this street and that, so that it was hard to know where the trouble was.

The truth was, he decided, there was trouble all over town. The riot was confined to no single place; there were a dozen riots going on. Some of the crowds who passed him were yelling about vengeance for Bagman Creech and death to the Dapplejacks, while others were demanding that the New Council do more to protect them from the Movement. Most, as far as he could tell, were just taking advantage of the general lawlessness to loot and rob and burn and bellow, safe in the knowledge that the Trained Bands had gone north to man the Moatway and could not be called out to stop them.

His best hope, as he reached Ludgate Hill, was that the mobs would have been too busy filling their pockets with the contents of the nearby techshops to trouble themselves with Kit Solent's house. But as he drew nearer to it he heard shouting and the smashing of glass, and realized that they had got there ahead of him. Fearing for the safety of the Solent children, he pulled his hat down tight to hide his shaved head and ran towards the noise.

By the time he reached the house the rioters had swept through it and away, bound for the Barbican where there was better loot to be had. Kit Solent's door, kicked off its hinges, lay skewed on the hallway floor. Grains of glass crunched under Dr Crumb's shoes as he crept cautiously inside. Someone had scrawled SCRIVEN LUVER on a wall. Things like dice skittered away from him at each step, and when he picked one up he found that it was a worn letter H from an Ancient keyboard – Solent's irrational house had been partly floored with the things, it seemed.

He let it fall. The house was quiet. Upstairs, the light came pale and wintry through crazed windows. Dr Crumb pushed open the door of one ransacked room after another, afraid of what he might find. "Children?" he called. (Kit Solent had told him their names, but in all the excitement he had forgotten them.) "Children?"

Below him, Ruan and Fern watched the ceiling, listening to the noises that he made as he prowled about the house. At first Ruan had felt glad when the terrible troll noises grew quieter. But in a way this new, quiet noise was worse. It made him think that someone sly and dangerous was creeping about looking for him and Fern, nosing into hiding places, maybe telling all the others to keep quiet so he could listen for the children's breathing. "Children!" they heard him call, but it was not a voice they knew. Not Daddy's voice.

Ruan tiptoed to the door on the far side of the basement and tried it. It was not locked. There was darkness on the other side, and he was scared of the dark, but he was more scared of whoever else was in the house, and at least there were lanterns lying about. He took a match solemnly out of the matchbox which he found on a shelf and carefully, carefully lit a lantern.

A padding of feet way up above the ceiling somewhere. A crash of something overturned.

He took Fern's hand. "Come on."

"Where are we going?"

"Somewhere where only Daddy will be able to find us. Only him and Miss Crumb know about this place." He tied the ends of his bedspread bundle across his chest so that he had one hand for the lantern and the other for his sister.

"It's dark in there," said Fern.

"It's all right. That's what the lantern's for. And I'll take spare matches and spare candles in case it goes out." He stuffed them into his pockets as he spoke.

Fern looked dubiously at the tunnel entrance. "Noodle Poodle's a little bit frightinged of the dark," she said.

"Then make sure you cuddle him up nice and tight," said Ruan.

And he took her hand, and picked up the lantern, and they went together into the tunnel.

"Children?" called Dr Crumb, one last time, into the quietness of the empty house. He knew there would be no answer. The children must have fled, or been taken.

209

He sat down on the bottom step, tore off his hat and held his head in his hands.

There was a dream which Dr Crumb had often dreamed when Fever was a baby, although it had come to him less and less frequently since she learned to walk and talk. In the dream, he was already dead. He had died in his sleep, and through some calamitous coincidence, everyone else in the Head had died too. Only baby Fever was left. She woke up crying, and there was nobody to hear her. She scrambled out of her plan-chest drawer and came and cried at Dr Crumb's bedside and clutched at him and tried to wake him, but he could not wake; he was dead. And Fever didn't understand. How could she? She was only a baby.

What could she do? How would she find food? How would she find help? He used to wake up in a panic, wondering what would become of her, alone and confused in the wide world. He felt the same sort of panic now, imagining what might have befallen Kit Solent's children.

It took him some time to control himself, and stow his emotions away. When he was ready he walked out calmly into the street, meaning to find his way back across the city to where the other Engineers were waiting.

He was almost at the corner of Cripplegate when he realized that he had left the Solent house without his hat. It must still be lying where he had thrown it, in the wrecked hallway. He was just wondering if he should turn back for it when a rough voice shouted, "It's another one of 'em! Grab him, lads!"

Dr Crumb started to run, but in his panic he ran the

210

wrong way, straight into the hands of the rioters. They grabbed and pinioned him. They lifted him off the ground. They jostled him round a corner and into the midst of a small crowd, and when he looked about he found that he was surrounded by his fellow Engineers, all prisoners too.

"Crumb!" said Griffin Whyre. "They caught us on our way out of Madame Lakshmi's tower. Perhaps we would have been less conspicuous if we had not all gone *en masse*. A most unreasonable woman, Crumb, but what equipment she possesses! 'Radio', I believe the Ancients would have called it. If that is an example of the Movement's technology, Stayling is right to side with them. . ."

Dr Crumb found that he was not remotely interested in Madame Lakshmi or her radio. He was more inclined to wonder why the Order had been seized, and why their grimy captors were shoving them uphill towards the Barbican. "What do they want with us?" he asked.

Whyre shrugged, but one of the roughs walking alongside overheard him and said, "You're needed at the Barbican, mate. Wormtimber's got himself squished, and the Mayor needs somebody who understands the old machines. . ."

"If Gilpin Wheen needs our help," protested Dr Crumb, "he could simply have requested it, like a civilized man."

"Who said anyfink about Gilpin Wheen? He's finished. It's Ted Swiney who's running this city now."

211

28

UNDER NEW MANAGEMENT

Ted Swiney hadn't meant to get himself a city that day. Everything was happening faster than he'd planned, thanks to Bagman Creech and the Patchskin girl. But the mob that surrounded Godshawk's Head and went storming up Slaughtergate afterwards to loot the fine houses on Ludgate Hill and seize the Barbican, well, they needed a leader to look to, didn't they? "Swiney!" they chanted, as they harried the frightened old councillors out of their homes. "Swiney!" they bellowed, ducking poor Gilpin Wheen in the horse trough outside the Barbican. "Swiney for Mayor!"

(A few tried yelling for Charley Shallow, him being Bagman Creech's heir and all, but Charley looked too young to be a mayor. Anyway, they didn't know his name, and yells of, "Bagman's Boy, You Know, The Little Skinny One With The Hat" didn't sound half so good as "Swiney!" when they echoed back at you off the Barbican walls.)

So they shouted for Swiney, and when the doors of the Barbican finally gave way and they surged inside it was Swiney whom they carried shoulder high, and Swiney whom they set down upon the ornate plastic and chromium throne of the Lord Mayor of London.

Swiney took it in his stride. He had a few of his trusty lads with him – Brickie Chapstick and Mutt

Gnarly and that crowd from the Mott and Hoople. Prowling around the mayor's apartments, he examined silver ornaments and squinted uncomprehendingly at antique paintings. Someone had fetched up a crate of vintage Frankish wine from the mayoral cellars, and he had a swig of that, but it tasted foreign, so he sent a few lads down to his brewery for a keg of decent London beer. A few more were dispatched to find Engineers – there was a lot of old-tech junk plonked on pedestals around the place, and he'd need somebody to tell him what it was worth. The rest of the lads he sent out to start quelling the riot. He'd been happy enough to see High London trashed while it belonged to old woofters like Wheen, but now it was his he wanted it to come through the night without being burned down. Mutt and Brickie and their mates knocked some heads together, and filled some others with dire visions of what happened to people who got on the wrong side of Ted.

Slowly, like a big, bad-tempered animal settling back to sleep, the brief disturbances wound down. It had been a little riot by London standards, with barely a hundred people killed, and only a half dozen buildings burning, somewhere down Cripplegate, but in its aftermath a carnival feeling filled the city. Happy looters gathered in the big square in front of the Barbican, clad in other people's hats and stolen ball gowns and tattered curtains ripped from the mansions of former councillors. The rain had stopped. In the smoky, slanting sunlight of late afternoon they waited for their new Lord Mayor to make his first proclamation.

Ted Swiney swaggered out on to the mayoral balcony, high above the throng. He'd buttoned his shirt up, and tied his mean little bow tie tight around his neck, which made his face redder than ever. "Swiney!" hollered the crowd.

Ted looked down at their upturned faces, smeared all across the square below him like the pattern on a carpet. A dim, rare doubt swam into his mind. How *did* you run a place like London? He had already sent the former councillors off to douse the fires, so he couldn't ask them. But then his usual confidence returned. He might not know how to run a city, but he knew how to run a pub all right. How different could it be?

He turned and said something to Mutt and Brickie, then looked at the crowd again and raised his fists for quiet. "Right," he bellowed. "First off, this gaff's under new management. You," (and here he turned to poor, wet, Gilpin Wheen, whom Brickie had just hauled out on to the balcony), "you're barred! Get out of my town, and don't come back!"

He waited till Wheen had scurried off and the mob's delight had quieted down a bit. "Right," he said, straightening his tie. Dealing with the old man had given him time to think about his own policies. What would his administration stand for? "Here's some new rules for you," he said. "From now on, no toffs, no misshapes, no foreigners, no spitting. Karaoke every Tuesday night, here at the Barbican. And live sports! Let's get Pickled Eel Circus rebuilt and have some proper fights again!"

A fond memory wafted back to him of the days when he had been the hero of Pickled Eel, using his fists and his wits to bludgeon flat all comers. He ought to get a muriel done of himself, he thought, forty feet high in his fighting togs, all up the side of the Barbican. But he

214

wouldn't announce that yet. What he needed was something that would please the crowd.

"And first off," he hollered, "since we've all had a busy day, I 'spect we could all use a *beer*."

Throughout his speech the crowd had heard a rumbling, low and hollow, growing louder. Now, down Cattermole Street and around the prow of the Barbican there came trundling an enormous barrel, rolled up the cobbled hill from Swiney's brewery in St Kylie by Mutt Gnarly and a regiment of eager, boozy helpers. The crowd parted to let them manoeuvre the huge keg to a spot below Ted's balcony, where they heaved and strained and manhandled it and finally managed to lift it up on two timber trestles. More men appeared, pulling a dray heaped high with mugs and tankards. Mutt used a lump hammer to drive a tap into the barrel, and drew off a pint of foaming amber beer, which he raised towards Ted while the rest of the crowd cheered.

"Brimstone Best!" yelled Swiney, above the din. "A barrel of my finest, big enough for all. Usually I stick a rusty horseshoe in each keg to give it a bit of bite, but this one's so big I had to use an anvil! So get stuck in. The first pint's free and after that it's half price till dawn. It's happy hour!"

And so it was. It was the happiest hour of Ted Swiney's entire reign. He leaned on the balcony and watched his followers get drunk, and the same half-contented, half-contemptuous look came over his face that he wore when he was standing behind his own bar. "Stupid cloots," he muttered to himself. "Booze and circuses, that'll keep 'em quiet." This mayoring lark was going to be a doddle.

But then, above the gusts of raucous singing that wafted from the square, he heard a new sound, softer and yet more menacing than the shouts of the drunken 'prentices fighting and spewing in the streets below.

A rumble and a roar it was, like beer kegs trundling into some vast cellar far away. Ted had never heard that sound before, but he knew it meant trouble. "What's that?" he asked Brickie Chapstick, but Brickie, too full of Brimstone Best, just said, "You're my best mate, you are," and fell over on the carpet.

Ted went and found a window and looked out of it. Northward, where the dim line of the Moatway stretched across the hazy heath, big lazy clouds of smoke were starting to sprawl across the land, and pulses of light kept flapping and flickering inside them, red and gold and white.

Even the revellers in the square had noticed it by then. "Shurrup," they told each other. "No, wha'sh'at, shurrup, *listen*. . ."

The sound came only dimly to them even then. Crackling volleys of musketry, the whoop of unlikely old energy weapons and the deep, steady, kettledrum boom of nomad cannon.

THE TRACTION CASTLE

he mono was an inefficient, fuel-hungry mode of transport, but it was fast. Fever looked out of the windows as it went rolling past the wrecked balloon and curved towards the breach which the Movement had made in the Moatway. As it climbed the steep bank she saw Stalkers at work there, pulling down the shattered palisades and heaping up the bodies of dead London soldiers. One of the Movement's armoured land barges was perched amid the ruins of a fort on the crest of the embankment, and she pressed her face close to the glass as the mono rolled past it, trying to peer between its armour plates to see which sort of engine it used, and whether it had wheels or tracks. Hatches on its hull were open and men in steel helmets and shining chain-mail vests were sitting on its upperworks.

Before she could make out much more the mono was careering down the steep northern face of the Moatway, crossing the nettle-filled dyke in front of it by means of a makeshift timber bridge. She could see other, smaller vehicles on the land ahead, and behind them something so high and dirty pale that she thought it might be the snout of a glacier. Could the ice really have come so far south?

And then she looked again at the thing, and slowly it

rearranged itself in her mind until she understood what it was.

It was a traction fortress, the great capital vehicle of the Movement, armoured in timber and metal, painted in dirty whitish dazzle-patterns which must have served as camouflage while it was lumbering across the ice wastes. Watchtowers and gun emplacements encrusted its hull, their hard edges softened by swags of camouflage netting. Huge, studded, barrel-shaped wheels showed dimly through the mist which hung about its skirts, the mist which was not mist at all but vapour from its hundreds of chimneys and exhaust stacks.

"It must be a hundred feet tall!" breathed Fever, peering up at its high prow, where a carved wooden dragon's head reared up, irrational, brutal and stained red by the evening sun.

The Stalkers, of course, did not reply.

In the fortress's flank an armoured gate stood open, and the mono rolled through it, up a ramp and into a hangar where a dozen others like it stood waiting or were being refuelled by crews of mechanics. Many of the machines had names, like *Rolling Thunder* or *The Wheel Thing*, but before Fever had time to take in any more details Lammergeier and Corvus were ordering her out of their mono. They marshalled her through a bulkhead door and up a spiral staircase, through more doors, along a passageway. The wooden walls, the low wooden ceilings, were all carved with serpentine patterns and the stylized forms of the gods and heroes of the old north. Fever and the Stalkers crossed a chamber where a huge cannon and its crew stood ready at an open gun port, and passed into another, more richly decorated, where evening light came through a score of slit-shaped windows to stripe the hanging tapestries and polished deck.

A man who had been sitting in a big chair there rose as she entered. There were others in the room with him – armoured warriors with swords and guns hanging from their thick belts, women in fur-trimmed robes – but Fever knew at once that the man in the chair was the important one, and she paid no attention to the rest.

"THE BALLOON HAS BEEN SECURED," said the Stalker Lammergeier. "ONE OF ITS OCCUPANTS IS DEAD, BUT THIS GIRL CONTINUES TO FUNCTION."

The man walked all round Fever with his hands folded behind his back, looking at her as if she were an exhibit.

"I am the Land Admiral Nikola Quercus," he said. He had the faintest trace of an accent. His eyes were narrow, slanted and stone grey. He wore a shabby, tall-collared tunic, breeches, boots. He didn't look like a warrior. He looked like a scholar. A mild young man, not big or tall, with fair hair cropped short and brushed forward around his high forehead.

"I am glad to see you safe, Miss Crumb," he said.

Fever could not hide the surprise she felt, that he should know her name. Quercus laughed softly. "Don't worry, I'm not a sorcerer. My agents have been in touch with Dr Stayling, and keep me informed by means of technomancy. It was a bold move of the Engineer's, putting you aboard that flying machine. Luckily he was able to warn us that you were coming. I am sorry about your companion, Master Salent."

"Solent," said Fever. "He died saving me. He was very brave."

Quercus nodded. "His soul is in the High Halls, then."

Fever thought she should tell him that there were no such things as souls, then decided that she had better not.

"He will be treated with honour," Quercus promised.

"He's *dead*."

"Nevertheless, we have certain rites and rituals with which we honour the bodies of the courageous dead, here in the Movement."

Fever bit her lip and supposed she should feel grateful. Funeral rites were silly religious nonsense, and it seemed pitiable that a man like Quercus should believe in gods and souls and rituals. But Kit Solent had not been an Engineer. She remembered the candles under Katie's portrait in his drawing room, and thought that perhaps it would have comforted him to know that the Movement would treat his remains with ceremony.

Quercus nodded, dismissing the matter. He held out his arm to Fever. "Come. I must take you to meet the Snow Leopard."

"Who?"

"My chief technomancer. We call her the Snow Leopard. You know her perhaps by a different name, as Wavey Godshawk."

"My mother?" said Fever, suddenly hesitant, afraid. "But that's. . ."

She stopped herself. She had been about to say, "That's impossible." But it was not impossible. When Dr

Crumb told her his story she had recognized that there must be a chance Wavey had survived. She had accepted that she might have a mother, somewhere in the world. She just had not expected to have the question resolved so soon. It was one thing to have a theoretical mother, quite another to be asked to meet her.

Quercus's smile grew broader as he watched the expressions flit across her face. "Come. She waits for you."

How long had it been travelling, that fortress of the Movement? Even the Movement had forgotten. Back when they were first driven from their homeland by ice and enemies it had been the ox-drawn wagon of their chieftain. It had grown as they moved on, acquiring first steam and then petrol engines from the cities that they conquered, putting on turrets and funnels, gun decks and cabins, spires and jaws and sally ports. It was too big now to be powered only by its primitive engines, and its under decks were filled with massive treadmills, worked by regiments of slaves.

But still the Movement recalled how, long ago, they had lived in Arctic oak forests during some brief, lost era of warmth, and worshipped the gods and spirits of the trees. They had brought one tree with them on their journeyings – age old, long dead – to remind them of their origins. It stood in a chamber of its own, near the castle's stern, a place which seemed quiet even when the engines were pounding and the big guns boomed. Centuries had passed since it last bore leaves or acorns, but the stumps of its branches were decorated with thousands of little scraps of coloured rag, the funeral ribbons of everyone who had died during the Movement's wanderings.

Beneath the oak that evening sat a woman. She wore one of the simple gowns that Movement women favoured, a grey gown which left her throat bare and displayed a curious sepia birthmark beneath her ear and another in the hollow above her collarbone, like a puddle of spilled ink. Nervously her long hands rose to tuck her hair behind her ears. Then she changed her mind and untucked it again. Her hair was grey-white, the colour of wood ash. There were faint crows' feet at the corners of her eyes. In every other way she looked just as she had on the day that Gideon Crumb rescued her from the crowd in St Kylie. Years lay lightly on the Scriven.

One of the big oak doors at the chamber's end opened. The girl came in, and Nikola Quercus came in behind her and softly shut the door again.

"Fever Crumb," he said.

Fever and her mother looked at one another.

"Fever," said Wavey Godshawk, after a little while.

She had thought of Fever often during the years since she fled London, but she had always pictured her as a little girl, like the little girl she had once been herself. She had not prepared herself to meet this spindly teenager with her shaven head and her strange, familiar face.

"My child," she said, after a little longer.

"You have grown up!" she said, wondering.

"What *have* you done to your *hair*?" she asked.

30

THE SNOW LEOPARD

y mother, thought Fever numbly. She went towards her, but did not take the slender hands which Wavey Godshawk stretched out to her. *My mother.* She could smell her perfume, a subtle, blue-grey scent which matched her dress. And what a strange face she had! It wasn't just those few small speckles. The cheekbones were too high, the eyes too large, the jaw too long, the wide mouth filled with far too many teeth (though very straight, thanks to the brace she'd worn when Dr Crumb had met her). It was easy to see why people had believed that the Scriven were a new species. It was easy to see why the Scriven had believed it themselves. *She isn't human,* Fever kept thinking. *And she is my mother. . .*

"You could have sent word," she said. "Dr Crumb doesn't even know that you are still alive!"

"I thought it better not to," said Wavey Godshawk. "What good could it have done? I could not return to London alone. I had to wait until Quercus was ready. Sit, my dear; sit. . ."

She patted the bench and Fever sat down beside her. She reached out and touched Fever's face, smoothing a thumb over her lips, brushing a smut from her forehead. Fever flinched away from her touch, feeling an irrational anger build inside her. What right did this stranger have to prod and stroke her, as if she was a pet, or a doll?

Wavey Godshawk sensed her feelings. "Oh, Fever," she said, sitting back and folding her hands in her lap, smiling. "Oh, but you must think me a terrible mother! To abandon you. To abandon your father before he even knew that he *was* a father. . . But I had to abandon him. Godshawk was furious when he found out I was in love with Gideon. He sent Gideon away, and he told me that if I tried to contact him he would be killed. He sent me away too; said he couldn't stand the sight of me, and packed me off to live at the Barbican.

"Then, when he learned that I was going to have a baby, he softened. I think that he had long been wanting me to have a child who would continue the House of Godshawk. He had spent years finding a good husband for me, and when Odo Bolventor rejected me perhaps he was glad that Gideon Crumb had been there to provide him with an heir. But still he would not let me contact Gideon."

Fever could picture her as she had looked in those days. The way she had worn her hair, the clothes she'd favoured. She had no memories of Wavey from her own babyhood, of course, but there were other memories, scores of them, from earlier times. Wavey as a little girl; and as a young woman. Wavey in her white coat, her hair tied back, careful and serious and the best laboratory assistant a man could ask for. Wavey fastening those thick leather wristbands, frowning as she tightened the screws of the helmet around Fever's head. . .

No, not my *head! Not* my *wrists! These aren't* my *memories. . .*

Wavey kept on smiling at her, and reached out impulsively to touch her hand. "You were never comfortable in my womb, Fever, dear. There was some mismatch between your human and your Scriven halves. How you struggled and squiggled! Elbows and heels jabbed me. I was feverish always. You arrived early, one spring night in my apartment at the Barbican, long before you were looked for. A small little purple monkey you looked, barely longer than my hand, and the Scrivener hadn't made even one single mark upon you. Nobody dreamed that you would live. But Godshawk took you away with him to his laboratories at Nonesuch House, and although I was too weak to go and see you there, he sent word to me by a servant every day.

"Every day I woke up fearing that they would tell me you were dead, but every day they said, 'She's still alive. She's still alive. Your father is doing all he can. Medical machines not seen since Ancient days. . .'

"And then, in early summer, when the blossom was still on the trees, he brought me home to you. You were in your little basket. Your eyes had changed – two different colours. He said it was a side effect of the surgery he had performed, and I did not complain. I was just so happy to see you. And so grateful to Godshawk for having saved you.

"But we had so little time together, Fever! There were riots in the city, and the mercenaries whom Godshawk had hired to protect us betrayed us and joined with the rioters instead.

"You and I were still living at the Barbican, and so were other Scriven, friends of Godshawk, sheltering from the riots. One morning he had us all gather in the basement and showed us the secret passage to Nonesuch House. We begged him to come with us, but he refused. He said he would stay and seal up the tunnel entrance, then organize a last stand against the Skinners. 'They can't kill me,' he said, as we set off along the tunnel. 'Just keep that baby safe, daughter!'

"That night, from the windows of Nonesuch House, we heard their horrid cheering drifting across the marshes, as if the whole of London was celebrating, and we knew that Godshawk was dead.

"We stayed there, hidden, for nearly two weeks. At first we felt sure that some Scriven noblemen would have survived the riots; that they'd retake London and come to rescue us. But slowly we realized we were alone.

"There was not much to eat. The others squabbled. Some said I should not keep you, Fever, that it was wrong to let a half-human hybrid eat food real Scriven needed. When they were not arguing and blaming each other and inventing hopeless schemes to win the city back, the men went out and cut the causeway to make sure no looters reached us, though there was enough loot on Ludgate Hill to keep the commons busy for a long time.

"At the end of the second week the Skinners came for us. My companions shot at them from the gardens and thought they'd killed them all – how they jeered and laughed, flinging stones at the bodies afloat in the lagoon! But one had survived, and that night he came to the house.

"As the panic grew, I took you from your basket and ran and hid. I snuggled down with you on the floor of a cupboard in one of the bedrooms and listened to the men as they shouted to each other, asking where the Skinner was, and the clang of his spring gun as he appeared out of the shadows to shoot them down one by one, and the screams. Gradually, the house grew quiet. A horrible silence. I whispered lullabies to you, and your little hands pulled at my nose and ears. And you made a sound. Not crying, just a little baby gurgle. And the Skinner heard you.

"I could sense him padding towards us through the house. I put my hand over your face, but I dared not hold it too tight for fear I'd smother you. And you were happy, Fever, snuggled up with me there in that place full of soft things. You started laughing. You made trilling sounds, and little wicked chuckles.

"And then, *Bang*. A hole appeared in the cupboard door, just in the place where my head would have been if I'd been standing up. Light was coming in. The force of the shot made the door swing open. I tried to stop it. I clawed at the wood, but my fingers couldn't find a purchase on it. The door swung wide open, and there outside it stood the Skinner, with his long black coat and his black hat and his pale eyes and his spring gun.

"I held you so tight, Fever. You sensed, I think, the danger we were in. Or else his first shot had shocked you quiet; quiet you were, anyway. I watched him, waiting for him to raise that gun. And I waited. And after a while he let out a long breath, and a cough – he'd been sunk in the marsh all day – and he put the gun away.

"'Well,' he said, looking around the room as if I

wasn't there. 'I suppose I'd better burn this place. It'll take me ten minutes, I reckon, to set the fire.'

"And he turned and went out of the room.

"For one whole minute I just sat there. Then I jumped up, and rummaged in the cupboard for an outdoor coat, and found some boots down on the floor – I'd been wondering what they were, digging into my bottom, all the time that we'd been hiding there. I pulled on the boots and wrapped that cloak around us both and I was off, down the hill and out across the marshes. And after ten minutes I looked back and there was fire in all the windows of Nonesuch House.

"When morning came I struck out for a dig I knew, owned by a man named Unthank who had worked for my father sometimes. He welcomed me, but he said he couldn't hide me long. I decided to go north and seek shelter among the nomad empires. But I knew I couldn't take you with me. You were too small for such a journey, and besides, what if my Skinner had regretted his mercifulness and told his friends of me? What if the Skinners' Guilds and the new guards on the Moatway were all looking out for a woman with a baby girl?

"There was only one thing to do, Fever, dear. I left you there with Unthank, and I told him to call Dr Crumb there on some pretence. 'Dr Crumb is a good man,' I told him. 'He'll take care of the child.'

"And he did, didn't he, Fever Crumb? Because look at you. You're a young woman, nearly. And I've no doubt you're just as sweet and clever as your father."

31

HIDDEN TREASURES

"M other," said Fever, very quietly and self-consciously, because it was the first time she'd ever used the word. "What did Godshawk do to me?"

Wavey's dark eyes darkened further; she glanced away. "What do you mean?"

"I remember things. Things that happened to him, not to me."

There was a little silence. They could hear people moving around somewhere below them in the fortress's engine rooms; the clangs and clatter of refuelling. Nikola Quercus stirred and shifted, over by the chamber door. "What does the girl mean?" he asked. "You never told me anything of this."

"Godshawk did something to me, didn't he?" Fever prompted. "He performed some operation on my brain, to give me his memories."

"Oh, Fever," said Wavey, wondering.

"Is this true?" asked Quercus, coming nearer. "She has the old man's knowledge in her? His thoughts?"

Wavey looked quickly at him, then back to Fever. "It might be. It is possible. . ."

"And you were keeping this secret to yourself perhaps, Snow Leopard?"

"I did not know," said Wavey. "At least, I could not be certain. I guessed that he had placed some engine in her head. There was that scar, still fresh when she came back to me. But I did not know what its purpose was. . ."

She pursed her lips, shook her head, looked down, looked up at Fever. She reached out to fondle the faint, scratchy stubble of the girl's regrowing hair. She said, "Godshawk spent decades studying the brains of Stalkers. He made expeditions to the uttermost north, where the old Stalker builders lived in the years after the Downsizing. He traded with the natives there for certain artefacts; rare Stalker brains of strange design taken from temples on the high ice. Things made in the long ago, by people for whom Stalkers were much more than the mere fighting machines we know today. Machines which could capture and curate memories; even the memories of the dead.

"For years Godshawk and his friend Unthank studied them, back at Nonesuch House. Godshawk did not want to die, you see. And he was convinced that he did not have to. He hoped to copy his consciousness into one of those ancient brains and install it in a new body when his old one failed. He talked of doing the same with all the Scriven. 'Then we truly will be *Homo superior*,' he used to say. 'Immortal, unperishing. Imagine the things a man might do if he had eternity to do them in, not just our present measly span of years!'"

"But it didn't work, did it?" Fever asked.

Another shrug. A shy, wry smile. "I helped him to imprint his mind on to the brains. *That* worked, as far as he could tell. But when he tried to put those brains in new bodies, something always went wrong. He placed them in dead men, and they remembered nothing, just like ordinary Stalkers. He put them into living men –

slaves and Skinner prisoners – and they simply died. I thought he had given up, moved on to other projects. . .

"But then. . ." said Fever, "he put one into *me*. . ."

Wavey nodded. The tears which had been forming in her eyes spilled out and trickled down her face. "And you did not die. A young body, perhaps that was what it required. A newborn body, where the Stalker brain would have plenty of time to bed in before it was activated by the tides of adolescence."

"He told you that?" said Fever, actually ducking to avoid a memory Wavey's words called up of Godshawk's own adolescence, and a girl he'd kissed at Rag Fair on a snowy afternoon.

"I'm guessing," said Wavey. "It might have been simple desperation that made him try it. The Skinners' Guilds had grown horribly strong by the time you were born, and he knew his days were numbered. You were on the brink of death anyway, poor little thing. What had he to lose by putting the device in your head? He would have injected you at the same time with microscopic machines which he harvested from the bodies of ancient Stalkers. They would have helped to repair the damage to your brain, and stop infections forming. At least, that was his belief. They never worked in his other subjects. But here you are, alive!"

"Here I am," said Fever numbly. But was she? Was this her, or was it Auric Godshawk? She reached behind her head and let her fingers trace the faint, rippled line of the scar, the zipper where Godshawk had opened her skull and slipped in his machine. The shape of a walnut, the size of an almond. The spring from which all those unfamiliar memories flowed. More washed over her now; memories of Wavey, mostly, pleasant memories, but still upsetting, because she wanted to get used to the idea that this woman was her *mother*, but she kept seeing her as someone younger than herself, a little girl, a favourite daughter, a workroom protégée.

She had no memories, thankfully, of the experiments Godshawk must have done, the operations he had carried out on both the living and the dead in an attempt to preserve his selfish self. She supposed his consciousness had been crammed into the Stalker brain at a time before those experiments were done. She was glad of that, for she could already sense things surfacing that made her feel giddy with disgust. The fights at Pickled Eel Circus, and Godshawk's excitement as he sat watching in the royal enclosure. His satisfaction as he viewed the progress of his huge portrait-head, ignoring what Fever could not ignore, the suffering of the slave gangs who were constructing it. She began to shudder, and suddenly hot tears were running down her face, and Wavey was reaching out to hold her, but she pulled away.

Wavey said, "Poor Fever! All these years you've been hidden in Godshawk's Head, and now you find out that he's been hiding in yours. . ."

Fever sniffled and choked and swallowed salty snot. She hadn't cried since she was tiny; it made her feel irrational and ashamed. "Can you get it out of me?" she whispered, clutching her head, battered by the storms of alien memories. "Can you turn it off?"

"I don't think so," said Wavey.

"We cannot," said Quercus, very firmly, sounding like a soldier for the first time. Fever saw his shiny boots

232

approach across the oak-planked deck. "If this is true, Miss Crumb, then we need the knowledge that you carry. My gods! All Godshawk's genius at our disposal. You're a greater treasure than any in that vault."

Fever looked sharply at him.

"Oh yes, Miss Crumb. We know about the vault."

"From Dr Stayling?" she asked.

The northerner shook his head. "I have not told Stayling of it. We could not risk having your Order of Engineers helping themselves to its contents. No, it was your mother who told me of it, many years ago. Back then, we had no reason to believe it still existed; we assumed that it had been looted or destroyed during your Skinners' Riots. Then one of my agents, the woman you know as Mistress Gloomstove, became aware of Master Solent's activities. That is what convinced me to advance on London."

Fever blinked. It felt strange, having to recast Mistress Gloomstove as a Movement spy, but stranger things had happened that day. She said, "What's in the vault anyway?"

Wavey did not answer her, but looked instead at Nikola Quercus.

"More Stalker stuff?" Fever prompted. "More things like this one inside me?"

"No, no," said Wavey. "Godshawk had given up that project long before you were born. He was working on something else. That statue he began to build was just a cover, an excuse to start constructing great factory sheds and importing tonnes of steel and raw materials. He was afraid that if he told people what he was *really* planning they would think it madness."

"What – madder than a mile-high statue of himself?" asked Fever.

Wavey ignored her, smiling shyly towards Quercus. "After I left you at Unthank's dig, Fever, I wandered for years, all through the Minarchies and up into the nomad empires, earning my living as a travelling technomancer. I never spoke to anyone of what I was, and who my father had been. I never hoped to return to London. But when I came aboard this castle and met Quercus I saw at once that here was a man who could appreciate Godshawk's vision. I told him about the vault and what it contained, and he decided that the Movement must have it."

Again her mother looked at Quercus, and Fever realized that she was waiting for him to decide whether they should share the secret of the vault with Fever.

"What is it?" she said. She thought of those loose pencil sketches of cogs and heat exchangers in the notebook on Kit Solent's library table, and dim memories of imaginary machines woke and whirred in her mind, but there was nothing that she could make sense of. "What was Godshawk working on? What is in the vault?"

Behind her, softly, Nikola Quercus said, "The future."

32

TECHNOMANCY

own on the under decks of the fortress, preparations were under way for the final assault on London. The technomancers who guarded the mysteries of its engines went about their work, opening the fuel cocks, oiling the pistons, coaxing the aged machinery into noisy motion, chanting prayers and incantations to keep it running. And at the same time, gangs of slaves from the barrack barges were marched aboard the fortress to take their places in the giant wooden drums which flanked the engine rooms. When forty men were shackled in each drum they too became engines of a kind; the energy they generated as they tramped endlessly along the rolling inner surface of their treadmills was transferred by means of cogs and camshafts to the drive wheels.

Slowly, as the lower decks filled with the smells of engine fumes and slave sweat, the fortress began to move. Barrel-shaped wheels, studded to grip the snows of the northern frost barrens, coped easily with the mud and scrub of Hamster's Heath. By the light of the rising moon it pushed its blunt prow through the Orbital Moatway, and from its funnels came a shrill, triumphant, *"WOOT!"* as, with its escort of armoured barges spread out like wings on either side of it, it began to roll towards the lights of London.

*

They let Fever have a little narrow cabin, and she lay down on the cot in the corner of it and tried to sleep. But how could she sleep, with the whole place shuddering and her mind a stew of someone else's memories? There seemed to be more of them every minute, and she was starting to be afraid that if they kept multiplying there would soon be no room left for her inside her own head. If the decisions she made about the future weren't based on her own experience but on Godshawk's, mightn't she start to behave more and more like him? Perhaps her own personality would fade completely, and she would be nothing but Godshawk's avatar; the evil old man reborn in a new body.

She climbed off the cot, which was really more like a padded shelf, space being precious in a traction fortress. She had not bothered to take off her trousers or shirt when she laid down. Quickly she pulled on her boots and the coat which Wavey Godshawk had brought to replace her own blood-stained, mud-stained one. It was a Movement woman's coat, cut long and slender out of red silk with a deeper red snowflake pattern and a fox-fur collar. Part of Fever thought it most irrational, but another part, the Godshawk part, thought she looked the bee's knees as she left the cabin.

There was a scent of smoke and metal in the cramped corridors. Movement warriors hurried to and fro, holding on to the handrails on the wall each time the fortress juddered over some obstacle. They stared at Fever as she passed, but none tried to stop or question her; she was the Land Admiral's guest, after all. She took a few wrong turnings, confused by the many

236

passageways and sub-levels, but she found her way at last to the big chamber where she had first met Quercus. He was there again, sitting in his big chair, listening to a report which one of his captains was shouting at him above the steady clangour of the fortress's progress. He had put on a coat of mail over his tunic, and there was steel armour on his neck and forearms. The other people in the chamber were all soldiers, armed and armoured; the women had been banished below.

Quercus looked round and saw Fever standing there. "Miss Crumb," he said. "You should not be here." He spoke politely, but in a way that made it plain that he did not expect her to argue. "It may get dangerous as we approach the city. There is trouble in London and our agents there are no longer sure who is in charge. There may be resistance, and you are too important to risk." He rose from his seat and came closer, looking curiously at Fever's face. "It will be one thing to capture Godshawk's invention, but quite another to make it work, and build replicas, and do all the thousand things that must be done. If you really have the old man's thoughts inside you, you will be invaluable. It will be like having Godshawk himself there to help us."

"You still haven't told me what is in the vault," said Fever. "What has my mother promised you, that made it worth bringing your castle all this way?"

Quercus laughed. "Look inside yourself, Miss Crumb. Search among the old man's memories!" Then he glanced past her and snapped his fingers. "Captain Andringa!" he shouted.

A young warrior came hurrying to take Fever by the

arm and escort her out of the command chamber. He was polite and respectful, but firm. "No women, no girls, not here, not when we are going into action. It is bad luck!"

"Is there going to be more fighting?" asked Fever.

"We hope not, but your people may have placed some artillery pieces among their northern suburbs. Don't worry. Our big guns can knock out their batteries before they do us any damage. May I help you back to your cabin?"

"Where is my mother?" asked Fever, who didn't want to be alone if there was to be a battle.

"The Snow Leopard?" He looked wary. "She is at work. In the Resurrectory."

"Where's that?"

The young man was doubtful. He looked back at the door of the command chamber as if he was thinking of asking permission from his Land Admiral. But Quercus had a battle to direct. He shrugged, and took Fever's arm again. "Come. I'll take you."

The Resurrectory was deep in the castle's rumbling innards, down among the engines and the straining slaves. Fever, recalling that her mother was a technomancer and that the nomads thought of technology as magic or a gift from the gods, imagined that it would be some sort of temple. When her guide showed her in through its heavy doors she saw at once that she'd been quite wrong.

It was a place of science. Science of a sort. The sort of science that felt almost like magic even to an Engineer; stuff that no one understood, but which stubbornly went on working anyway. A 'lectric lamp swung from the centre of the low roof, lighting up a bench where Wavey Godshawk and two red-robed assistants bent over a dead man, turning him patiently and carefully into another Stalker for the Movement's army.

Wavey turned from her work as her daughter came in. She pushed up the brass goggles which she wore and smiled, as if there was no corpse lying on the zinc-topped slab in front of her. But there was, and because it was not yet fully sheathed in its Stalker armour, Fever could see that it was the corpse of Kit Solent.

She put a hand to her mouth, and backed against the door, which the man who led her there had closed behind him as he left. Her Engineer upbringing had never been so tested. Her reason told her that Kit Solent was dead, and that it did not matter what happened to his remains. Her instincts all screamed at her that it was wrong, wrong, wrong to strip and mutilate him like that, and fill the hollow of his chest with whatever those weird, gleaming devices were; to fit those flashlights in the craters where his eyes had been.

"Fever!" said Wavey, pulling off soiled rubber gloves as she came round the worktable to greet her daughter. "Are you all right? You look quite pale. Don't be afraid. Quercus has fought ever so many battles, and always brings us safely through."

Fever could not stop staring at what was left of Kit. Plastic tubes led from his veins, pumping out blood, pumping in chemicals. The robed assistants were busy fitting clumsy-looking metal hands to the armour which encased his arms. His real hands, discarded, stuck out of a soggy basket on the deck, looking pale and stupid and unreal.

"Quercus said he would be treated with honour," she said, in a tiny voice.

"But this *is* an honour, Fever, according to the customs of the Movement," replied her mother. "Only the best fighters are reborn as Stalkers, so that their bodies may go on serving the Movement even after their souls have gone to the High Halls. It is a privilege extended to very few enemies. Your Master Solent was a brave man, and this is Quercus's way of acknowledging that bravery." She put a comforting arm around Fever's shoulders, but Fever shrugged it off. She hated being touched, and she didn't want comfort. She had done quite well without a mother for fourteen years; why did Wavey think that she suddenly needed so much stroking and hugging?

She mastered her feeling of nausea and stepped closer to the horrid table. She saw that the machines that had been packed into Kit's torso were already old; Ancient technology recycled down the centuries in Stalker after Stalker, just as she and Dr Crumb had recycled the New Council's stock of brains and claws and eyes into generations of paper boys. In some ways, she supposed, this was a fitting end for an archaeologist. "I didn't know you did this," she said thinly.

"How do you think I managed to become Quercus's technomancer in the first place?" asked Wavey. "I spent so long assisting Godshawk that I can build Stalkers in my sleep. Though not for much longer, I fear. Our supplies of Stalker brains are running out, and the art of making new ones is long lost. That makes it even grander, in a way, that Quercus has ordered your friend to be Resurrected. The new brain in Master Solent's head is the best we have in stock, brought from a Snowmad trader who found it high, high upon the northern ice. I think you really impressed him, Fever; Quercus, I mean. I'm sure he likes you. We really *must* try and do something with your hair. . ."

"But will he remember anything?" asked Fever.

"Quercus?"

"No, Master Solent!"

"Nothing," Wavey promised her. "Your friend is dead. This new warrior we are building will not be Master Solent at all, but a Stalker, implacable and undying."

"What power source keeps all those devices running inside him? How is he fuelled?"

"No fuel is required."

"But that would break the first law of thermo-dynamics. . ."

"Oh, you Engineers and your laws," said her mother. "They *work*, Fever. What does it matter how? They draw the power they need from the environment somehow. Godshawk called it 'Molecular Clockwork', but even he could not discover how it was done. Yet the Stalkers go on. Your friend Solent may still be stalking around long after you and I and the Movement are forgotten."

Fever stood with her and watched while Kit's chest was closed, and a plate of armour fitted over the dead flesh. The red-robed mechanics then set to work upon his helmet, attaching a complicated sliding visor

241

arrangement to the metal skull-piece which now sheathed his head. They had just finished stencilling his new name on it when the body began to stir, making small restless movements with its feet and fingers. A green light flared up in its eyes. The mechanics drew back.

"What is happening?" asked Fever.

Wavey drew her carefully away from the creature. "It is quickening. The Stalker brain is taking control of its new body. It is. . ."

With a hard clang, sharp, steel-blue blades extended from the Stalker's hands. It began to thrash its arms about. Its mouth opened and a terrible, deep, wordless cry came from it. One of the mechanics ran to a red locker on the wall and took out a clumsy-looking gun with a thick copper disc in place of a muzzle. He trained the weapon on the new Stalker's head and looked up at Wavey, waiting for her order.

"No," said Wavey. Avoiding the flailing blades she went close to the Stalker and laid her hand upon its chest. "Listen to me!" she shouted, over the ceaseless scream. "You are a Stalker of the Lazarus Brigade. You are not yet operational. You will be quiet, and lie still, while you are made ready. Obey."

The Stalker fell quiet. After a moment more the blades slid back into its hands, and it lowered its arms. Wavey Godshawk looked up at her assistants, and the one with the gun returned it to its locker.

"That happens sometimes," she told Fever. "A side-effect of quickening. Some become violent and have to be destroyed with the magneto pistol. I'm glad that didn't happen to Master Solent."

But the thing on the bench was not Kit Solent any more. It was a Stalker of the Lazarus Brigade, and all it remembered, as it lay there waiting for the mechanics to finish work, was that it wanted to destroy the Movement's enemies. It didn't even know its own name yet, the stencilled name which was drying white upon its brow. It had been given a bird name, like all that year's recruits to the Lazarus Brigade. It was called Shrike.

33

LONDON FALLING

here was a plan to hold the Movement on the northern edge of the city. It wasn't much of a plan, but it was the best that anyone had been able to come up with in the circumstances, and Ted Swiney had decided it would have to do. He got the old Clerks of Council to toll Big Brian, the ancient bell which summoned all able-bodied men to defend the city. He sent criers out into the streets to jangle their handbells and holler, "Get up the Barbican, you cloots!"

But no citizen army presented itself in the square below Ted's balcony. Those men of the Trained Bands who had escaped when the Moatway was breached had returned to London with no desire to face the Movement again; they had stopped just long enough to gather their families and a few possessions, then fled south. As for Ted's own supporters, they had been disappointed that the riots had ended so soon and were spoiling for another fight, but rumours soon spread among them of the Movement's armoured land barges, their Stalkers and their old-tech guns.

"Is this all?" demanded Ted, when he stalked out on to his balcony to review the troops. The only people in the square were those who'd had too much of his free booze to leave. He spat over the balcony rail and cursed. (Spitting was banned now, of course, but what was the point of being Mayor at all if you had to live by your own rules?) Snatching up the telescope someone had nicked for him, he squinted through it at the tatty rooftops of the north boroughs and the land beyond. What looked like a wall of mist billowing across the moonlit heath was really smoke and dust flung up by the Movement's traction fortress as it rumbled towards London. He could see the lines of little lighted squares that were its open gun ports, and the lights of dozens of smaller vehicles spread out on either flank.

Cheesers! Who'd have thought the nomads would be so tooled up? Swiney had been brought up believing that Londoners were automatically superior to every other kind of people on the Earth, and that they'd proved it once and for all by dishing the Patchskins. He'd never dreamed this Movement riff-raff, this bunch of . . . of . . . of *foreigners* would have the nerve or nous to bust the Moatway down.

He went back inside and stomped through the Barbican's big rooms in a haze of rage, issuing orders that no one paid any attention to, sometimes kicking things to ease his temper (which didn't work). At last there was a pummelling of feet up the stair carpets and Mutt appeared with some of his lads, herding Dr Crumb and the rest of the frightened Order of Engineers ahead of him.

"About time," snarled Swiney. "Who's in charge? Never mind, you can all come. Come on."

He led the way to the Chamber of Devices on the upper floor, where the clerks had told him London's most precious and destructive old-tech weaponry was stored, ready for use in just such times as these.

Wormtimber had been in charge of it, of course, and he'd taken the key with him when Godshawk's statue nutted him six feet down, but Swiney had found a spare, and had already had a look into the secret arsenal. The stuff in there hadn't made a speck of sense to him, which was why he'd sent Mutt to drag the Engineers out of the basement where they'd been penned.

He kicked the door open again and stood aside so that Dr Stayling and his colleagues could file past him into the chamber. It was high, and lined with shelves, and some of the shelves had things on: batteries and spools of wire and crated machinery from other eras.

"Well?" he demanded impatiently, as the Engineers looked about. "What do we use? What have we got that will stop that fortress thing?" He snatched up a promising looking artefact. "What's this? A ray gun?"

"I think that's part of what the Ancients called a 'Hoover'," said Dr Stayling, taking it from him and flipping the switch on its handle, which made all the other Engineers dive for cover. "It doesn't work."

Ted grunted. "What about those, those silver balls there?"

Dr Stayling picked one up. "A ball bearing," he said. "Quite a large one, though. I suppose it could be fired from a slingshot or some type of catapult. . ."

"Will it explode?"

"Of course not."

"Then it's no bloggin' use to me, is it?" raged Ted. "What else we got?"

The Engineers peeped into boxes and opened the lids of crates. "I don't understand it," said Dr Collihole, who had once been Master of Devices himself, before

Wormtimber ousted him. "There used to be all *sorts* of things stored here. A kind of hand-held cannon with the most ingenious sights. A big rockety kind of a thing. A very curious energy gun from the Electric Empire Era. . ."

"The Trained Bands took that north, apparently," said Swiney. "It blew up."

"And there should be some paper boys, of course," said Dr Whyre, opening the empty plan chest drawer where they'd been stored.

Ted understood. "Wormtimber!" he muttered. "That greedy little goblin snitched the whole lot for himself! He's left us nothing!"

Dr Crumb raised a hand. "Could we not simply go to Wormtimber's establishment? He may not yet have sold on everything he stole. . ."

"It's on fire, innit," said Ted, glancing poisonously at the Engineers as if he thought they were deliberately mocking him. "Some of the lads got carried away and half the bottom end of Cripplegate's gone up in flames." He turned his wide back on them and stalked out of the chamber, pausing just outside the doorway to look back and shout, "Well? Get thinking! When these cloots get here I want something I can throw at 'em! I'm not going to be kicked out of my own town by a mob of foreigners!"

"Ted!" shouted Brickie Chapstick, appearing at a run from the far end of the long corridor. "Ted, the nomads have stopped!"

"What? Where?"

"Just short of Finnsbry."

Ted hurried towards the nearest window. The Engineers went after him, joining other men – liveried

247

servants of the fallen council and Ted's scruffy hangers-on – in a general rush.

North of the city the lights of the Movement's fortress rose above the roofs of Finnsbry like an unsightly new block of flats.

"Brickie's right," someone said. "It's stopped."

Ted grinned. "They've seen sense, ain't they? They must have heard that things have changed, and there's a real man running London now. They know we'll wipe the floor with them if they try it on." He slung the window wide and shouted, "Go on, hop it! Leave it! It ain't worth it!"

Everyone else watched the motionless fortress, waiting for its banks of guns to fire and send some colossal broadside slamming into the Barbican. *This could be the last thing I ever see*, thought Dr Crumb. *I may die here, without ever seeing Fever again, without ever even knowing if she is alive or dead. . .*

But the fortress did not open fire, and in a few moments more there was something else to look at. A terrible, thin, rising screech drew everyone's eyes towards Bishopsgate, that long road which led down the slope of Ludgate Hill towards the north boroughs. Sparks of reflected moonlight were being flung across the house fronts there; across the sails of a wind tram abandoned on Finnsbry viaduct. Swift shapes flicked across gaps between buildings. "Vehicles!" said one of the Engineers.

Seconds more, and a dozen monos came bowling like bashed-off hubcaps into the littered square before the Barbican.

*

Charley Shallow was not there to see the northerners arrive. He had slunk off as night fell, making his lonely way by quiet streets back to Ketch Causeway and the Skinner's house. He hadn't a key for Bagman's place, but the Skinner had never needed to lock his door. Not only had the house not been burgled, there were little offerings of flowers and teddy bears all up the steps, and candles burning down in bottles, and little scrawly notes, which Charley couldn't read, tied to the railings. Food, too; pies and loaves and joints of meat, left as offerings to the Skinner's memory, or gifts for his boy.

Charley stepped over it all, too tired to eat, too tired to care. He went into the house and fell down in his nest on the floor of the front room and he was asleep before he even had time to think.

It was late when he woke. Cold bluish moonlight was creeping round the edges of the blinds. No coughing from Bagman's room, not this night nor ever more again. He wondered why that made him so sad. He'd only known the old man for about a day and a half. But it had been the only day and a half in Charley's life when he'd felt as if somebody cared for him, and thought he might amount to something.

He lit a candle and went and found the eggs and stuff he'd brought for breakfast that morning. While they were cooking he looked for clean clothes. His own were so stiff with mud and sweat that he doubted they could ever get clean. He went into the old man's room and found a cupboard, and clothes inside it. There were good black breeks and a black long-tunic that Bagman must have kept for wearing to the funerals of his fellow

Skinners. The breeks fitted Charley all right round the waist as long as he belted them tight, and if he left them unbuckled they hung so far down his skinny legs that it didn't matter when he couldn't find any stockings. He found a shirt, a bit yellowish round the neck but clean enough. In a wooden box on the floor of the cupboard he found a spare spring gun and a half dozen bolts wrapped up in an oily rag. He cleaned the gun carefully, stuck it through his belt, and filled his pockets with the bolts. But when he went to put the tunic on he saw that there was a little enamel badge on the lapel; the crossed knives of the Skinners' Guilds.

Who am I kidding? thought Charley. He took off the tunic and sat on the edge of Bagman's bed. He wasn't a Skinner. He wasn't fit to inherit the old man's gear, let alone his title. He'd let Bagman down. "Finish it," Bagman had told him. But he'd bottled it when he had the chance to shoot the Crumb girl. And now she'd escaped him, blown away in that flying thing.

He shut his eyes and Bagman Creech appeared as a cheap blue ghost, whispering, *"She's Scriven, boy. It ain't like killing a human being. You do what's needful. It's all up to you now."*

He sat there for a long time feeling guilty and sorry for himself, until he heard a rising babble of voices outside. For a moment he was afraid that it was the people of the neighbourhood coming to ask him why he'd failed in his duty. But when he went and looked out the window he saw the crowd in the street weren't interested in the Skinner's house at all. They were hurrying past without even looking at it.

He opened the window a crack, his own worries

250

forgotten in his eagerness to hear what they were shouting.

"The nomads are here!" he heard a man yell. "They're at the Barbican!"

34

MAYOR VS MAYOR

ondon had always loved a show. A bit of spectacle; something a little different; preferably the chance of violence. . . The arrival of the Movement was almost better than a riot. Once they realized the city was not to be pulverized people came out to line the pavements and peer down from balconies at the screeching monos as they went racketing towards the Barbican. Gangs of children ran behind, but not too close, because along beside the wheels came detachments of the Lazarus Brigade, big, battle-battered Stalkers, moving at a clanking jog-trot with their finger blades bared.

Fever rode with her mother in the third mono from the front, the vehicle behind the Land Admiral's. Looking out through the glass of the cabin windows as it bowled up Bishopsgate she saw the watching faces of the Londoners lit up by its lights and shivered, wondering if some of them were the same people who had encircled Godshawk's Head the day before, chanting for her blood. But they looked cowed now, even the roughest of them punch-drunk by the speed of the Movement's arrival. And there was little chance that they would recognize her, in her red silk coat with its collar turned up and a fur hat pulled down to her eyebrows.

In Barbican Square the monos halted. They lowered

their parking props, which also served as ladders, and let out more Stalkers, along with mortal warriors carrying big multi-barrelled muskets or holding up the banner of the wheeled tower on skull-topped poles. The mono pilots left all their lights burning, and the warriors lit flaming torches and held them high, so that the square and the broad frontage of the Barbican were lit up brightly. They stared about them, curious and ill at ease among these immobile buildings. Usually when the Movement took a static settlement it was looted and then destroyed and its population sent to man the slavemills, but Quercus had different plans for this place; they'd been told to tread lightly. Two-man arquebus teams rested their guns on stands and swept them across the balconies and upper windows of the houses on the square, across the viaducts and rooftops. The Stalkers stood poised, blades a-twitch, ready to rush in and slaughter any lurking Londoners who offered resistance. But no shots were fired.

After a few moments Quercus himself emerged from his mono, fastening his cloak, and Wavey Godshawk took Fever's hand and said, "Come, dear, let's step down."

The night air felt cool and fresh after the stuffiness of the mono cabin. Fever went down the ladder behind her mother, watching her gaze about at the city, wondering what she was feeling. Would any of those Londoners, looking on from their windows and the doorways of shops and houses, recognize Godshawk's daughter from all those years ago?

"What do you want?" bawled a big, rough voice, echoing off the house fronts. Fever looked up at the balcony above the Barbican's prow, and saw that it was not Gilpin Wheen who stood there but Ted Swiney. She stepped behind her mother, not wanting him to see her. But Swiney was not looking at her; his mean little eyes were fixed on Quercus.

Quercus looked up at him. "Do you have the authority to speak for London?" he called.

"*Speak* for London?" Swiney swelled like a cockney toad, flushed with pride and hatred. "*Speak* for London? I *am* London!"

Quercus turned around slowly, taking in the watchers in the square. "This city," he said loudly, "is now a possession of the Movement. We have plans for it. Great plans, which you may share in. Offer no resistance, and you have nothing to fear."

"That's a load of blog!" shouted Ted Swiney, as the echoes faded. "I bet that's what the Dapplejacks said when *they* took over. We're Londoners, we are! We won't be ruled by some jumped up gypsy like you!"

He looked triumphantly at his people. He'd expected his words to raise a cheer, but apart from a half-hearted "Yeah!" from Mutt Gnarly, no one reacted at all. The truth was, most Londoners didn't much care who ruled them. The ones who had had their property burned or looted the day before were inclined to think that Quercus might be an improvement, and there were many important men who had, like Dr Stayling, already been swayed by Movement agents. Meanwhile, the thugs and wastrels who had shoehorned Ted into the Barbican were too wary of the nomads' weaponry to show him much support.

Quercus came up the steps in front of the Barbican,

past the giant beer keg which still waited there, lofted up on its trestles. He stood directly below Ted, and called loudly up at him. "Your army is scattered, and your city lies under my guns," he said. "I am not even asking you to surrender. It is over. I am Mayor of London now."

"Are you, now?" said Ted, through his small, square, tight-clamped teeth. He lacked most virtues, but he did have a fierce, stupid, cornered-rat kind of courage. Hadn't he battled gladiators and Godshawk's death-machines in Pickled Eel Circus? He was a fighter, and he wasn't going to give up the city he'd won to this pale little twig of a man. And wasn't that how they settled things, up in the nomad hunting grounds? You had to give them that; they didn't muck about with elections and speeches; if there was two nomads who both wanted power, they settled it like men.

"I'll fight you for it," he said. "You and me. Right here. With all London as our witness. Winner takes the city."

Quercus scratched his nose. "Hand to hand? Unarmed? No weapons?"

"A fair fight," said Ted proudly, grinning down at him, this little northerner he could snap with his bare hands.

The arquebus men fingered their firing levers. Several Movement chieftains came hurrying forward to warn Quercus that he need not accept Ted's challenge, but he waved them away. He seemed amused.

"You're on," he said.

Down in the square, Londoners and nomads alike were drawn towards the Barbican, magnetized by the prospect of the duel. But Wavey Godshawk took her daughter by the hand and started to pull her in the opposite direction. She was carrying a bulky canvas satchel over one shoulder, and a 'lectric lantern.

"Come now," she said. "We don't have time to watch this foolishness. The important thing is to make sure that Godshawk's vault is secured. . ."

"But what about Quercus?" asked Fever. She looked back at the Barbican steps where the Land Admiral was stripping off his cloak and armour and handing his sword belt to a second. "Aren't you worried about this fight?"

"Of course not. It will make no difference. The city is ours. It is just Quercus's silly pride that makes him want to indulge in this gesture. He's a fighting man and this was all too easy for him. He wants it to feel like a real victory."

"But that's irrational! He might be killed!" protested Fever.

Wavey shrugged. "It will make no difference. Another man can take his place and the Movement will still have London. You are not *worried* for him, are you?"

Fever felt her ears turn pink, and was glad that she was still wearing the hat. "I would not wish him to be killed," she said.

Wavey squeezed her hand. "He is only a common human, Fever. Their kind are two-a-penny, you know. *We* are the ones who matter; you and me and Godshawk's legacy. Come, let's go and see if it's still intact."

The edges of the square were filling fast with people

256

as word of Swiney's challenge spread down Ludgate Hill. Wavey called out to some nearby Stalkers to come with her and clear a way for her. Lammergeier, Corvus and Shrike.

"Do we have to have *him* with us?" asked Fever, still uneasy in the presence of the new Stalker. Despite his armour and his towering height she could not stop thinking of him as Kit Solent.

"It would hardly be wise to go wandering about this town without a bodyguard," said Wavey. "Quercus agreed that I could take Corvus and Lammergeier, but he cannot spare many of his experienced warriors, so Shrike will come too. Besides, who could be more appropriate?"

She shone the beam of her lantern ahead of them and the crowd parted nervously to let them through. The Londoners' eyes were all upon the Stalkers and not upon the woman and the girl who followed them. Fever watched Shrike, trying to forget who he'd been the day before, trying to ignore her feelings of pity and disgust.

She did not see Charley Shallow standing in the crowd. She did not see his gaze slip from the Stalker's face to hers.

A storm had blown through the Solent house. At least, that's what it looked like; blasted the front door in and roared right through, overturning furniture and wrenching down curtains, smashing the scent lanterns and spilling perfumes across the floors, filling the wrecked rooms with drifts of clashing scent.

The Stalker Shrike strode through it all quite unmoved, following Corvus and Lammergeier. His visor was up and his bloodless face was the face of Kit Solent, but as his electric eyes slid over portraits of his wife and father, his children and his former self, he gave no sign of recognizing anything. *He has no memories at all,* thought Fever. *And me, I've far too many.*

There was no sign of Fern or Ruan as they walked towards the hidden basement and the passageway. Fever thought of calling out their names, but stopped herself. She would not want them to meet their father in his new form, not unwarned. Anyway, it seemed unlikely that they would have remained in this place, with its broken windows and torn-off doors. Even though she worked for the Movement, Mistress Gloomstove surely wouldn't have left them alone to face the rioters, would she?

They stopped before the bookcase. Wavey shone her lantern-beam over it, and Fever reached up and pressed the stud to open it. As it slid aside she half thought she heard another sound, behind her. She turned, but saw nothing there. The house was probably full of small meaningless noises as the wind whisked through it.

She didn't notice Charley Shallow dart behind the door jamb. But he was there all right, and he had watched the bookcase open, and he had seen how it was done.

In Barbican Square Quercus and Swiney circled each other, crouched and wary. Spectators pressed in on all sides. There was a silence which was not quite silence; rather the sound of a thousand people trying not to make a sound. Sometimes a burning torch flapped and roared as the breeze caught it. The short stood on tiptoe to peek over the shoulders of taller Londoners. Movement warriors lowered their guns and stood watching. Mono pilots gazed from the open hatchways of their vehicles. Children were held aloft by their parents – "It'll be educational, this. When you're grown you'll be able to say, 'I was there, on Ludgate Hill, the day Swiney did battle for the city against . . . against . . . what's this bloke's name again?'"

"Quercus!" shouted a warrior suddenly, and the others around him took up the chant, cheering on their leader. "Quercus! Quercus!"

For a moment it was only the invaders' voices that went echoing about the square. Then a Londoner called out, "Swiney!" The rest all looked at him with interest, waiting to see if the Movement or their Stalkers would punish him. When no harm came to him, others started to join in. "Swiney! Come on, Ted! Swiney for London!"

Quercus lunged forward, feinting to the right, then driving his left fist hard at Swiney's head. But Swiney was ready for him. Caught him by the forearm and slung him past, swung his leg up in a kick that missed, because Quercus was tougher than he looked and recovered faster than Swiney had expected. His bony fist smashed into Ted's face once, twice, blood squirting sudden and red from Ted's nose, Ted staggering backwards, shaking his head as if he was shaking off the pain. . .

"He's tapped Ted's ketchup," they said in the crowd.

"He's hard all right."

"It's a good thing we put Ted in instead of old Gilpin Wheen. Gilpin Wheen wouldn't have lasted ten seconds against this geezer."

"Gilpin Wheen wouldn't have asked him for a fight in the first place, you great soft blogger."

And the shouts going on all the time, booming off the walls all round the square, while pigeons scattered into the sky, and the two men grappled and went rolling in one another's arms down the Barbican steps.

Inside the Barbican, everyone had forgotten Dr Crumb. He came out on to a high balcony and peered down into the square with the sort of concentration he usually reserved for Petri dishes and bits of alum paper.

Below him, Ted had gained the upper hand. But it was only for a moment. Quercus was as slippery as an elver, and the brisk blows he kept landing on Ted's ears and jaw were making the pub keeper slow and stupid. There was blood on both men's faces now, blood spotting the steps and the cobbles of the square, and Ted had spat out a couple of teeth that he could ill afford to lose. But he kept fighting. He was glad, in a way, that the northerner hadn't proved as fragile as he'd expected. This way all London could see the fight was fair, and when he won it they'd rise up and turf these nomads out and carry him shoulder high, the way the crowds at Pickled Eel used to when he laid out one of the Patchskin's champions.

But he knew that he was flagging. It was time to end this punch-up. Grabbing Quercus by his upper body, Swiney started manoeuvring him towards the trestles which supported that giant barrel of Brimstone Best. A few men had climbed up on to the trestles as the fight began, and anyone who wasn't in the know would have thought they were just up there for a better view. But one of them was Mutt Gnarly and another was Brickie Chapstick, and Ted had given secret orders to them both.

35

MEMENTOES

ever was walking through memories, following her mother and the Stalker Shrike along the tunnel, with Corvus and Lammergeier marching behind her. It was so like the first time she'd walked there, with Kit Solent. And so like other times, when Godshawk had come this way, hurrying off to spend a few quiet hours in his workroom between meetings at the Barbican. The old man's memories were pouring into her mind, and the further she went along that winding way the more frequently she caught herself believing that she *was* Godshawk, and that the woman who strode ahead of her was her daughter.

She remembered standing outside Nonesuch House, looking north to London. But instead of the real city she saw the future London which Godshawk had imagined. The Barbican was repaired. It had wheels and tracks again, as it had when it first brought the Scriven south, but it was ten times larger than it had been then. Even Fever's own memories of the Movement's traction fortress couldn't compete with it. In Godshawk's vision the whole of London had been stripped and cannibalized to build three tall tiers of houses, parks and manufactories on its back, and the thunder from its giant engines drummed across the Brick Marsh, startling up wildfowl from the reed beds as the whole structure began dragging itself laboriously across the earth on banks of huge wheels. . .

"A moving city!" she said, stopping short. "I— I mean *he* – he meant to move London. . . The thing in the vault, it's an engine, isn't it?" She remembered the designs she had seen in the notebook at Kit Solent's place. She remembered drawing them now. Just doodles, they had been; the first inklings of an idea. "An external combustion engine, based on an Ancient device called a Stirling engine, but far more efficient. . ."

Wavey had stopped walking too. She stood with her lantern raised, her face turned back to look at Fever. "Godshawk believed that with a few dozen such engines he could move London. He had time to build only one before the Skinners murdered him."

Fever shook her head, clearing away the memories. "But why would anyone want a moving city?"

Wavey laughed. "Perhaps it takes a nomad to see the beauty of it. Godshawk only envisaged moving London once. He meant it to carry the Scriven to the shores of the Middle Sea where they would settle down again, far from angry Londoners and the spreading ice. Quercus has other plans. He means to make London the first true nomad city. He means it to keep on travelling the world, taking whatever it needs from other cities that haven't the means to get out of his path."

"That's not what I intended!" said Fever, Godshawkishly. And then, more like herself, "That's irrational! It's deranged!"

Her mother made a pretty, dismissive movement with one long white hand in the lantern light. "I suppose it's a nomad thing. Who cares? By telling Quercus about

Godshawk's plans and Godshawk's engines I made him the instrument of my revenge. Thanks to him, London will be humbled; its streets will be torn down to provide raw materials, its people will be forced to toil at building Godshawk's dream. A thousand years from now the Scriven will be forgotten, but the world will still remember Auric Godshawk, the man who set a city moving!"

It seemed to Fever much more likely that it would be Quercus who got the credit, should the unlikely scheme succeed. But she did not say so, and Wavey, after smiling fiercely at her for a moment turned and walked on. Fever and the Stalkers went with her. And perhaps because she now knew each twist and dip of the way so well, or perhaps because she was so taken up with Godshawk's salvaged memories that she was not aware of much else, it seemed to Fever only a little time before the passage widened into the antechamber where the vault door waited.

The Stalkers' green eyes swept the walls of the antechamber, and their beam came to rest on the other door, the door with the ivory handle, which led to the upper world.

It was open. And when Wavey went and opened it still wider and looked up the long throat of the stairway there was a dim hint of daylight high above which told them that the outer door was open, too. Fever supposed that she and Kit had forgotten to shut them when they came back inside after Creech was shot. That had been less than twenty-four hours ago, but so much had happened since then that the memory felt more ancient than one of Godshawk's.

Wavey returned to the vault door. She lifted her lantern again. Fever looked at the lock. For a moment she was afraid that all her misfortunes would have driven the number that opened it out of her head, but she just had to stop thinking for a second and it was there. She closed her eyes and carefully pressed each key in turn, watching Auric Godshawk's old speckled fingers type out the sequence. *2519364085*.

The lock ticked. The door gave a little shiver, like something waking itself from sleep. Fever heard her mother make a soft sound, deep in her throat, almost a purr. Then the door slid swiftly up into the roof. Behind it was another, but that was already sliding to the right, and behind that was a third which went left.

And behind that, darkness, and faint shifting shards of lantern light bouncing back from dusty metal surfaces.

Wavey took out a pencil and a note tablet and carefully wrote down the code while her Stalkers dragged Kit's heavy toolbox halfway across the doorsill and left it there to stop the door from closing behind them. Wavey had loved her father, but she did not trust him, and Fever, knowing how the old man's mind had worked, knew that it would have been just like him to install some trap or trick that would slam the doors behind them and leave them both entombed.

They picked up their lanterns and stepped across the threshold, cautious and curious as a pair of cats.

Roaring with the rage of the fight, Ted slammed his fists and knees against Quercus's thinner, fitter body, driving him backwards. Quercus fought back, landing a blow on Ted's right ear that jarred his skull and sent pain spiking through his head. He grabbed Quercus's hand, his shoulder, brought his head down like a hammer on the younger man's face. Quercus started to fall, but Ted grabbed him by his belt and hair and flung him bodily down in the shadow of the mighty keg.

"Swiney!" roared the crowd, the voice of London drowning out the shouts of the nomads.

Ted looked at him lying there, between the trestles which held the fat barrel up. The cobbles all round it were puddled with the beer that last night's revellers had spilled. The fumes alone were probably enough to set Quercus's head reeling. He would go to meet his gods stinking like a bar-room rug.

Ted lifted his swollen, bloodied head and nodded at Mutt and Brickie, up on the trestles. And Mutt and Brickie, just as he'd told them to, kicked hard against the chocks they'd driven in between the trestle and the keg while everyone was watching the fight, and jumped clear.

Except, like the stupid, drunken cloots they were, they didn't do it quite at the same time, the way Ted had told them. Instead of coming down square and mashing Quercus like a cockroach, one end of the barrel smashed down before the other, missing him by inches. The nomad squirmed swiftly backwards, shouting something furious and foreign at Ted.

That was Ted's last sight of him. A half second later the other end of the barrel came down, hiding him from sight. Beer spurted between the staves, but the hoops held it in shape, and the slight camber of the square set it rolling, and its own huge weight kept it coming, straight towards Ted.

"Oh, Cheesers *Crice*," he said, not scared, just furious at the never-ending uselessness of Mutt and Brickie. He eyed the barrel sullenly as it rumbled towards him, taller than three men, beer sloshing about inside and the old anvil he'd added for flavouring going dunk, dunk, dunk in there somewhere like the clapper of a wooden bell. Ted waited till it was close before he stepped sideways out of its path with that surprising, prizefighter's grace that he'd used in the old days to dodge charging Stalkers and mounted gladiators.

Only in the ring at Pickled Eel Circus there had always been sawdust to stand on, not smooth cobbles slippery with spilled beer. His heel came down in a puddle of Brimstone Best, and slid from under him. He fell heavily, and before he could rise, the barrel with its heavy planks and thick iron hoops was upon him.

It looked, as it came down on him, rather like a huge wheel.

There was a thick crunch, and a sudden silence in the square. The barrel rolled on, drawing a long red stripe across the pavement until it came to a gentle stop against the water trough. Men were running forward to help Quercus to his feet. Mutt and Brickie and a few other London lads hurried to where Ted lay, but they'd have needed spatulas to get him off the cobbles. The barrel had ironed him as flat as a paper boy.

The silence lasted just a heartbeat more. Then everyone was shouting again. "Quercus! Quercus!" they chanted, as the battered nomad hobbled up the steps, turning at the top to raise both fists in victory. And it wasn't just the men he'd brought with him who were cheering him. Because, say what you will about Londoners, they enjoyed a good, fair fight, and they had always loved a winner.

36

THE STALKER'S QUESTION

 low, unwindowed room, ribbed with stone buttresses. Brass lamps shaped like lilies hanging from the roof. If you ignored the dust, the vault had the look of a place only lately abandoned. Piles of papers lay waiting to be filed on shelves. A cup stood on a desk, and when Fever peered into it she saw the brown, crystallized dregs of Godshawk's morning coffee.

Tall figures stood in a rank along the farthest wall, and seemed to move when she lifted her lantern to look at them. Corvus, Lammergeier and Shrike all bared their claws while Wavey instantly darted a hand into her bag and brought it out clutching that clumsy gun, the magneto pistol from the Resurrectory. But it was only shadows which had moved; thick, solid-seeming shadows which swung through the dusty air as the lanterns shifted. The Stalkers that stood against the wall were old and lightless-eyed and they wore veils and trains of dusty cobwebs like a row of jilted brides. A few were without their heads. Dimly, from the back of Fever's memory, their names came wafting. *Salvage. Rusty. Clockwork Joe.*

"There's another chamber," she said. "And then another beyond that. . ."

They moved towards the dead Stalkers. There was a narrow door in the wall behind them. They wove a path to it between the spiky, silent figures, and Wavey kept her strange gun ready.

Corvus shoved open the door and pushed through it into a second chamber, identical in size and shape to the first. Fever, Wavey and the other Stalkers went after him. These rooms were hexagonal, fitted together like the cells of a honeycomb. In this one were shelves of strange old medical devices, and a slab just like the one on which Kit Solent had been remade as Shrike. Fever remembered being Godshawk, standing at that slab to fumble in the brains of the living and the dead. She remembered the sharp, off-white smell of the chemicals, the deep copper tang of blood. She did not remember the little cot which her torch revealed in the shadows behind it. Here, in this room, she too had been remade.

She let her light go wandering over the rows of vials and syringes, the ranked bottles with their dusty, unreadable labels, the cobwebbed trays of catlins and retractors. How hard and patiently the old man must have worked down here to save his tiny granddaughter! And for the first time it occurred to her that perhaps he had not simply done it out of a desire to fill her head with his own thoughts and memories. Perhaps Godshawk's consciousness was not inside her after all. Maybe he had failed to transfer more than a few fragments of himself into those old Stalker brains he'd brought back from the north. And maybe he had *known* he'd failed. When he put that machine in baby Fever's brain it might not have been an attempt to preserve his own personality. It might have been just a last, desperate effort to save his daughter's child. An old man, alone with a dying baby, grabbing up an abandoned experiment and thinking, *let's see if this does any good. . .*

Perhaps he realized, there at the end, that immortality wasn't won by designing engines or building sky-high statues or stuffing your thoughts into other heads, but just by keeping your children and their children safe, so that they could carry something of you on into the future. Not your opinions, or your silly memories of pools and parties and kissing people in parks, but the deeper memories, written in your genes; the shape of a nose, the curve of an eyebrow, the little habits and mannerisms which endure through families, through history.

Perhaps he hadn't even known, when he placed that device in baby Fever's brain, that it contained anything of himself at all. And Fever, standing in his workroom now, felt for the first time a sort of affection for him, and a sort of gratitude.

She looked up. Shrike stood nearby, the green light from his eyes flickering as he studied the slab where Godshawk had tinkered with his Stalkers. Was he remembering his own creation, in Wavey's Resurrectory? Or was some deeper feeling stirring in him? Fever watched uneasily as his bared claws flinched. Told herself not to be silly. *He's not Kit Solent. He's just a machine now. . .*

Wavey, meanwhile, had crossed the room along with Corvus and Lammergeier and thrown open another door. "Fever!" she said excitedly "Come and look! Wait till Quercus sees *this*!"

But as Fever started to move towards the doorway, the Stalker Shrike barred her way.

"WHAT AM I?" he asked.

She hadn't heard him speak before. He had the same flat, awful voice as the other Stalkers, nothing at all like Kit Solent's. The bladed hand he raised in front of her was trembling. "WHO AM I? WHAT HAS BEEN DONE TO ME?"

"I don't . . . I don't. . ." said Fever, not knowing what to say.

But before she could say anything Shrike's fellow Stalkers had reacted. She saw their heads whip round at the sound of his voice, visors down and green light flaring through the eye-slits. In the Lazarus Brigade it sometimes happened that a battle-damaged Stalker would go mad, lashing out at his comrades, even claiming to remember his mortal life. They knew what had to be done. They turned towards Shrike, and the crash of armour against armour echoed from the low roof. Fever threw herself sideways as Shrike stepped back out of the way of Corvus's blades. Whatever had gone wrong inside his Stalker's brain, it had not slowed or weakened him. He recovered in an instant, slammed Corvus's second blow aside, and drove his own blades through the other Stalker's armour, deep into the organs and machinery beneath. There were sparks and a glittering spray of fluids. Corvus gave a grating roar, and Shrike drew back and struck again. Corvus fell sideways, spewing smoke and a smell of burned wiring, the green glow of his eyes going out. Lammergeier circled warily just beyond the reach of Shrike's talons. In the doorway of the inner chamber Wavey Godshawk appeared, the magneto pistol in her hands.

"Something's gone wrong with him!" Fever screamed. "Stop him!"

Her mother raised the pistol, pointing it at Shrike's head. Shrike lunged forward, seizing Lammergeier by his armoured wrists. The vault was too small a space for such large creatures to fight in. An upended shelf spilled laboratory glassware; a cabinet was kicked into splinters. Shrike twisted Lammergeier sideways, shielding himself with the other Stalker's body as Wavey pulled the pistol's trigger. The pistol made a thin whining sound, almost lost in the clash and scuffle of the struggling Stalkers. Lammergeier, caught by its blast, went rigid, juddering. Shrike levered his head off, shoved the body aside and strode towards the door, where Wavey stood fumbling with the magneto pistol.

"Wavey!" screamed Fever.

She saw Wavey look up, and watched her realize that she had not time to recharge the pistol. Her face was a ghastly green in the light from the Stalker's eyes. He smashed her aside, looked through the doorway into the far room, then turned back. The beams of his eyes swept past Fever, but he was not interested in her. He looked again at Godshawk's cobwebby equipment, then turned and went striding from the chamber. Fever heard him go crashing through the first room, blundering out into the antechamber. Heard his heavy footfalls go stamping up the stairs and into silence.

For a moment she felt too frightened to move, but she shut her eyes tight and repeated the Laws of Motion until she felt stronger. Then she picked up her lantern and stepped over the wreckage of Lammergeier and Corvus to the inner door.

She had prepared herself to see her mother dead, like Kit Solent on the heath. But Wavey was still moving, sprawled on the stone floor of the inner room. Above her, forgotten, Godshawk's giant city-shifting engine stood like a huge totem, reflecting gleams of lamplight from a hundred dusty fins and ducts.

Fever knelt down by her mother, and a sudden Godshawk-memory showed her Wavey as a little girl, fallen over on the drive and crying, "Ow, ow, ow!"

"Ow," said Wavey, shifting, trying to find comfort on the hard, dusty floor. She found none. The Stalker's blades had not ripped her, but his armoured fist had struck her like a hammer and flung her hard against the engine. Bones had shattered. Tears of pain shone on her face, and the sight of them filled Fever with panic. What should she do? What should she do?

"Go back to London, quickly!" her mother said, reaching up and touching her, stroking her face with a shaking hand. "There is something wrong with that Stalker; the brain I put into him must have some fault. I should not have brought him here. . ."

"It is irrational to build machines whose principles you do not understand and whose actions you cannot predict," said Fever, her Engineer's attitudes spilling out in spite of herself. "This mobile city you propose will be the same. Where will it lead?"

Wavey wasn't listening. "Go, Fever!" she said. "What if the Stalker returns?"

Fever looked sideways and saw the magneto pistol lying on the floor. A small green light shone like a sequin on its handle to let her know that it was charged. She picked it up and it felt odd and heavy in her hand.

"Leave me that," begged Wavey. "Go!"

"I'm going to go and find Master Solent," said Fever. "It would be unwise to leave him alone up there."

"Why can't you do as you're told? He could kill you!" Wavey struggled to raise herself, but the pain was too much and she fell back half fainting. "Great Scrivener!"

Fever stood up, backing away from her. "Someone else will come soon. Quercus will come, won't he, when his fight is won?"

It felt wrong to leave her mother there, weeping with pain and unable to move. *But feelings mean nothing*, Fever reminded herself. She gripped the magneto pistol and went quickly out of the vault and up the stairs which led to the old garden.

37

THE MAGNETO GUN

uan had promised that it was going to be fun, but Ruan was silly because it wasn't fun at all. They had come all through that horrid tunnel, scared of ghosties and Dapplejacks all the way, and the walk had made their legs ache very badly and at the end of it there was just a horrid room with boxes in, and they couldn't sleep there because it smelled funny and they were scared the ghosties might come for them out of the tunnel. So Ruan had found this door and they'd sneaked up the steps and reached another door and gone out through it into open air and there'd been trees and the moon. And Ruan had said, "Now it will be fun! We'll sleep under the stars, like children in a story!" But it still wasn't fun, because he'd made her climb all up a horrible steep hill and her shoes had got wet and she'd dropped Noodle Poodle and they'd had to find him in the dark and at the hill's top there was a horrid ruin just *full* of ghosties so they didn't go in there but went round it instead and found a sort of summer house with moss and ivy instead of a roof and they went in there and Ruan covered them over with leaves the way the Helpful Birds did to the children in the storybook, only it didn't work because the wind blew through all the holes in the summer house and the leaves that were dry blew away and rustled like ghosties in the corner and the leaves that were wet were cold and clammy. So she'd cried and said she wanted to go home, and Ruan had cried too, and they'd been afraid to put the candle out, and he'd read them a story out of the red storybook and somehow they had fallen asleep.

Now Fern was awake, all cold and stiff. It was horrible sleeping outside. She wanted Daddy, and she wanted to go home. Ruan was still sleeping, with his hair flopped over his face. "Wake up, Ruan," she said, but he just grunted at her and stayed sleeping. She rummaged in the bedspread bundle and found a bit of cake for breakfast and went outside with it, breaking off crumbs to give to Noodle Poodle.

It was just starting to get light, and it was very quiet because even the birds were still asleep. There was mist all round the hill and the hill stuck out of the top of it in sunlight and little jewels of water were shining on the grass. And up the hill, out of the mist, came a man made all out of metal, with knives for fingernails.

Fern looked at him. He looked at Fern. Fern smiled at him. "It's Daddy!" she shouted, and ran towards him as fast as her fat little legs would carry her.

There were footprints all the way up the stairs. The new Stalker's huge, blank prints, and Fever's scuffly bootmarks from the day before, and here and there a tiny print, like the print of a child's shoe. Fever, running towards daylight and the open air, was so confused by Godshawk's crowding memories that she imagined those footprints might be Wavey's, and Wavey still a little girl.

The door at the top of the stairs still stood wide open where the Stalker Shrike had shouldered his way out.

Outside, mist hung thick and white above the dripping bushes. Fever started climbing and stopped on the first terrace, near one of the pools. The mist pressed close all round her, as if she were something precious, wrapped in cotton wool. The pool in front of her was green with weed, but at the same time, superimposed upon it, she could see it as it had looked twenty years before. She went down on her hands and knees on the mossy concrete at the edge of it and looked down, and she saw *a)* a surface of small green leaves, packed so tight that the water was hidden, and *b)* a clear pool, six feet deep, with speckled carp drifting lazily beneath the lily pads.

She pinched herself, trying to dim the insistent memories. She was not Godshawk. And nor was she the daughter Wavey wanted her to be, or the Engineer Dr Crumb had wanted to turn her into. She was sick of being the vessel for other people's hopes. . .

The weight of the strange gun in her hand made her think of Kit Solent and the thing he had become. If she could just find him, and use the gun on him, at least she would have achieved something for herself. But how was she to find him in this fog, with Godshawk's memories flitting between the trees like phantoms?

She was about to shout his name when she heard another voice, a child's voice, high above her in the mist.

"Daddy!"

She knew then who it was that had come through the tunnel ahead of her and opened the door. She knew who had made those small footprints on the stairs. She knew that Fern and Ruan had come to Nonesuch Hill, and that the new Stalker had found them there.

But at the same moment, and before she could react

to that new knowledge, she heard someone come out of the doorway below her and start running uphill towards her.

"Quick," she said urgently, turning, imagining that it was Quercus or some of his men, freshly arrived through the tunnel.

But it was Charley Shallow.

All through the dark of that tunnel Charley had crept, following their voices and the light of their lanterns, far ahead. He'd kept urging himself to go faster and catch them up, but he was scared of the machine men, and he knew he couldn't bring himself to shoot the girl when she was close to that older lady; she might not even know that Fever Crumb was a Scriven, and it would be terrible to kill a proper human by mistake. So he hung back. He hung so far back that he heard the crash and clatter of the Stalkers fighting while he was still sneaking along the tunnel, and of course he could not know what it was. When he reached the tunnel's end he saw the big door opposite him standing open. He could see nothing of his quarry, but there were faint voices, and lights and shadows moving in some deep, inner chamber.

It was a strange place, all right. Full of old tech and old magic. It scared him. So he waited at the tunnel's end, watching the open doorway of the vault and wondering what to do. And after a while his vigilance was rewarded, because the girl came out, just her alone. He had the spring gun ready but he hadn't time to steady his nerves and shoot, and she went past him and through that other door without even looking at him.

He was still scared, but he knew that this was the best chance he was likely to get, and he had to jump at it, for Bagman's sake. He crept past the vault entrance and then pelted up the stairs.

Emerging into the mist he felt a heartbeat's dismay – how was he to find her? Then he thought of the ruin on the hilltop. That was where she would be. Something about the old house drew her. He looked down, and there were her footprints, dark green on the dewy grass. Following them, he ran up the hill, scanning the mist ahead of him. But he was looking for someone his own height or taller; he didn't see Fever crouched in front of him until she shouted, "Quick!"

By then he was almost on top of her. Fever tried to scramble out of his way but he swerved to miss her at the same moment, and he went the same way as her. "Sorry!" he heard her say, as he crashed into her, tripped over her, fell. He landed hard on the grass and the spring gun was jarred out of his hand. He saw it go. It went slowly, like something in a bad dream. It skipped once off the concrete on the side of the pool, and dropped over the edge with a plop like a big frog jumping. He could see little individual leaves of duckweed in the spurt of water it threw up. When he reached the pool's edge himself there was a gun-shaped hole of dark water in the surface of the weed. He plunged his hand in, shoulder deep and groping, but he could not touch bottom. And all the time the girl was behind him, and he turned and saw her standing, staring down at him with her ill-matched eyes, her mouth opening to say something or scream for help or something. And she started to run and then hesitated, looking down for something she'd dropped in the grass and he looked too and saw it first. It was this other gun, a weird looking one, all wires and stuff. And he grabbed it quick before she could, and rolled over, and pointed it up at her.

"Oh, don't be ridiculous!" said Fever. "That's not a – that won't harm me—" And then she remembered the machine in her head, and realized that it *might*. The boy was shaking, terrified, and the magneto pistol was shaking too, but not enough to make him miss. She watched him pull the trigger.

There was an astonishing pain; a hard white flash; then nothing at all.

38

WE ARE THE DEAD

he fell on the grass. She lay on the grass with her feet turned in and her arms thrown out to either side, her right arm stretched across the concrete at the pool's edge, her right hand hanging down into the water. Charley scrambled up and wiped his nose on his sleeve and looked at the gun, wondering if there was another shot in it. But he didn't need another. Fever lay still. Her eyes were open very wide, as if in amazement at what he'd done, and they didn't blink. You could hardly tell any more that they didn't match because the pupils had flared huge and owlish, two wells you could look down into the dark unknown. When he reached out and touched her face her head flopped sideways and a leak of blood like a thick red worm came out of one nostril and started to creep across her face.

That was when, too late, Charley realized that Bagman had been wrong. Not just Bagman, but all the Skinners, wrong, wrong, wrong. Maybe Fever Crumb had been a Scriven and maybe she hadn't, but what would it have mattered if she'd lived? What difference would it have made to the world if she'd grown up and had sons and daughters just like her? None, he thought, or any rate, not enough to make it worth doing the thing that he'd just done. She'd been a person like him, and he had killed her.

He threw her gun away as he went running down the hill. He lost Bagman's hat somewhere too. He ran into those trees that broke like green surf around the hill's foot and hid himself there, trying to get the memory of Fever's dead face out of his head, knowing that it would keep coming back to him for ever.

On Nonesuch hill, the boy's running footsteps faded into the mist. Inside Fever's body, machines no larger than germs swarmed in her blood and in the clear reaches of her spinal fluid. Many drifted powerless, destroyed by the magnetic pulse which had disabled the old machine nested in the root of her brain. But there were multitudes of them, and the ones which had survived went on with their patient, endless work, repairing damage and harvesting waste energy from her muscles and synapses. Some clustered round the machine, while others busied themselves with her stilled heart. They were brisk, and mindless, and very good at what they did.

Thirty seconds after the magneto pistol fired, twenty seconds after Charley Shallow turned tail and ran, Fever shuddered and flailed her arms and swallowed a gulp of air and started coughing. She wiped her eyes and looked for the boy. She didn't know she'd been unconscious. To her, it seemed as if he'd vanished. She saw the magneto pistol lying in the grass and picked it up and thought at once of the child she'd heard on the hilltop. She staggered to her feet and started climbing. She felt vague and groggy, and she had sprained her knee in falling, which made her limp. She was halfway up the hill before she realized that her nose was bleeding. She had almost reached the top before it occurred to her that this one hillside in the damp present was all she could see; this overgrown garden, this mist. She remembered the old garden, the float lamps and the carp ponds, but the memories had no weight any more; they were just the memories of memories, already growing colourless and fragmentary, like spent dreams.

The flash of the magneto pistol had driven Godshawk from her head.

Was she glad, or was it grief she felt? She wasn't sure, and nor was there any time to think about it. For as she climbed the mist had thinned, and now she stepped out of it altogether, up into the dawn sunlight on the hill's top and the sharp shadows stretching from the ruined walls. A little way from her Fern and Ruan were waiting hand in hand. And a little way from *them*, with all his blades unsheathed and dazzling in the sun, there stood the Stalker.

"Stop!" she shouted, and "No!", the words tumbling over one another in her haste to get them spoken. She went as fast as she could on her sprained leg towards the children, and as she went she lifted up the magneto pistol, wondering how close to the Stalker and his terrible knives she had to be for it to work.

But the Stalker, though he looked round at her, did not move. Nor did he move towards the children. He had unsheathed his blades, but he had not used them. Did that mean that there was some trace of Kit Solent still inside him somewhere? Was it possible that some residual memory in his brain recognized Fern and Ruan, and could not harm them? He had closed his visor, as if to shield them from the sight of his dead face.

The children looked at Fever. "Miss Crumb!" said Ruan.

She lowered the pistol. She had wanted to destroy Shrike, but she didn't now, not if he meant the children no harm. He was too fine a piece of engineering, and she felt a sort of kinship with him. Perhaps one day, inside his mind, Kit's memories would ignite again. But still in the sunshine those blades gleamed, twitching restlessly now and then, and she could not quite trust him. She let the gun hang by her side and held out her empty hand to Ruan. "Ruan, come here. . ."

"It's Daddy!" said Fern excitedly, pointing at the Stalker.

Fever shook her head. "This isn't your father. Come away from him."

Obediently, the children came to her. Ruan was carrying a big bundle, wrapped up in a very dirty cloth. The little girl held Noodle Poodle tight and kept looking back at the Stalker, who turned to watch her go past him. "Why did he look like Daddy if he isn't Daddy?" she asked loudly.

"People do look like other people sometimes," said Fever, picking her up and turning away, listening all the time for the sound of the Stalker coming after her.

But the Stalker just stood there watching as Fever, with the girl in her arms and the boy beside her, went down the steep slope of the garden and walked into the mist like someone walking into a white sea. He was going to live a long time, that Stalker. The Movement would send him north, where he would become one of the fiercest warriors of the Lazarus Brigade, and in later years he would serve many other masters, until his battered armour was a palimpsest of stencilled insignia. And always there would be this flaw in him, this softness when it came to small children, and he would never understand why.

So he stood and watched them walk away from him into the mist, and just before it hid them from him the little girl raised her hand and waved goodbye.

While she was up in the sunshine Fever had felt very clear about what to do. Once she was down in the mist again she grew uncertain. Where was she to take the children? What future would there be for them in Quercus's London?

"Are we going to find Daddy?" asked Ruan.

"Your father is dead," said Fever.

The children accepted it quietly. Fever stopped to get a better grip on Fern, and went on through the mist. Ruan walked trustingly beside her. "What will happen to us?" he asked, in a small voice.

"I do not know. Do you have any relatives who might look after you?"

"No," he said, holding back tears.

Fever thought, *I'll take them to Dr Crumb. Dr Crumb will know what to do.* But he wouldn't, would he? He would tell her to do the rational thing, which would be to give Fern and Ruan to the civic orphanage to care for. Or he would make them shave their heads and bury their feelings and try to turn them into little Engineers.

She stopped walking. They were close to the door which led into the hill, and sounds were coming out of it. Tramping footsteps and echoey, military shouts in northern accents. The Movement were coming through the tunnel to Godshawk's vault, and she felt relieved that there would be help for Wavey, and then unhappy, because she didn't want to be any part of Quercus's strange plans for London, and she didn't want Fern and Ruan taken from her, as she was sure they would be.

"Miss Crumb?" said Ruan, sensing her confusion and starting to grow afraid.

"It is all right," she promised him. "Come this way. . ."

She turned away from the door and pushed downhill through scrub and long grass till she saw reeds ahead of her, and water beyond the reeds. Turning right at random, she walked along the edge of the lagoon for a way, and there ahead of her, as if she'd planned to find it, there was a wooden jetty, and drawn up on the bank beside it the little round boat that had brought Bagman Creech and his boy to Nonesuch House.

She thought, *I can't go off in that. What will Wavey think, when she sends people out to look for me and I am gone? And Dr Crumb, what of Dr Crumb?* And then she got into the boat anyway; shoved it into the water and got into it and had Ruan hand Fern down to her and then get in himself. "The water's coming in," said Ruan, but Fever said it was all right; they would not sink unless a lot more water came in, and if a lot more water *did* come in, then Ruan would be allowed to bail.

She found the paddle under the seat and started paddling them away from the jetty, which faded quickly into the mist behind. She still half believed that she was going back to London, to find Dr Crumb. But she knew that if she did he would want everything to go on as before. The Order would have new premises, and the

Engineers would all be busy working on the new city, bolting the Movement's traction fortress on to the Barbican and fitting wheels and the new engines. And she wasn't sure she wanted to be a part of that. She wasn't sure that she was ready to go back to being just an Engineer, and she wasn't sure she was ready to be Wavey Godshawk's daughter, either.

39

CRUMBS OF COMFORT

hile London was distracted by the duel at the Barbican, more and more of the Movement's soldiery had been arriving on Ludgate Hill. Now that the duel was ended they were suddenly everywhere. Up Bishopsgate came more vehicles; not just monos but land barges and traction bunkers, some so wide that they bashed balconies and drainpipes off the houses as they rumbled by.

Quercus's doctors attended to him in the open, on the Barbican steps, where his new subjects could see that he was not too badly hurt. Meanwhile his warriors started rounding up former councillors and other Londoners who would be able to help them restore order and keep the city working. It was not long before they tracked down the Order of Engineers, and not long after that that Dr Stayling and Dr Crumb were hurrying, along with a band of soldiers and Stalkers, through the tunnel that led to Nonesuch House.

"Extraordinary!" said Dr Crumb, as their way took them deeper and deeper under the Brick Marsh. "To think no one knew that this was here!"

Dr Stayling was not listening to him. He was too full of Nikola Quercus and his plans. He'd had a brief conversation with the Land Admiral before setting out, and it had left him as giddy as a schoolgirl. "He has remarkable ideas, Crumb!" he kept saying. "Remarkable!

There is an engine of some sort in Godshawk's vault, apparently, and Quercus reckons that with a bank of them he will be able to power a mobile city! Think of it! A whole traction city!"

Dr Crumb thought of it, and was not much impressed. "It hardly seems a very rational idea. Trundling about the world, snapping up the things one needs from other cities. And what if those other cities follow suit, and start to move themselves? Then only the fittest and fastest would survive. It would be an absurd way to live. . . A sort of municipal Darwinism. . ."

"But what a spur to progress, eh?" chuckled Stayling, who seemed to be finding it hard to control his emotions. "And this Quercus seems a fine fellow. London will support him, I am sure of that. I believe he should alter his name to something more Londonish, though. Kirk, perhaps?"

It was Dr Crumb's turn not to listen. For Stayling had told him before they left Ludgate Hill that Quercus had already sent his technomancer with an advance party along this tunnel, and that it had included Fever. Now he was nearing the tunnel's end; he could hear the voices of the Movement's warriors echoing in a new way as they stepped into a larger space. He felt his heart beginning to beat faster and faster at the thought of seeing his daughter again. He was going to embrace her, he decided. He didn't care what Stayling said; he was never going to hide his feelings from Fever again.

And then, as he stepped out into the antechamber, he heard shouts of alarm from inside the open vault. "Stay back!" warned an officer, but Dr Crumb said, "Let me through, I'm an Engineer," and pushed past him.

He barely noticed the scientific treasures heaped up in the vault's first chamber. He hurried through into the second, and saw Movement warriors stooping over the wreckage of two Stalkers, asking each other in scared voices, "What can have happened here?"

He went through the doorway into the third chamber, with men behind him holding up hurricane lamps, Stayling saying, "Crumb! Look there! The engine!" Dr Crumb glanced at it, but without much interest. He had seen the woman lying on the floor beside it, and he went closer to her and saw who she was.

He thought she was dead. He wondered if she had been lying down here ever since the riots, her body preserved by some quality of the vault. But when he dropped to his knees beside her she stirred and groaned and half opened her eyes, and he understood that *she* was Quercus's technomancer.

"Wavey," he said.

She frowned, and smiled weakly as she recognized him. "Dr Crumb! Always coming to my rescue. . ."

He wanted to pick her up and hold her tight, but he could see that she was hurt, so he contented himself with leaning down and kissing her. "I say, Crumb! Steady on!" warned Dr Stayling.

"Oh, shut up, Stayling!" he retorted. And then, "Wavey, where is Fever?"

"She went outside. The new Stalker ran mad, and she took the magneto pistol and went outside after him. . ."

One of the Movement soldiers, a medical orderly with a canvas satchel of supplies, was waiting to

291

examine the injured woman. Dr Crumb waved him forward, gave Wavey's hand an encouraging squeeze and made his way quickly back through the now-crowded vault. "There is a deranged Stalker outside!" he shouted.

He had not even noticed the door that led to the gardens, but he found it easily enough. Three warriors and a pair of Stalkers came with him up the stairs. Outside, in the thinning, sun-bright mist they spread out across the ragged gardens, climbing past the ponds towards the hilltop and the ruins of the house which Dr Crumb remembered so well.

"Fever!" he shouted as he climbed. "Fever!" But there was no answer.

He reached the hilltop, and there was no one there except the men who had come out with him, and a tall, new-looking Stalker standing silent with his visor down.

"Is he the mad one?" Dr Crumb asked.

The young officer, Captain Andringa, said, "He seems quiet enough now."

One of the other men had found a fat, unlikely pistol lying in the grass. He held it up. "Stalker gun here, sir. Shall I decommission him?"

Andringa shook his head. "Best not, as he's calmed down. We have few enough left. We'll send him north to the oil country. He can take out his rage on the Arkangelsk shock-troops at Hill 60."

More Stalkers came clanking up the steep lawns. They had been searching the reed beds around the hill's foot. One of them carried a thing that looked like a bundle of soggy clothes, but which turned out to be a boy, wet and trembling and terrified. "SIR, WE FOUND THIS FUGITIVE. HE IS UNARMED."

"Who are you, boy?" asked Andringa.

Dr Crumb looked at the boy. He knew that crossed-knife badge on his tunic. Of course – this must be the boy whom Fever had told him about, the Skinner's boy!

He grabbed Charley by his wet shoulders and wrenched him upright. "What have you done? What have you done with my daughter?"

"Your daughter, sir?" asked Charley, shivering.

"With Fever Crumb!"

Charley swallowed. He'd never imagined Scriven having parents. He saw the magneto pistol in a warrior's hand and nodded at it. "I killed her, sir. With that fat gun there."

Dr Crumb felt a terrifying anger rise up in him, and on the far side of the anger, only emptiness. But before he knew what to do with those wild emotions Captain Andringa said brusquely, "He's lying. That's not a real gun. It's technomancy. It shuts down Stalkers, but wouldn't harm a human being."

"Well, I still killed her," said Charley bleakly. "I'm sorry I did, but I did. I fired that thing at her and she fell down dead."

Tears were spilling down his thin little face. Dr Crumb let go of him. He quietly recited the prime numbers up to seventy-nine and then said, "Show me."

Charley looked round, frightened of the men and their guns and their Stalkers. He nodded, and started leading the way back down the hill. The mist was clearing now, but it still took him a while to find the pool where he'd left Fever.

"Well?" asked Dr Crumb. He knelt down, looking critically at the grass around the pool. It was flattened in one place, as if someone had lain there for a little while not long before.

Charley shook his head. "I don't understand, sir. This is the place. See that scrape in the moss? That's where I dropped my own gun. She lay there sir, and she was dead. I killed her."

He started to cry, big, weary, miserable sobs shaking his thin body. Dr Crumb put an arm around him, then both arms, remembering how he used to comfort Fever when she was little. "It's all right," he said. He was thinking fast, and as he thought, he smiled. He could hear Andringa and the other men spreading out across the gardens again, shouting, "Miss Crumb! Fever!" He didn't expect them to get an answer.

"It's all right," he told Charley again. "She wasn't harmed. She just laid here for a time, and then when you'd gone she got up and went away."

Charley sniffed hopefully, glad to learn that he was not a killer after all. "We'll find her, then. . ."

"No, no," said Dr Crumb. He straightened up, staring into the mist. He had never been good at understanding other people, but he had been observing Fever for fourteen years and he felt he had enough evidence to construct a hypothesis. "If she wanted to be found she would have waited near here for us to find her. She wants to be alone. She needs it; needs a chance to think." And he looked out across the marshes, where treetops and the sunlit golden waters of lagoons were showing through the mist, and he felt enormously happy that he could understand what his daughter was feeling.

"She can look after herself," he said. "And when she is ready, she'll come back."

He let go of Charley and turned away, towards the door that would lead him back to Wavey. Before he stepped through it he stopped and looked back and saw the boy still standing there. "What about you?" he asked. "Do you have somewhere to go?"

Charley shrugged.

"Best come with me, then," said Dr Crumb. "There is an injured woman to be taken back to Ludgate Hill, and all manner of equipment to be moved. Yes, come with me; that would be the rational thing."

He went back into the hill, and after a while Charley followed him.

40

THE PASSING SHOW

ever paddled for what felt like a long way, and saw nothing but a circle of water about ten feet across with the coracle in the middle. The children sat in the damp bottom of the coracle and watched her trustingly. Fern said, "Will Daddy come back?"

"No, Fern," she explained gently. "He is dead."

"Has he gone to the Sunless Country?"

"There is no such place," said Fever firmly, because she did not believe in telling lies, not even white ones, not even to little girls. "Dead people are dead; they do not live on, and they do not come back, except in our memories."

"I want to go home," said Ruan.

"I'm afraid that is not possible," Fever told him.

Fern hugged Noodle Poodle tightly and started to cry. It occurred to Fever that she had no idea how to cope with these two children. But then her father had had no idea how to cope with the baby he found in the basket, and *he* had managed all right. . .

Soon after that, the sun appeared, like a flat white hole poked in the mist. There were trees ahead; reed beds; the ruins of a mill. Beyond it, a high embankment. It was not the landfall that Fever had expected. In the mist she had turned west instead of north. But at least she knew where she was. On top of that embankment was the Great South Road, up which the land hoys came from Chunnel and Brighton and the south-coast ports.

She brought the boat ashore there, helped the children out and together they scrambled up the steep bank. On the top was a wide roadway made of packed, crushed chalk. The mist was thinning steadily; you could see it blowing across the road like smoke, and Fever and the children cast shadows now on the grey-white ground. On either side of the embankment, stretches of water gleamed like battered metal. From the north there came a sound of engines.

Out of the mist, moving slow and steady, a lone land barge appeared. The brightening sunlight struck little brilliant highlights from the spikes and stars of its decorated upperworks, and lit up all the colours of its painted bodywork. It jingled with bells and jangled with good luck charms, and statues of at least two dozen gods gazed out from a niche above the driver's cabin to ward off collisions. Above them, in gilded script, were the words *Persimmon's Ambulatory Lyceum*.

Fever remembered faintly the play which she had stopped to watch at Summertown, and how the travelling theatre had seemed to her to sum up all the unreason of the unreasonable world. But it felt like immense good luck that had brought it down the Great South Road at that precise moment, so, telling Fern and Ruan to wait on the verge, she stepped out in front of it and raised both arms.

Shrill horns sounded. The driver inside his cabin waved frantically until Fever stepped aside. The barge slowed, but it did not stop. "Can't stop, dear!" shouted a woman leaning over a handrail on the upper deck. "If you knew the trouble we'd had to get our old engines started, you'd never make us stop! But if it's passage to the coast that you're after, climb aboard!"

Fever wasn't sure that that *was* what she was after. She just wanted a little distance between herself and London; a time and space to think. But there was no time to consider possibilities, with the gaudy barge growling past her at a steady five or six miles per hour. She ran to the verge and picked up Fern, calling for Ruan to follow. A man came out on to the open platform at the barge's stern where the plays were performed and reached out to help them all aboard.

He was a big man, tall and portly and broad-shouldered. He had side whiskers and a rosy, sunburned face, and religious trinkets hung in tangles round his neck and were stitched into all the seams of his silk coat. He bowed low and smiled a wide, warm smile and announced, "Ambrose Persimmon, Tragedian, and Manager of this humble company. How may we help you, my dear?"

Fever remembered seeing Master Persimmon dressed in cardboard armour and a woollen beard only two days before. She looked warily at him, and then past him at the faces of his company, who stared out at her from various portholes and windows and open hatchways. Wondering if she had made the right choice she said, "You are bound for the south ports?"

"The south ports and then onwards," boomed Persimmon, in a voice used to speaking over the cheers and jeers of a rowdy audience as well as the din of barge engines. "First to Chunnel, then east to Hamsterdam, and after that Frankland or the Plains or . . . who knows? Where'er the Muses lead us! All the way to the Middle Sea, perhaps! I'll take you where you like, my friends. Though I, ah, take it you've coin to pay your passage with?"

Fever shook her head. She had forgotten that things had to be paid for, in the world outside the Order. She hadn't a penny to her name, and she didn't think the children had, either.

"Well, never mind!" said Persimmon. "You can work your passage. These children will melt the hearts of any crowd – I can just see them in *Babes in the Mall* or *The Poor Orphans of Dunster* – I think we still have the backdrops for that in the hold. And what of yourself, miss? Have you never tried your hand at acting? You've a winning face, and with the right wig. . ."

Fever shook her head. She knew that she could no more act than fly. But she thought sideways past the problem and said, "I can help you with your engines."

"What's that? Speak up! Project!"

"I can help with the engines!" shouted Fever. "I was trained by the Order of Engineers."

"So *that's* what happened to your hair!" Persimmon laughed. "One hardly liked to ask. . ."

Fever touched her fuzzy scalp, and tried out a smile. "I'm planning to grow it," she called. She had been planning nothing of the sort, but saying it made it true. She would not have a lot of hair, she decided, just enough to hide her ears, and keep her neck warm at the back. She held Fern tight and followed the actor up a tiny, twisting stairway to the open upper deck. Ruan came after them, dragging his bundle. Two actresses who had been rehearsing up there set down their playscripts and came at once to fuss over the children. "May I present my dear wife and greatest helper," said Master Persimmon reverently, indicating the older of the two, the same handsome lady who had called down to Fever before she came aboard. "Mistress Persimmon's *Diana* is still spoken of in tones of awe and gratitude by all those who appreciate great acting."

"Master Persimmon is too kind," replied his wife, blushing as she heaved bales and baskets about and wrestled out some folding chairs for the newcomers to sit on. The younger woman, helping her, shot Fever a frank and friendly smile, as if to say, *You'll be all right with us.*

"There has been trouble in London," Master Persimmon confided in a whisper that was still loud enough to cut clearly through the engine racket. He took Fever's arm and guided her gently forward to a clear space near the bows. "A new man in charge. Big plans, they say. A New Era dawns. It could be good for business. But I'd rather be well away till things are settled down."

"Me too," said Fever. She would go to Chunnel, she thought. She could write to Dr Crumb from there, and after that. . .

Well, after that, who could say? She had only just found out who she was. She had no idea what she wanted to do with the rest of her life.

"And what are we to call you, dear?" Mistress Persimmon asked.

Fever set Fern down beside her brother. The wind tousled the children's hair and the silver lagoons slid by on either side of the road and she stood holding the handrail and looking out into the misty, sunlit land ahead. And as loudly as she could, she said the one thing about herself that she was certain of:

"My name is Fever Crumb."

ACKNOWLEDGEMENTS

My grateful thanks to everyone at Scholastic, and to all those people whose encouragement and advice has helped to shape this book; Kirsten Stansfield, Elv Moody, Marion Lloyd and Alice Swan. Also, of course, to Kjartan Poskitt, the discoverer of Molecular Clockwork.

Philip Reeve, Dartmoor, 2009

THE WORLD OF MORTAL ENGINES

Fever Crumb's adventures
are continued in

A WEB OF AIR

THE SECRETS OF FLIGHT HAVE BEEN LOST FOR THOUSANDS OF YEARS

But in a faraway corner of a ruined world, a mysterious
boy is building a flying machine. Birds help him, and
so does a beautiful, brilliant engineer called Fever
Crumb. But powerful enemies stalk them – either to
posess their fantastic invention, or to destroy the
secrets of flight forever.

Read more from

THE WORLD OF
MORTAL
ENGINES

There are four more
great books, set centuries
after *Fever Crumb*.

Mortal Engines
Predator's Gold
Infernal Devices
A Darkling Plain